FOR WORSE

FOR WORSE

L. K. BOWEN

BLACK STONE
PUBLISHING

Printed in the United States of America

First edition: 2024
ISBN 979-8-212-63116-7
Fiction / Thrillers / Psychological

Version 1

Blackstone Publishing
31 Mistletoe Rd.
Ashland, OR 97520

www.BlackstonePublishing.com

For M. and E.
With more love than you can imagine.

I, _____, take you, _____, to be my lawfully wedded husband/wife, to have and to hold, from this day forward, for better, for worse, for richer, for poorer, in sickness and in health, until death do us part.

—Traditional Marriage Vow

CONTENTS

CHAPTER ONE
SHE'S LEAVING HOME

DIVORCED WOMEN OVER FIFTY CHAT ROOM
SEPTEMBER 2, 2018
3:14 P.M.

Welcome to Divorced Women over Fifty Chat Room,
or as we affectionately call it, DWOF.

Here you'll be able to talk with women aged fifty-plus who
are going through the challenges of separation, divorce, and
the rebooting of their lives in the aftermath of marriages that
have sometimes lasted more than half their lives.

Please click the link below to get to our registration page,
where you can choose a username and password.

Divorced Women over Fifty—**LOG IN/REGISTER**

ELLESBELLES:
I'm leaving my husband.

GINGERBEAR:
Good for you!

ELLESBELLES:
. . . again.

FREEATLAST:
Girl, you come sit by me.

MAIRZYDOATS (DWOF MODERATOR):
Are you safe? Are you or your children in any danger? PM me
(that's private message, like an email or IM) if you need any
immediate help.

ELLESBELLES:
Yes, thank you, I'm perfectly safe. Our daughter is at college
in Boston. I mean, it's just me and him at home now, and
it sucks, but . . . I just really need to do it this time. The last
time was just practice.

SUZYQ:
Welcome!!!! You are safe here, and can always count on a
friendly ear to listen and a soft shoulder to cry on! We are all
for one and one for all here!

ELLESBELLES:
Is it okay that I'm here???? I mean, I'm not divorced yet,
but . . .????

MAIRZYDOATS (DWOF MODERATOR):
Of course, that's fine! There are women here in all stages of
what can be a very attenuated process.

FREEATLAST:
So, you left him before? Why'd you go back?

ELLESBELLES:
I ran out of money. And . . . nerve, I guess. I've only been back about five months, but it just feels . . . wrong. The thing is, it's not like I can say, he does drugs, or he's unfaithful, or he beats me up. Something cut and dried, that anyone would understand. He never pushed me or hit me or our daughter— he never did any of that. He was, is, just—intolerable. It's a thousand little things a day that . . . I don't know.

LORELEI:
Ah. Marriage by a thousand cuts. We're all familiar with that syndrome.

MAIRZYDOATS (DWOF MODERATOR):
Do you have a lawyer? A therapist? You'll definitely need the first and probably the second.

ELLESBELLES:
We're just about to start couples therapy, probably too little too late. At the risk of sounding crazy, I'm not the crazy one here.

MAIRZYDOATS (DWOF MODERATOR):
I was a divorced divorce lawyer, and now I'm a reasonably sane therapist. I can help you with any resources you might need.

LORELEI:
How did he react when you left?

ELLESBELLES:
Oh, he was surprised. He never saw it coming, because there's not really anything real for him outside of himself, if you know what I mean. Told me I was ridiculous, didn't know

what I was doing, would come back as soon as I realized how stupid I looked to all our friends . . .

SuzyQ:
When I left, I just texted C. He didn't check his texts for three days cause he was in Canada selling tires, by then I was back with my momma.

Ellesbelles:
I'm vision impaired, so I don't drive, which made it kind of awkward. I had my bags in my friend's car, and she waited outside the house like a getaway driver while I told him. Never ran so fast in my life as I did from the front door to her car!

Gingerbear:
What's with your vision?

Ellesbelles:
I have an eye disease called retinitis pigmentosa, which nuked my peripheral vision. Central vision's fine, I can see what I look at, but nothing above, below or to the sides. It's sort of like looking at life through a pair of binoculars. Plus, total night blindness. So, I had to stop driving a few years ago.

Mairzydoats (DWOF Moderator):
Where do you live, if you feel okay to answer that?

Ellesbelles:
Northern California. Kinda hard not to drive here.

Freeatlast:
How do you get around?

ELLESBELLES:
Well—mostly my husband. Except if he's pissed off at me, or if I've done something he thinks is wrong.

LORELEI:
Define "done something wrong."

ELLESBELLES:
Oh, you know—really horrible stuff, like not refolding the newspaper correctly or taking his suggestion when I was doing something that he knew how to do better.

FREEATLAST:
Oh, we know this guy. The Anal-Retentive Micromanaging Control Freak Asshole. Or, as Gingerbear would say:

GINGERBEAR:
The Fucker.

FREEATLAST:
How long have you been in for? Married, I mean?

ELLESBELLES:
Well, counting the six months last year that I was gone— 22 years. Of my life.

FREEATLAST:
Yeah, you won't get those back again.

SUZYQ:
You're gonna be okay. If I'm okay, you will to!

LORELEI:
Suzy's right. You come talk to us, love, we'll get you sorted.
Someone's always around to chat at all hours—usually me!
You'll be surprised how much it helps.

ELLESBELLES:
Thank you, Gingerbear, SuzyQ and Lorelei.

FREEATLAST:
Oh, what am I, chopped liver?

ELLESBELLES:
Oh, and Freeatlast! How could I forget THAT username?

FREEATLAST:
That's okay, girl. Second time's the charm! You make your
plan and get the hell away from him!

GINGERBEAR:
The Fucker.

———

**PM TO MAIRZYDOATS FROM ELLESBELLES
4:02 P.M.**

Hi, am I doing this right? —Ellesbelles

Hi, Ellesbelles, there's no right way to do this. There are some
common denominators, the most usual being, I Just Can't Take It
Anymore, but everyone leaves in their own way.—Mairzydoats

No, actually, I meant, am I doing this PM thing right?—Ellesbelles

LOL, yes, sorry, this is fine. So what's making you so miserable in your marriage?—Mairzydoats

Him! LOL (not). He's obsessively controlling. Has to be right. No perspective but his own, and that's revisionist and sometimes impervious to reality. How do you stay married with that?—Ellesbelles

It sounds like you're talking about emotional abuse. That's a big category and it covers a lot of ground, but that fact is, if someone's inhibiting your natural self-expression or your physical movements, or making you feel unsafe, you are being abused.—Mairzydoats

I hate the word abuse. I do not want to be a victim, of abuse or anything else.—Ellesbelles

You left before and you'll leave again. That's not being a victim.—Mairzydoats

Took me 22 years.—Ellesbelles

Yes, well, that's how long it takes sometimes. If he'd been beating the crap out of you, you would have left sooner. The emotional stuff is usually easier to put up with, so women with that issue stay longer.—Mairzydoats

I was so *angry* from all the years of shit. I didn't think ahead, I just *left*. I want to do it better this time. Smarter.—Ellesbelles

You will. Take your time and make your plan. It's good you're in therapy, though. You're both going to be the parents of your daughter for the rest of your lives, you need to find some way to be comfortable with each other.—Mairzydoats

I guess. I sort of wish he'd just . . . disappear. —Ellesbelles

I get it. He won't, though. Well—most likely. —Mairzydoats

———

DIVORCED WOMEN OVER FIFTY CHAT ROOM
SEPTEMBER 3, 2018
2:15 A.M.

LORELEI:
Ellesbelles, my love, you're lurking. I can see your name on the list of who's on. Come out come out and say hello.

ELLESBELLES:
Oops, sorry. I'm here. I've actually snuck—sneaked?—into the guest bathroom so I can get on here without him knowing. I can't sleep. I think I'm anxious.

MOREOFME:
Hi, Ellesbelles, welcome! I saw your posts from earlier today. You should get your doctor to prescribe something for anxiety. I find Ativan is a very nice drug, but a lot of the girls here like Xanax or Valium. Klonopin is excellent for a longer lasting effect. I wouldn't hesitate to recommend Ambien or Lunesta for sleep.

ELLESBELLES:
Wow. Okay. Thanks, Moreofme. Are you a doctor?

MOREOFME:

Oh, gosh, no! I work in a Joanne's Fabric store in Topeka. My husband left me because I gained 75 pounds after our son was born and have been having a hard time taking it off (our son is 32 now). So I'm an expert on anxiety attacks and sleepless nights. Also eating LOL (if you're fat it helps to have a sense of humor!)

LORELEI:

EB, why don't you just pull up a chair and chat with us. You're in NorCal, right? What time is it there?

ELLESBELLES:

It's . . . 2:17 a.m. My mind is buzzing with things I should do, have to do, and don't want to do. Like start the leaving process all over again. It's exhausting.

LORELEI:

It is. You must remain strong and resolved, my love. Never doubt yourself for an instant. You're an intelligent woman, and you have good reason to leave.

ELLESBELLES:

I'm gonna put that on a t-shirt. I'm starting to feel better. Where are you, Lorelei?

LORELEI:

Sweden. It's mid-morning here, I thought I'd check in on my tea break.

ELLESBELLES:

Sweden! Do you live there?

LORELEI:
No, I'm working on a movie.

ELLESBELLES:
Are you an actress?

LORELEI:
Yes.

ELLESBELLES:
Wow. That's cool. Do you have a good part? Is it a good movie? Do I sound like an idiot?

LORELEI:
LOL. No, you don't sound like an idiot, and yes, I have a brilliant part in a good movie. Not easy at my age.

MOREOFME:
Lorelei (Not Her Real Name) is a famous actress, Ellesbelles! We are very proud to have her in our little chat room. I think I know who she is but I respect DWOF's anonymity policy and would never say.

ELLESBELLES:
No way. Really? Wait, am I being gullible here?

LORELEI:
No, it's true. I like DWOF because I can vent all I want and my publicist need never know. In public, of course, you must be oh so very conciliatory and working-it-out and all that rot. Don't ever be conciliatory, Ellesbelles. Stand your ground and don't let the bastard gain an inch. Shit, now I'm crying.

ELLESBELLES:
Oh, Lorelei! I'm so sorry!

MOREOFME:
Lorelei, your makeup will run! Blot your eyes with a wet wipe
and take some Tylenol prophylactically—it'll keep you from
getting a headache (I always get a headache when I cry).

LORELEI:
Ugh, somebody distract me, or I will be an absolute
wretched mess when I'm called. Ellesbelles, tell us about
your particular bastard and how pure sweet love went so
disastrously off the rails. I never tire of the tale.

MOREOFME:
No, tell us how you met. I think it's always better to think
sweet thoughts before you go to sleep, EB. Especially if
you're not taking anything.

ELLESBELLES:
Okay.

ELLESBELLES:
Are either of you Beatles fans?

CHAPTER TWO
I'VE JUST SEEN A FACE

NEW YORK CITY
MARCH 1995

As soon as Jeff walks into Starbucks, he can see the line is long—as usual—but the coffee here is unbelievable, so it's worth it. He's been telling everyone about this place, and he's proud to be a regular, on a first-name basis with the baristas, who know his preferences and will get his venti latte with a shot started as soon as they see him. This is very cool.

He deftly maneuvers himself so that he's behind the girl with the long red hair. He can't see her face, but he's pretty confident it wouldn't disappoint. He likes anything that has a mark of distinction, and he's never been with a red-haired woman before—wait, has he? No, he doesn't think he has.

The Girl with the Long Red Hair is bopping to the music piped over the sound system. It's the Beatles, "She Said, She Said." He can hear her singing, and he feels a jolt of joy. She is word-perfect.

So am I, he thinks.

"She said, 'I know what it's like to be dead.'"

He can hear her singing, but it isn't obnoxiously loud. He joins in on the next line. *"I know what it is to be sad."*

She stills a second in front of him as the short guitar riff whines in. He grins to himself. He starts lustily (he thinks) on the next line.

She joins him and turns around, smiling. His heart does a thing as he takes in brown eyes, the redhead's inevitable freckles and a dimple only on one side (he thinks symmetry is overrated anyway). Not to be crass about it, but she clearly has a great set under her T-shirt—not that that's a deal-breaker, but still.

They hit the next verse in unison.

She belts out the lyrics with feeling. Harrison's guitar chimes like church bells.

They stand facing one another. She fixes her brown eyes on him, at once confident and mischievous and naive.

He thinks she must be younger than him, about thirty, give or take. He gives her his professorial smile—not that he's a professor—the one where he crinkles his blue eyes. He has a modest faith in his blue eyes and his height (he is a gangly six foot), but beyond that he feels appropriately mild mannered about his average looks, ears too big, chin a little weak. Listen, a guy has to compensate, at least until she knows what he does for a living.

"Wow," he says. "You really know your Beatles."

"That was the Beatles?!" she says, wide-eyed, then laughs at his look of horror.

"Yes, I know my Beatles. *Rubber Soul.* Second side, first track."

She is so adorable. Wrong, but adorable.

Don't say anything, he tells himself. Himself doesn't listen.

"Nope," he counters, even though he wishes he'd just shut the hell up. "*Revolver.* First side, last track."

She cocks her head. "Mmm. Don't think so." She turns to the barista. "A large coffee, please, to go. With room for cream."

He feels a wisp of panic as he clocks her order; she obviously doesn't know you don't come to Starbucks just to order a cup of coffee.

"Well," he says, "there's only one way to solve this."

She looks around. "Is there a problem?" To his relief, she seems more amused than pissed off.

"Jeff!" calls the second barista, who'd seen him in line. "Got your venti latte with a shot right here, man!"

"Thanks, Doug!" Jeff is pleased that Little Red-Haired Girl's (golden-brown) eyebrow goes up a bit as she takes in that he's a regular and knows what he's doing here. He grabs his drink and heads over to the condiments table right behind her.

"So, okay, we're both Beatles fans, but you say *Rubber Soul*, and I say *Revolver*. Obviously, we're going to have to head over to Sam Goody's and get this thing straightened out like men."

She laughs.

"Oh, are we?"

"Yeah, but here's the thing." He takes a breath and metaphorically stretches one foot over the precipice. "If you're right, I will admit defeat and be humiliated. But if I'm right—I get to take you out for dinner and a movie. How's that? Is that okay?"

She tilts her head. Caught in the sun, filaments of her hair crinkle electrically. That dimple is driving him crazy.

She's a keeper. He's a goner.

CHAPTER THREE
THINGS WE SAID TODAY

NEW YORK CITY
MAY 1995

When Ellie was young, whenever she went out on a date with a new boy, her mother would say to her, as a joke, "Is he tall? Does he have blue eyes?"

Now, looking into Jeff's pale blue eyes while she cuddles next to him in bed, she feels like she's finally giving Betty her dream son-in-law—well, potentially.

(The fact that he's an investment banker at Morgan Stanley made her father all but levitate with joy. That was satisfying.)

Jeff's breathing quickly settles as he drifts into sleep, but Ellie is awake and thoughtful, staring up at his ceiling fan, making its lazy circles in the warm late spring night. The make-up sex they'd just had was amazing, so she's trying not to think that, after only two months of dating, it's a little early to have had a fight that warrants it.

His opening gambit in Starbucks was funny and charming, and though she was mortified to learn that she was actually wrong about it being *Rubber Soul*, he was gracious about it. It only took a few more dates to make Ellie realize that Jeff is the One.

He ticks all her boxes.

He has a goofball sense of humor, and more importantly, thinks she's hilarious. Ellie is very proud of the way Jeff will stop walking and throw his head back, laughing, when she's whipped off an example of her deadpan wit. He loves showing her off to his friends, a few obnoxious bro-type Masters of the Universe guys but mostly couples, reassuringly nice and apparently devoted to him, who also laugh at her jokes and profess to be very relieved that Jeff has finally found himself a good woman and will settle down appropriately. Jeff is forty-two, twelve years older than Ellie.

Should she be nervous that he's in his forties and not married, not even divorced? Is it a sign that he's troubled? Or has he just been waiting for her, Ellie, his soulmate?

Other boxes he checks:

Reading. He's a big reader, possibly the only guy she'd ever dated who knows that Beth dies in *Little Women*, and is still upset about it. Like her, his tastes are eclectic: a huge fan of David McCullough, Nick Hornby, and Charles Dickens, he howled with delight at her own favorite, Kingsley Amis's *Lucky Jim*. She's looking forward to someday cozily reading in bed with him before they go to sleep, though that's hardly what they're doing in bed these days.

Sex. What they *are* doing in bed these days. She knows not to put too much stock on the staying power of sex, that they're in the halcyon honeymoon period of romantic sexual delirium, when just a random thought of him makes her literally weak in the knees, or more accurately somewhat higher. But it's delicious and addictive, and who is she to deny them both great sex on the remote possibility that the whole thing might not work out?

He likes going shopping. She hadn't been aware this was even a box. She thought it was very cool when, a few days ago, he said he'd help her find a dress for a family wedding. He went, willingly, to Macy's with her, after briefly trying to convince her to go to the more upscale and unaffordable (for her) Bergdorf Goodman.

She'd felt like she was in the *Pretty Woman* shopping montage, with her man waiting outside the dressing room as she came out to show him every new outfit she tried on (she didn't twirl though; she's not a twirler). Unfortunately, when she'd put on the dress he picked out—a wrap dress in a gorgeous shimmery brown gold—she wasn't that crazy about it.

Jeff had thought it looked great on her and had told her she wasn't looking at herself at the right angle, that she wasn't really seeing how the highlights in the dress brought out her eyes, how the wrap made her waist look *tiny*. Delighted by his fervor, Ellie had thought he must be right, and let him buy the dress for her, floating out of the store on the wave of his adoration.

"It's kind of like having a boyfriend who's also a girlfriend," she'd gushed later on the phone to her sister, Wendy, who immediately told her that he was gay. Wendy's gay and always points out people who seem straight but are probably gay. "Nope," Ellie had confidently told her, "This guy ain't gay. He's just highly evolved."

But when she'd tried the dress on again at her apartment that night, her roommate, Liz, said, "Um, no. Color's gorgeous, but you know you can't wear wrap dresses. Your boobs look like missiles." Oh well. Win some, lose some. She took it back to Macy's.

She's probably not going to tell Wendy or Liz about the huge fight she and Jeff had at dinner last night when she told him she'd taken the dress back. She'd been shocked at how angry he was ("Why did you let me buy it, then, if you didn't like it? What was *that* about? What, did *Liz* tell you it didn't look good, and you believed her instead of me?") and how sullen he became when she'd told him, rather firmly, that she appreciated the fact that he bought it for her but that she simply didn't feel comfortable in it ("Fine. I know I have excellent taste, and I gave you a gift I thought would make you happy").

She felt slightly derailed by the lopsided nonlogic of his argument, but he seemed to have cooled off by the time they walked back to his apartment, and she didn't want to escalate things, so she let it go. And, of course, after they'd kissed and made up, and then made up again, all seemed right with the world once more.

Now, as she lies against his warm chest amid the wreckage of his bed (with the one-thousand-thread-count sheets—he really does have excellent taste), she calms herself—what's one fight?

CHAPTER FOUR
YOU CAN'T DO THAT

SEPTEMBER 9, 2018

Ellie's having a lovely Saturday morning.

She's out for breakfast with her best friend, Jane, who picked her up and took her out to their favorite overpriced deli. Ellie had told herself sternly that she was not going to complain about Jeff, and then, of course, she complained about him the whole time. (She's decided not to tell Jane about her first foray onto the "DWOF" forum. She knows Jane is all for support groups, but for some reason Ellie wants to keep DWOF to herself, a secret just for her.)

This week's event in, as Jane calls it, "Jeff's Cavalcade of Shit," was his unilateral decision to take to Goodwill all the stuff Ellie had bought for her own apartment during the six months she'd left him—her boxes of dishes, wineglasses, silverware, dish towels, and linens. "That was my stuff," Ellie says hotly to Jane over their eggs Benedict. "Not his. Not ours. Mine. I loved those dishes and glasses, and I'm going to need them when I move out again, whenever the fuck that will be."

"That schmuckball," Jane declares with a passion that's never faltered, despite the constant litany of Jeff's outrages over the past dozen years of their friendship. Jane was a stalwart support when

Ellie left last year. She'd taken her shopping and waited with her at her little apartment for the beds to be delivered and spent hours on the phone with her to dispel her loneliness and panic.

Jane wants to go right to Goodwill and rebuy all the stuff Jeff had taken over there, and Ellie laughs with delight at the idea. But they both knew she won't. Something inside always prevents her from shoving Jeff's face in his mess and saying, "This is not okay." Was it cowardice? Laziness? She wonders aloud if it maybe it isn't, in fact, some deeply buried wellspring of enduring love. Jane snorts. "More like Stockholm syndrome. Face it, Ellie, it was a bovine move on his part."

Bovine is Ellie and Jane's code word for an irredeemable Jeff gaff. It comes from an incident years ago, before they had met, when Hannah was an infant going through what even the pediatrician called "an epic bout of colic." On this infamous day, a bedraggled, unwashed, catatonic Ellie (who was nevertheless madly in love with her baby) sat nursing a finally quiet Hannah at the dining-room table, her entire body flaccid except for the arm that held the baby. Jeff, to be fair ("Why?" Jane said here when Ellie first told her the story. "Why be fair?"), had been staying up with the baby too, and then had to go to work the next day, so he was also pretty tired. But this was a Saturday, and he'd showered and shaved and was resting comfortably on the couch, when he looked over at his exhausted, nursing, postpartum wife with mild disgust. "You look . . . bovine," he said.

("You should have killed him right then," Jane had interrupted again, "No jury would convict you.")

Ellie very carefully set baby Hannah in her bassinet by their bed and came back into the living room to rip Jeff a new asshole. New-mommy hormones eclipsed rational thought and dignity, and Ellie heard herself screeching in a way that she didn't recognize, though she understood that it came from the deep, dark place where she sucked down all her real feelings every time the charming, devoted Jeff was replaced with his icy, unreasonable doppelgänger. She gave in to the luxury of screaming invectives she'd bottled up during their four-year marriage, after always graciously conceding to whatever self-righteous bullshit point Jeff made.

The relief was short-lived, as, of course, Hannah woke up crying. Jeff threw Ellie a withering look and went off to comfort the baby, leaving Ellie shaking and ashamed of herself.

The memory of the story reverberates silently between them. Then Jane says, "Listen, I know it was bad. But you guys had some good times in between the crap."

Ellie throws her an incredulous "who-are-you-and-what-have-you-done-with-my-friend-Jane" look.

Jane continues, "Ellie, you've got a special circumstance with your vision. If you decide you need to live with Jeff so that you can have someone around to drive you, help around the house, keep you safe, no one's gonna judge you for that. Not even me."

Ellie nods. Jane is outspoken and opinionated, but she's fair. For a second, Ellie envisions a life with Jeff and her steadily diminishing vision, which had, in many ways, made living on her own a lot more difficult than living with him. It seemed appealing for about a split second. Then she circles back to the realization that she's been settling for twenty-two years, and she's over it.

After breakfast, they head over to CVS so Ellie can pick up some new mascara. Jane waits in the car on her phone, ironing out some recent catastrophe with one of her children, while Ellie wanders happily around the store on her own, without someone breathing down her neck to hurry up and finish what she's doing.

Since Ellie stopped driving several years ago, both Jeff and

Hannah have repeatedly told her that they're there for her to run any errand or take her anywhere she'd like to go. And then, of course, when she took them up on it, they'd either put her off, want to do it themselves, or make it clear she had fifteen minutes before their heads would blow up while waiting for her. Ellie remembers sadly the days when she could just drive over to Bed Bath & Beyond to pick out a dish towel, then hang out and look at bedding for forty-five minutes, and then maybe, if she felt like it, go get a cup of goddamn coffee. Without her own transportation, she was always *accountable*, to whoever drove her, dropped her off, or picked her up. It was suffocating.

(In her nostalgia for her driving days, Ellie has forgotten that even then she was accountable to Jeff, whose first question when she came home from anywhere was always, "How come it took you so long?")

But Jane had breezily told her to take her time ("I'm gonna be screaming at this one for a while"), and Ellie feels pleasantly untethered as she chooses a new mascara, picks out some pretty blue nail polish, which she thinks is kind of cool and knows Jeff will hate, and then wanders over to try on some cute sunglasses.

Which is where Jeff finds her.

"Hey!" he says. "Those look good on you! Are you sure they're dark enough?"

The joy drains out of Ellie so fast she's sure it leaves a puddle on the floor.

"What are you doing here?" she says flatly. She yanks off the sunglasses; the tag gets stuck in her hair. Jeff leans over to help her extricate it. She smacks his hand away and pulls it out herself.

"I was in the neighborhood, and I stopped in to get some ChapStick and some of that Dove dark chocolate you like," he says, using the jovial tone he'd taken to using since she'd returned, as if he's trying to cajole an insane person into a better mood. "I had no idea you were here. I just saw you in the aisle. C'mon, I'll take you home."

"Jane is taking me home."

"Why?"

"Because we made plans. She's taking me home."

"Does that make sense? You've already had breakfast, you did your shopping, and anyway, I saw her in the parking lot. She's on the phone looking pretty intense about something. Why do you want to bother her? After all"—he smiles at her, but his point is pointed—"you live with me. It's not like it's inconvenient."

Ellie looks toward the large front window of the store and can indeed see Jane, phone to her ear, gesticulating wildly with her other arm. She sighs. It is the lot of the disabled to be a burden to others.

Ellie pays for her items and tamps down the simmering rage, as is her custom. She goes home with her husband, comforted by the knowledge that she's a short-timer in this marriage anyway.

CHAPTER FIVE
I'LL BE BACK

DIVORCED WOMEN OVER FIFTY CHAT ROOM
SEPTEMBER 13, 2018
11:35 P.M.

GINGERBEAR:
8. On a good day.

FREEATLAST:
I'm gonna say 6. The Catholic Church says 7 is the age of reason—you know, knowing right from wrong—so I'd have to put him below that by at least a year.

ELLESBELLES:
4.

GINGERBEAR:
Jeez, EB! LOL!

ELLESBELLES:
I know. It's like dealing with an unpredictable toddler. Not all the time, but enough of it.

LORELEI:

17. Brilliant fuck, otherwise clueless.

SUZYQ:

Just got on, what THE HECK are yall talking about?

ELLESBELLES:

The emotional ages of our exes. Or future exes.

SUZYQ:

413, because he's a vampire, he never sleeps he sucks my blood and he'll live forever so at least he'll outlive me and I'll have some peace when I'm dead

FREEATLAST:

LOL, Suzy!

SUZYQ:

Is that funny? You know, there's LOL and ROFL, but Momma and I came up with SMKL, which means Slap My Knee Laughing isn't that cute?

GINGERBEAR:

Very southern.

LORELEI:

Suzy, my love, how's your mother doing?

SUZYQ:

Oh she's real sick. She's dying actually, going in inches, she's got lung cancer cause she was a smoker so it's bad but thank you for asking!

ELLESBELLES:
Suzy, I'm so sorry. Is she in hospice?

SUZYQ:
The hospice folks came and went, LOL or maybe I should say SMKL, because she never died so she's home with me bless her heart. I'd say I could kill her but that's REDUNDANT so I won't—FORGET I SAID THAT

FREEATLAST:
It's all right, it's damn hard taking care of a sick parent. Been there, done that.

GINGERBEAR:
At least that asshole Chas is out of your hair.

SUZYQ:
Well Chas has actually been pretty helpful

FREEATLAST:
NO!

GINGERBEAR:
SUZYQ!!! WTF?? Or should I say, WT"SMK"F?

SUZYQ:
What, its ok!! Guys hes been SO HELPFUL he brings groceries and watches Momma so I can go get my nails done or take a hike or whatever

GINGERBEAR:
But this guy, jeez. I remember back when you first got on

here, you said he said something like, "You should use your vagina more than your head," something like that. Only he didn't use the word "vagina."

SuzyQ:
Ew I don't remember THAT

SuzyQ:
Oh, wait, he said, You have more brains in your _____ (I NEVER say THAT word) than your head . . . yeah Chas can be uncuth (sp?)

Lorelei:
I would put my boot in his bum and kick his bum to the curb if anyone ever said that to me.

Lorelei:
So sorry, Suzy, that was rude of me. I'm taking that comment down.

SuzyQ:
Noworries! I did kick him to the curb twice Now he's back maybe third times the charm ha ha!

Freeatlast:
Don't count on it. I took the Male Chauvinist Pig back twice, then married him again, then divorced him again. Then moved out of state.

Ellesbelles:
Wait, does that happen a lot? Women get *divorced* and then go back?

GINGERBEAR:
Like ping pong balls.

ELLESBELLES:
Shit. That makes me nervous. I don't want to ping pong. I feel stupid enough going back once.

LORELEI:
You're under stress with your mother, Suzy. Don't beat yourself up.

SUZYQ:
I don't ever beat myself up, I had my daddy for that. chas never ever hit me either I would not of put up with that for a split second.

LORELEI:
Is there anyone else—a neighbor, an old friend—who can help you so you don't have to rely on him? Even a hated relative might be better than bringing Chas back.

SUZYQ:
I don't know when he's not being an asshole excuse my French he's not so bad. I just ignore the stuff he says most of the time.

ELLESBELLES:
Do you still love him?

SUZYQ:
no

SUZYQ:
but what else can i do

CHAPTER SIX
DON'T LET ME DOWN

SEPTEMBER 15, 2018

Ellie's standing outside the giant Cineplex, waiting while Jeff gets the car from the parking garage. He'd suggested it so she wouldn't have to navigate the dimly lit garage, and, he'd added, he could move faster without her. The reality hits her that waiting outside in the dark late at night in a strangely unpopulated area is possibly not the lesser of the two evils.

She liked the movie—at least, what she could see of it. Why are movies so dark all of a sudden? Why can't they tell the same story in a brightly lit sunshine-y field somewhere? Then maybe she could have seen the whole damn thing instead of trying to follow a story whose visuals were always on whatever part of the screen she *wasn't* looking at, with Jeff "translating" for her the whole time. She cringes, thinking about the last two hours. "Did you see that?" he'd whispered loudly to her every five minutes.

"Yes," she'd said quietly back to him, whether she had any idea if she saw it or not.

"Okay, what was it?" he'd challenge her, irritated by the angry shushes from the people around them.

Ellie feels a little depressed. She realizes that, in all likelihood, she's probably just seen the last movie she will ever see in a movie theater. *The Wife.* Ellie had been chilled to the bone by the movie's dysfunctional family dynamic, which reverberated on her psyche like a plucked string.

She peers around her, barely making out shapes in the darkness outside the lit funnels of the streetlamps. She can dimly make out a bunch of people across the street—a family waiting for the bus or a group of troublemakers eyeing a defenseless blind woman? She startles as a sudden shout and then laughter erupts from the distant group. Amid the shadows, she can make out the red-orange tip of a lit cigarette, going in and out of her field of vision like a firefly.

The street is otherwise empty, as far as she can see. Which isn't that far.

She starts to get anxious. She texts Jeff.

ELLIE

Where are you? It's been ten minutes.

He texts back immediately.

JEFF

Long line to get out. Be patient.

A light somewhere goes off—maybe one of the Cineplex's outside lights? She's not sure, and only knows the darkness is a little darker than before, almost palpable. Sometimes she gets panicky in the darkness, knowing that someday she'll be living her whole life inside it. She strains what's left of her vision, the grimy light that her retinas' receptors can no longer correctly process. *Fuck Jeff,* she thinks, and wonders why she doesn't just get herself an Uber right this goddamn minute. Jane would. What's wrong with her?

———

Jeff watches Ellie as she huddles by the wall of the complex on the street.

He's been there for about twenty minutes, waiting for his irritation to subside. He's not going to take her to the movies again anytime soon, that's for sure. He can't understand why she's so stubborn, and why she won't let him help her, simply by explaining what's happening on the movie screen when she clearly cannot see it herself. Is it pride? Defiance? Some stupid need for independence when she so obviously needs assistance?

Whatever it is, it infuriates him. So now he's sitting in his darkened car, about thirty yards down the street from her, munching on their leftover popcorn as he watches his wife twist in the wind, so to speak. She wants to be independent? *Go ahead, Ellie. Let's see how you do.*

Obviously, he's there in case anything really bad happens. He's not going to put his wife in any danger, for God's sake, but he wants to teach her a lesson. Make her appreciate what she's got in him, her husband, who's always standing by to help. Does she not see that this is love? That he's there for her, would do anything for her? Is it too much to expect a little consideration instead of that attitude she's thrown at him since she came back from that godforsaken apartment?

Another text, an empty Uber threat. He knows she's not going to call an Uber; it's too cumbersome for her in the dark to navigate the app. He calls her.

———

"Listen, I'm out," Ellie's relieved to hear him say, finally. "Turn to your right and go about thirty yards, then around the corner—I'll be there in two minutes!"

He hangs up. She calms down. He's on his way. No harm, no foul. She obediently turns to her right and walks to the corner, swearing briefly as her cane snags for a second in a sidewalk grate. She takes the corner and continues on, cane wagging before her till it connects brusquely with a small bus stop bench, which she carefully walks around. She goes for what she thinks is about thirty yards—she has no idea—and stops to wait.

Another five minutes. I hate my life, she thinks, where going to the movies and getting home again in one piece is one long, drawn-out, never-fucking-ending episode after another of humiliation and inconvenience. She wonders if other people experience life this way, or if it's merely the province of the disabled.

Jeff calls. She hates him too.

"Where are you?" he starts in.

Wearily, she responds, "Where you told me to wait. Walked to my right, around the corner, thirty yards down. There's a bus bench—"

"No, Ellie," he responds, exaggeratedly patient, as if to a child (*Oh, add infantilization to the list of humiliations, why dontcha?* she thinks). "I said turn left. Not right, left."

She can't even. She taps her way back to the bus stop bench and sits.

"Look," he goes on quickly, like he doesn't want to argue, "I can figure out where you are. Just stay there, and I'll come get you. Okay? Just stay where you are."

"Yeah, okay, I will," she manages to croak out. She feels her throat fill, doesn't want to cry.

She waits on the bench, for Jeff or death—she doesn't much

care which. In a few minutes, she hears footsteps. Oh shit. Some survival instinct gets her to her feet, her cane before her, a slender bastion of aluminum between herself and assault.

The steps grow nearer. She walks away from them, briskly but not, she thinks, revealing panic.

"Hey!" she hears, an instant terror in her heart before she realizes she knows the voice.

"Ellie!" Jeff yells, and she turns back to meet him, still a hazy figure in the darkness.

"Good to see you," she yells back wryly.

They walk toward each other.

"Car's around the corner," he says as they near each other. "It's a one-way street here; I couldn't drive down it." He looks at her. "You okay? You look a little . . . feeble."

Feeble. Thanks, Jeff, you old fuckwad. Now she wants to cry, and to hit him. She has a nanosecond vision in which she's a crabby old Dickensian lady who swats people with her cane regularly without recrimination. She hopes that's in her future.

"I'm fine. Let's go home," she says.

"You want to stop for frozen yogurt?" he asks brightly.

"*No*. I just want to go home!"

"Jeez. No need to be crabby."

She doesn't say another word and pretends to fall asleep in the car on the way home, even when Jeff stops for frozen yogurt.

CHAPTER SEVEN
A DAY IN THE LIFE

Her daughter's warm, slightly sticky hand in hers, Ellie carefully navigates the uneven pavement of Eighty-Third Street. Even at age three, Hannah knows that Mommy can't see things above, below, and to the side, so she's adept at yelling, "Mommy! Door!" though she's not entirely reliable and can't tell left from right. Ellie frequently has to spin her head wildly to figure out where the obstacle is, by which time she's either already hit it, or it's long gone. Jeff would rather Hannah not know about her mother's "affliction," as he calls it in a grim attempt at humor, and Ellie would rather not be afflicted, but it is what it is. Ellie doesn't ever want to be a burden to her little girl, but she loves that Hannah looks out for her mommy, just as Ellie looks out for her.

It's a perfectly blue-skied September morning, so beautiful on the Upper West Side that Ellie can barely imagine the dark hell that is unfolding seven miles downtown. On a bright day like this, the retinitis pigmentosa doesn't bother her too much, and her field of vision seems like that of a normally sighted person, wide open and unbounded.

She had raced to get Hannah at her Montessori preschool

for an early dismissal after the Twin Towers were hit, and she's not sure how much Hannah knows. Ellie's not exactly sure what she knows either, other than that Jeff had started to walk down from his Morgan Stanley office on the seventy-fourth floor of the South Tower, and then had been told he could go back to work.

Did he?

She'd managed to get through to him on his cell, but after only a few seconds of Jeff's terrified bravado they were cut off amid sounds of static and chaos. She's been having a little trouble regulating her breathing ever since, but she doesn't want to transmit her panic to Hannah.

In their building lobby, they bump into their neighbor Carly, a bubbly actress and waitress who sometimes babysits for Hannah. She and Hannah do their secret handshake, but not before Carly sends a worried glance at Ellie, who can only shrug slightly in response.

She doesn't want to turn on the TV in front of Hannah, who quietly colors her *Little Mermaid* paper dolls in her room, but a little after ten, Ellie's sister, Wendy, calls from Boston to say that the South Tower has collapsed. There is no word from Jeff. All calls to his cell go to voice mail. Ellie feels her heart squeeze inside her chest like a blood-pressure cuff. *Please, God*, she thinks, *not a heart attack. If I'm Hannah's only surviving parent, I have to stay alive.*

Wendy's call is the first of many, the news relentless, terrible, incomprehensible, the callers full of fear and empty reassurances. She tells Hannah what she hopes is a child-friendly version of what's happening: "Some bad men tried to hurt some people in Daddy's building, but so far we think he's okay."

"I don't want to not have a daddy," Hannah says, and Ellie aches for her daughter.

Despite the intermittent blood-pressure cuff around her

heart, despite the breath that speeds and slows as the helpless waiting works into her body, Ellie manages to move purposefully and calmly about the condo, setting, she thinks, a good model for Hannah of Grace under Pressure. If the worst should happen, she feels comforted knowing that there are tried-and-true behaviors one can always fall back on, keeping a lid on grief or hysteria or whatever. They even had titles. She'd already finessed Glowing Bride, Contented Wife, and Ecstatic Mother, and if she had to, she'd damn well knock Grieving Widow out of the park.

The morning wears on, a pall inside the condo as the normally ebullient Hannah is subdued and clingy. She snuggles on Ellie's lap in a tight ball, and Ellie wonders if this is the first day of the rest of their lives, if it will be just the two of them from now on. She rests her chin on Hannah's red head (almost the same shade as her own), and the part of her heart that isn't numb grieves for those in harm's way and the people who genuinely love them.

Ellie and Hannah have just finished tuna sandwiches, carrot sticks, and Pringles when Jeff walks in, shaky, covered in gray dust, scraped up the side of his face where he'd skimmed the pavement after the implosion sent him flying along Liberty Street. Dazed and bleeding slightly, he'd walked all the way uptown.

Hannah flings herself into her daddy's arms.

Ellie falls to her knees, weeping.

The bastard is still alive.

CHAPTER EIGHT
ANY TIME AT ALL

SEPTEMBER 16, 2018

Jeff settles back in the chair in his home office. Ellie's asleep in the bedroom upstairs. At least, she better be. He doesn't know what the hell she was doing in the guest bathroom at midnight the other night, but he was damn sure he'd figure it out eventually.

He activates the Find My Phone app on his iPhone, which he'd set it up when Hannah went off to college so that he could track her without her knowing it. He'd made the same arrangement on Ellie's phone, though, of course, he'd done that when she'd still been the Good Wife and vision impaired to boot, so he'd never thought to use it—she was either home or at the office, maybe out with a girlfriend for coffee or a mani-pedi. He had to hand it to himself though—it sure came in handy when she lost her mind and left him last winter. She wouldn't tell him where she'd moved at first? Fine! It took him less than a minute to figure out exactly where she was—that crappy apartment building in Campbell.

And he was able to swoop in on her at CVS the other morning so she wouldn't wind up spending the whole day with Jane, whom he considers a bad influence.

Jane. He knows she's the reason Ellie left, the secret traitorous buzz in Ellie's ear that made her suddenly think it was okay to leave twenty-two years of a good, solid marriage. He remembers that surreal moment she stood in the little hallway by the front door, looking up at him, a huge bag slung over her arm, and told him she was leaving. And then she walked out.

He catches his breath as the memory of that pain hits him. He'd never told her how sick he had been, how he'd cried and couldn't eat for days, how he had called Hannah several times a day just so he could reassure himself that he hadn't lost his entire family. How humiliating it was, how depressing to consider himself a failure in this one simple staple of a happy life. Yes, he knew 50 percent of all marriages ended in divorce, but he refused to be a statistic—at least, not a negative one. And although he never let her know his anguish—why give her an advantage over him?—he was so relieved when she finally came back, so thankful that he didn't have to join the rank and file of divorced, lonely, pathetic old men. That was not how he saw himself.

He would not go through that again.

Just before she "left," some instinct prompted him to further modify the whole iPhone thing by setting her screen to stay unlocked for up to four hours, so he had ample time to hop on her phone and check out her calls.

Which is how he knew she'd been lying to him for a while, because he'd looked up a few of the strange numbers he found on her cell phone. One was to a therapist—no surprise there. Ellie was always on him to go to therapy, so periodically she called a few of them around town. He never made a stink about it, since he was very clear that he was not now, nor was he ever, going to see a shrink. If he hadn't done it after 9/11, why the hell would he do it now?

She had come to her senses and returned, thank God, but

frankly, he knew all along she would. Ellie is a fine person and a good wife, but she's weak and hates confrontation (he could never understand her success as a sales rep for TriState since she lacks, at least at home, the killer instinct that's essential for sales). And let's face it: she can't drive herself anywhere, can't go shopping, can't fend for herself—she obviously shouldn't be independent. Jeff thinks of her waiting outside the movie theater the other night, alone and in the dark; she'd looked addled. The fact is, Jeff muses, she should be *more* dependent, on him and Hannah, the older and blinder she got.

Jeff is irritated that Ellie has been depressed since she came back home, and no amount of dark chocolate or jollying her out of it seems to work. He finds depression in anyone but himself self-indulgent. He has alternated between leaving her alone and doing what he thinks is some pretty good cheerleading, which, annoyingly, annoys her. She seemed to perk up toward the end of the summer, a few weeks before Hannah went back to school, but she also had a kind of brusque efficiency that wasn't like her. None of this boded well for his marriage, and he realized he'd have to make good on his promise to go to couples therapy, so he wouldn't have to live with Debbie Downer for the rest of his life.

He can feel his blood pressure rise just from thinking about her past transgressions. He takes a few calming breaths, until his fury abates. There's no point in dredging all that up again, especially since he knows that it *is* all going to be dredged up *in therapy.* He'd stalled as long as he could—she's been back for over five months—but after rejecting all her choices, he finally picked some guy in Saratoga who didn't sound like a total moron, and now he's grimly anticipating their first appointment.

His iPhone glows with the map of Boston, the little icon of Hannah's precious face right where it should be—in her dorm room, either asleep or studying. He checks the history, an advanced function he was glad he enabled, and tracks where she's been around town: that ice cream place she's been going to a lot lately (he hopes she's not gaining weight); then hours in the theater (he's so proud of her, a theater major, now with a lead in the university's musical); and some place that pops up as the Friendly Toast. He cross-checks it on Google Maps; it's a brunch spot. He maps the route Hannah would have taken from her dorm to the restaurant. It looks safe enough, and anyway Boston on a weekend morning is mobbed with kids. He shuts the app down; he doesn't have to worry about Hannah.

He checks his emails, then types in Ellie's Gmail address. He doesn't think of email as real mail; he figures if it's hackable, anyone can see it. Of course, he opens everyone's snail mail if he thinks it's something to do with business, money, or technology, but he'd never open anything that looked personal. He doesn't even open their birthday cards. And he wouldn't mind if Ellie opened *his* mail; he has nothing to hide.

But apparently, she does, because she's changed her password since the last time he logged on to her account.

CHAPTER NINE
YOU WON'T SEE ME

DIVORCED WOMEN OVER FIFTY CHAT ROOM
SEPTEMBER 18, 2018
8:16 P.M.

LORY:
Hi. New here.

ELLESBELLES:
Hi, Lory. Welcome!

MAIRZYDOATS (DWOF MODERATOR):
Are you safe? Are you or your children in any danger?

LORY:
No, I'm all right, thank you. Not really sure what happens here.

MAIRZYDOATS (DWOF MODERATOR):
This is where women 50+ who are facing divorce—or who are separated or already divorced—can come to talk about their particular issues, find support, vent their anger, discover solutions and become part of a community.

SuzyQ:
Hey Lory you will like it here, these women are the BEST!

Lorelei:
Greetings, Lory. Do you feel like telling us a bit of your story?

Lorelei:
No pressure.

Lory:
Thanks.

Lory:
So, everyone here is divorced?

Ellesbelles:
I'm not divorced. Yet. Still trying to get up the courage/
money. I'm pretty new here myself. This is a great place to
find women who know just what you're going through.

SuzyQ:
I'm common law divorced like common law marriage SMKL!
I haven't lived with chas for three years but not divorced so I
guess just seperated

Lorelei:
 . . . and I suppose I should confess I'm not divorced either,
actually, just in the middle—or please God, maybe near the
end—of the world's longest running soap opera.

Mairzydoats (DWOF Moderator):
Do you have children, Lory?

LORY:
A son. He's in college. My husband left me.

GINGERBEAR:
The Fucker.

ELLESBELLES:
Lory, I have a child in college also. People often wait till the kids are out of the house to start this process. I know that was my thought.

MAIRZYDOATS (DWOF MODERATOR):
Lory, you can PM me (that's a Private Message, like an email or IM) if you have any questions or concerns you don't want to air on the forum. I'm a divorced former divorce attorney and a family therapist—have been through the wars and came out relatively unscarred.

LORY:
I just don't understand why he would leave. Sure, we had our issues, but I thought things were going along pretty good. Especially with our son in college. It was just us. I feel stunned, like I've been hit over the head with a brick.

ELLESBELLES:
Are you and your husband in therapy?

LORY:
Do you really think that would help?

ELLESBELLES:
I think if you get a good therapist, it can help to sort of clear the air. Maybe you'll learn why he left.

FREEATLAST:
A therapist is like a referee. I think all marriages should have three people—two spouses and an onsite referee for all those damned stalemates.

GINGERBEAR:
Yeah, only if the referee/therapist agrees with you, though, right?

FREEATLAST:
Goes without saying. I'm not interested in being fair, I'm interested in being right. Or at least, vindicated.

LORELEI:
I'd take some of that. As far as my children are concerned, anyway.

LORY:
I would like to tell my part of the story. I'm afraid he's been telling all our friends terrible things about me, things that aren't true.

LORELEI:
A familiar tale, my love! My bastard—I'm sorry, did I say bastard? I meant to say my scum-sucking lying sonofabitch soon-to-be-ex bastard—has completely turned my children against me. Because I was always off working. I admit, I work a lot, thank God, and yes, I was gone a lot, but . . . they are my children. They shouldn't hate me.

ELLESBELLES:
Oh, Lorelei. I am so sorry, how awful.

LORELEI:
Sorry, I don't usually go on like that. It's my son's birthday today. He's thirty. I sent him a beautiful suede jacket and a card—one of my more coherent ones, I'm proud to say, rather than my usual blithering about how much I love him and his sisters and miss them every single minute of every day—but there was no response.

SUZYQ:
That is so wrong

LORELEI:
I kept hoping that once they were adults they'd perhaps give me another chance. But they can't be compelled to spend time with me now, and he seems to have upped the vitriol against me. And it's hard to argue with a doting father (*in* his dotage, I profoundly hope, the man is eighty-two) who has limitless cash, a seventy-foot yacht and vacation houses in Malibu and Lake Como. So they remain gone. The rest is silence.

SUZYQ:
Well Lorelei my momma says where there's life there's hope so hopefully your life will be long and your babies will come back to you. I will pray they do

LORELEI:
Thank you.

LORY:
I don't think he would turn my son against me.

MAIRZYDOATS (DWOF MODERATOR):
It can get unexpectedly nasty, Lory. I know you might be too
stunned right now to think, but if you're still in contact with
your husband you might want to think about therapy, as
Ellesbelles suggested. And perhaps a lawyer.

LORY:
You all sound so mad at your husbands. I love mine. I don't
want to be divorced.

FREEATLAST:
Would you take him back?

LORY:
In a heartbeat.

MAIRZYDOATS (DWOF MODERATOR):
Then go to therapy if he'll agree. Express your love and see if
you can work things out. There have been many women on
this board who wind up going back to their husbands, and
have a whole new chapter of their marriage.

SUZYQ:
I say go for it Lory!!! Whoo-hoo! We are all behind you here,
go Get your man back !!!!!

GINGERBEAR:
And then beat the shit out of him.

GINGERBEAR:
Just kidding.

FREEATLAST:

No you're not.

LORY:

Boy, you gals are tough!

CHAPTER TEN
DR. ROBERT

SEPTEMBER 25, 2018

Jeff makes no secret of the fact that he's not happy about going to therapy, and Ellie sits with grim determination in the passenger seat, praying that Joseph—Jeff's choice, not hers—won't be a total asshole.

She tries not to think about the thing with Hannah last summer—"the thing," God, she can't even articulate it—nervous that she might somehow be tripped up into revealing this secret in the heat of some truth-telling therapeutic moment. Ellie's a good compartmentalizer and hopes that will serve her now.

Joseph begins by asking Ellie to tell Jeff why she left him last year—if there's anything specific she'd like to say to him. She's loaded for bear, having had considerable time to hone her bullet points (like twenty-two years).

"For starters, stay the fuck off my cell phone."

Joseph's eyes widen, as if he's not quite sure what he's hearing, and Jeff blows out air through his pursed lips, as he realizes the gloves are coming off.

She goes on: "I know you set up the screen to stay unlocked for a while so you can get on and see my calls. That ends now."

Ellie sees she's made an impression and continues with her list, punctuated by Jeff's increasingly feeble defenses.

"Don't follow me in the car when I go out for my walk in the morning."

"I only did that once," he replies.

"No, you do it a lot."

"That's because I'm out anyway getting coffee"—he tries for a joke here—"think of it as your security detail!"

"Don't stand behind me when I'm on my computer."

"I don't do that."

"Yes, you do! And you do it when I cook and clean up and make the bed without those fucking hospital corners that nobody in the world cares about except you."

"Okay, I'm sorry. It just drives me crazy when—"

At this point Joseph weighs in. "Jeff. Let Ellie speak. You'll get your turn."

Ellie immediately falls a little bit in love with her therapist.

She enjoys the pleasure of being able to speak out to a reasonable human being after two decades of Jeff. She could tell Joseph *got* Jeff right away, noticing the way he wouldn't let her finish a thought before jumping in with corrections and explanations and defenses. She luxuriates in the sensation of being understood, of having someone finally nail Jeff on his bullshit. She can see why people get addicted to therapy; it's like slipping into a nice hot bath after a lifetime of cold showers.

"All right. Thank you, Ellie," says Joseph, nodding to her. She nods back, the good student with the right answer, like she used to be until her marriage. "Now, Jeff, you tell us in your own words what Ellie said, and then you'll get your turn to speak your piece."

"Well," Jeff starts, "she's angry. I can see that. I don't

understand a lot of what she said, because I don't see it that way, and I really think she's overreacting—"

"Jeff," Joseph says patiently, "we'll get to your feelings in a minute. For now, just tell us what Ellie said. This is the exercise. It's a measure of how well you listen to each other."

Ellie feels bad for a second. She knows she doesn't listen very well to Jeff. She started blocking him out about seven or eight years ago.

"Okay"—Jeff takes a breath—"she says she thinks I try to, I don't know, oversee what she's doing. And can I just say, why the hell shouldn't I? We're a couple. We do things for each other. I mean, look at her. She's *blind*—"

"Okay." Joseph is a touch less patient. "Ellie listed specific incidents in which she felt you exerted a control over her that she didn't appreciate. Can you name any of them?"

Jeff grapples with some internal conversation, then offers, "Don't stand behind her when she's on her computer. Don't follow her in the car when she walks. Don't tell her how to do things at home."

Joseph nods, opens his mouth; Jeff beats him to it.

"Seriously? Two decades of marriage come down to not telling her how I like to do something in my own house? We are a *team*! Suppose I wanted to go buy a car without her input. Would that be okay?"

Ellie has to interrupt here herself. "You bought Hannah's car without telling me anything about it"—she rushes to get this in because her blood is starting to boil—"and I'm not *blind*. I'm vision impaired."

Jeff opens his mouth, clearly about to protest that Ellie interrupted him.

Ellie can see Joseph calculating that this tumor is going to be more difficult to extract than he thought. She feels a pang of pure hatred for Jeff, wants to hurt him, snap a finger till it breaks, stick a pencil in his ear, then feels bad: Can her own mental pain really be relieved by physical violence? That's not who she is. Is it?

As Joseph ushers them to the door at the end of the session, Jeff turns back for one final salvo.

"We have a good marriage here, and I'm not planning on ending it anytime soon. I'm a good man. I'm a good husband"—he looks pointedly at Ellie, then at Joseph, almost accusingly—"and a good father. And I know that for a fact."

Ellie throws Joseph an apologetic look as she follows her husband out, her brain now seared with a memory of Jeff, the Good Father.

CHAPTER ELEVEN
MEAN MISTER MUSTARD

"In her room," Jeff says, grinning. "I had to do some parenting with a capital *P*."

Ellie had just walked in from work, surprised that Hannah hadn't run to greet her at the door to the apartment like usual.

Ellie's tired but getting used to working full-time. Jeff hasn't worked since 9/11, which is understandable since he still had what they were calling survivors' PTSD.

Jeff had told Ellie that first night the harrowing story of how he scrambled down seventy-four floors and was expelled onto the street just as the South Tower collapsed, his body skimming and scraping along the concrete, somehow just ahead of the ultimate catastrophe. She was horrified and in awe of the terror that he and so many, many others had endured that day.

And horribly guilty about her disappointment that he came home alive that terrible day. What had she been thinking? (Well, she knew what she'd been thinking. It was not nice.) She had been ashamed of herself and vowed she'd be a better wife to the man who'd come home to her, when so many had not.

And at first Ellie had smiled with the requisite pride and

relief as Jeff told their friends and family his story, masking her discomfort every time the story got a little longer, with the fictitious addition of Jeff's going back up to help save his crew, and the firefighter who wouldn't let him go, who told him to go back to his family and tell the story of what it was like in the Towers. People hung on his every word, and she could see the attention puffed him up, that he basked in the light of their hero worship.

As time went on, she felt terrible about the rising bile, the tension in her neck every time he told the story to yet another stranger, the endless cabbies, the ticket takers, the delivery guys, and the painters who came to paint their living room. The way he went up to every firefighter in Manhattan—still does even now, two years later—to personally thank them for saving his life that day so that he could go home to his wife and family. (She figured he thought she'd appreciate making Hannah and herself a part of the Greatest Thing That Ever Happened to Me.) Ellie knew she had to tread carefully with this new Jeff, the Jeff Smalls Who Was Now Part of History. He'd always been big on self-aggrandizement—or, as she put it privately to herself, bragging—whether it was about his brilliant investment acumen or how he'd expertly taught a friend a better way to hold a tennis racket; it was something she found increasingly obnoxious as the years went by. But now Jeff's self-importance had some legitimacy because 9/11 ran deep with New Yorkers, and rightfully so. But if you asked her, she'd rather he stopped talking about it and go out and get a job.

Jeff's savings from his hedge fund days flew by in a heartbeat. The workman's comp settlement he got from Morgan Stanley would hold them for a considerable amount of time, but only if she brought in a salary as well. Jeff was also working on trying to get one of the really big payouts that went to the families of those who had perished. He'd been told repeatedly that it was impossible, that he'd gotten all that he was ever going to get, but Jeff was a firm believer in getting what he felt was owed to him.

Not that Ellie minded working; she liked the gang over at the TriState Auto Insurance Company, who were friendly and kind and had, rather to her surprise, some very funny auto insurance stories. She'd been promoted from secretary to sales rep and quickly signed up new clients, who paid on time with checks that didn't bounce and, on the whole, didn't seem to be terribly accident-prone. She found she liked spending the day with adults after years of the baby/toddler routine, and she and her sales manager, Jane Warren, a working mom herself, became fast friends. Ellie enjoyed talking to her clients and was genuinely interested in their needs, whether for a new policy for a teenage driver or a reassuring voice after a fender bender. She had a good client renewal rate and was successful and respected.

But she missed the day-to-day free-for-all with Hannah, and she was a little jealous of Jeff getting to be the stay-at-home parent. She knew he was good at it; he adored Hannah and was very serious about his "parenting." But it made her a little sad and, okay, resentful that when she came home from work at six thirty the two of them had had a whole day together, which, let's face it, was a significant portion of Hannah's life. Hannah was always bubbling with stories, eager to debrief the minute Ellie walked through the door, Jeff proudly nodding in agreement as he and Hannah laughed over that silly parrot in the bakery or the mix-up with Hannah's cubby at school, like it was a private joke that Ellie couldn't get.

Tonight Ellie is amused when Jeff tells her that he had to get tough with five-year-old Hannah for refusing to wear her sweatshirt outside. Ellie's guard is down because Jeff's laughing as he tells her the story, and she falls into the comfort of their familiar banter.

Jeff says, "I gave her a choice, you know, like you're supposed to: she could wear the *Lilo & Stitch* hoodie or the *Nemo* hoodie."

"That's parenting," Ellie says approvingly.

"That's parenting," he agrees. "So then she throws both sweatshirts in my face and makes an end run for the door. I run after her and slam my hand on the door, and then I say, in my best Father Knows Best Voice, 'Young lady, there's going to be consequences!'"

Ellie starts laughing.

"I know. It just came out. I sound like a real dad, right?"

"Well, you are a real dad. You're a real good dad."

"Yes, I am."

"So, what were the consequences?"

Jeff smiles. "Well, I made her pick up all her toys that were thrown around in her room and put them in the toy box. But I timed her."

"You *timed* her?"

"Yeah. If she didn't get 'em all in within fifteen seconds, I made her take them all out and do it all again. Only the next time, I only gave her fourteen seconds. And the next time, twelve seconds. So she could never really finish the job. She's a trooper though—she kept at it!"

Ellie feels the sands shift. "Why would you keep giving her less time to do the same job?"

"It keeps her off-balance. Also made her tired—she took a great nap."

"Why would you want to keep your five-year-old off-balance?"

Ellie feels her rage absorb her rational ability to argue.

Jeff isn't smiling. "Ellie, you have to back me up on this. We can't have two parents disagreeing on punishment. That's counterproductive."

"She's five years old! How would you feel if someone gave you a job to do and then kept calling time on you every time you got close to finishing? Don't you get how unfair that is?"

"Well, if that's the system, that's the system. This is my system. You're not here during the day; I'm the one doing the parenting. You just said I was a real good dad."

Ellie marches off to Hannah's bedroom and finds her daughter on her bed holding *American Idol* tryouts for her Cinderella doll, with three stuffed animals as the panel of judges. Hannah looks up happily as Ellie comes to the door.

"Mommy, Mommy, Mommy, you're home!"

Could there ever be, in this world or the next, anything as fabulous as an exultant five-year-old greeting you at the door with an excess of mommy love?

Ellie feels her feathers deruffle as she wraps up Hannah, who certainly doesn't seem the worse for wear for her "consequences."

"Cinderella just got sent through to the next round! She's crying, she's so happy!"

"That's fantastic. What did she sing?"

Hannah gets very serious. "She sang 'My Heart Will Go On' by Celine, and Simon said she was *superb*."

"Tell Cinderella I'm really happy for her!"

"I will! Mommy, we counted up to one hundred today in school, but I *already knew that*, and so did Alex and Jessica, so we were invited to help our classmates who were learning it for the first time. They did great!"

"Well, you're a good teacher! You taught me how to use the TV remote, remember?"

"Yes, I'm going to be a teacher when I grow up. And a singer. Or maybe a fireman. Can I be a firegirl, or is it only for boys?"

Ellie considers this. "I think anything a boy can do a girl can do. Maybe you could be a fireperson?"

Hannah giggles and whispers, "That sounds like I have magic fire powers though. Maybe that's not good."

Ellie giggles also, agreeing with her. Then gets down to business. "Listen, Hannah—Daddy says you had"—Ellie pauses; she doesn't like the word *punishment*—"to accept some consequences for not doing what he told you to do."

"I know! Daddy said it was like the Family Olympics! I had to put all my toys and stuff back in the box, and I had to run around and run around, and if I didn't do it in time, I had to do it all over again!"

Grinning, Hannah falls back on the bed dramatically. Ellie is relieved, feeling she just made a psychological mountain out of a molehill. Then Hannah lowers her eyes and says, "It was fun at first, but then it was stupid, and then I got tired, and he wouldn't let me stop and told me to stop whining."

Ellie holds her breath as Hannah whispers, "And for a second, I hated Daddy." The dagger goes into Ellie's heart until Hannah resumes, cheerfully: "But—he's my daddy, so I don't hate him anymore."

Ellie can't move, envisioning with painful clarity the long road of Hannah's relationship with her father as it scrolls out before her.

"Hey, what have you two gals been doing in here? Dinner's almost ready. There's garlic bread!"

Jeff's in the doorway, smiling.

Hannah immediately bops up, singing, "My garlic bread will go on and on!" and runs off to wash her hands.

Jeff taps Ellie on her arm. "C'mon, I made the pesto sauce you like."

Ellie waits a split second before thinking, *She's fine. She will be fine.* She puts on a smile and goes off to cheerfully join her family for dinner.

CHAPTER TWELVE
BABY, YOU CAN DRIVE MY CAR

PM TO MAIRZYDOATS FROM ELLESBELLES
OCTOBER 3, 2018
8:35 P.M.

So we're in therapy.—**ELLESBELLES**

That's good.—**MAIRZYDOATS**

Do you like your therapist?—**MAIRZYDOATS**

I do. I think he can tell that my husband's the problem
here, and I can see that Joseph, he's the therapist, is getting
frustrated. But he's also very patient and fair with him, and I
just hate that. I wish he'd just rake him over the coals on my
behalf.—**ELLESBELLES**

It takes two to make a marriage, EB. Even a bad one.
—**MAIRZYDOATS**

I know, I know, but I'm just not in the goddamned mood
to accept any blame for this fiasco. What was I thinking?

I saw every signal from jump, and I just thought—oh, he's
just eccentric, oh, it'll be better when we're married, oh,
I'll be able to jolly him out of it when he sees how loving,
reasonable, and fun I am. Oh, it won't matter that I don't drive
and I am becoming marginalized in my own home without my
even seeing it. Oh, I was such an idiot.—**ELLESBELLES**

I'm angry.—**ELLESBELLES**

I can see that.—**MAIRZYDOATS**

I was so depressed when I came back, I thought, fuck this, I'll
just be a Stepford wife for the rest of my life, how hard could
that be?—**ELLESBELLES**

And how'd that work out for you?—**MAIRZYDOATS**

Let me tell you something, it's HARD being a Stepford Wife!
Three days of that "Oh, honey, you're so wonderful" shit, and
I was ready to kill somebody. Believe me, I have new respect
for those Stepford Wives!—**ELLESBELLES**

LOL. I know. I tried being a SW for about ten minutes. Then
I cracked and threw a phone at his head. But it's good to be
angry. It will galvanize you.—**MAIRZYDOATS**

You know . . . I think it has.—**ELLESBELLES**

My therapist (yes, I still have one) says, Suffering leads to
Change which leads to Action. Or maybe it's Action leads to
Change, I never remember. But I think you're on your way to
getting the life you want. And deserve.—**MAIRZYDOATS**

I hope so.—**ELLESBELLES**

My real name is Ellie.—**ELLESBELLES**

Nice to meet you, Ellie. I'm Marilyn.—**MAIRZYDOATS**

Hi, Marilyn.—**ELLESBELLES**

When did you stop driving, if you don't mind my asking?
—**MAIRZYDOATS**

———

Ellie stops typing and leans back against her headboard in bed, the laptop balanced on her knees (Jeff is out grocery shopping). She doesn't mind Marilyn asking, but it's a large question that she tries not to think about too much because it's just . . . too much.

Retinitis pigmentosa is a hereditary degenerative retinal disease, but Ellie is the only member of her family to have won this particular lottery. It's not fatal, and it doesn't hurt, as Jeff likes to point out, but when you only have a fifteen-degree field of central vision—most normally sighted people have about sixty—and can see nothing above, below, or to the side, you are in fact vision impaired and shouldn't drive or operate heavy machinery.

Ellie sees the world in sections, a tantalizing snippet at a time, from which she has to construct a concept of the whole. If she's going downstairs, she can see the step she's on and the one before and after; beyond that, she must suppose, there be dragons. She's very careful going into an unfamiliar home or building since walls and doors and furniture lurch into her path unexpectedly, and if she's looking into your eyes, she has no idea what your mouth is doing, though, bizarrely, she may be able to get a vague sense of the color of your shirt.

Even in her own home, her thighs and shins are constantly bruised from unseen (to her) open drawers and invisible (to her) bedposts and sofa arms. It's a joke, but no joke that in her kitchen, if someone opens the dishwasher, he or she has to announce, "The dishwasher is open!" or she'll fall right over it. She will stand for seconds a few feet away from the bathroom door in the hallway, not quite sure if it's to her left or her right, since the blank wall she's staring at stretches as far as her eye can see, and she must turn her head—left, right, left—to finally catch the elusive doorframe. There are times when the handle to the front door escapes her completely. Times when she can't tell if there's another person in the room with her, or if she's alone.

Everything is better in bright daylight, and she can seem fully sighted, for the most part. She has all sorts of tricks for making it appear as though she's like everyone else. She knows to look for the credit card handed back to her after paying for groceries; she can follow the line of a person's arm when she's first introduced, and a handshake is inevitable.

But at night the lights go out, and she relies on her cane or the guiding arm of someone who doesn't mind, or who minds but does it anyway.

She likes using her cane; it makes her feel secure and graceful and fast. People see it and get out of her way. Without it, she moves like an old person afraid of breaking a hip, since she's had enough experience slamming her head into a low-lying tree branch or pitching forward on an uneven sidewalk to make her shuffle along like—well, a blind person, expecting the worst with every step.

Hannah doesn't like her mother using her cane. She thinks it's an acknowledgment of defeat, that Ellie should rage, rage against the dying of the light and try to move through the world unaided till the last possible moment. She has trouble with the fact that Ellie uses her cane but doesn't always look blind, since she still has some remnants of vision. Hannah worries that people will think she's faking it.

"It's true," Ellie says to her. "Many people fake blindness because it opens so many doors in life." What she really means is, "You think this is easy? I'm a wreck!" But she'd never say that to her daughter.

Ellie stopped driving when Hannah was twelve. Jeff had been telling her for years to stop, ever since they moved to California, fearing that she was putting Hannah in danger. Ellie never felt her driving was a threat to Hannah. For some reason, driving was easier for her than walking down a crowded street; she may not have been able to see the person sitting next to her, but beyond the windshield, her parameters seemed to broaden, and the world stretched reassuringly out before her. But then she began narrowly missing people in crosswalks on left turns and nearly sideswiping cars while changing lanes. "Almost doesn't count!" her mother would cheerily say when she was a (fully sighted) kid and had a close call of some sort, but "almost" was beginning to fray her nerves, and she knew she couldn't live with herself if she ever hit a person with her car.

She can't remember the trigger that made her give up the keys to her Camry; it may have been the time she missed by inches a mother with her stroller in a crosswalk, which was bad enough without the self-righteous prick coming from the other direction, who loudly thought she (and everyone within a two-block radius) should know what she'd nearly done through her stupidity and carelessness. Shaking, she wanted to yell back, "I'm vision impaired, you prick!" but that's not a good thing to announce if you're driving.

In a way, it was a relief to give it up, to finally admit there was a problem, like saying, "Hello, my name is Ellie, and I've got retinitis pigmentosa," to a sympathetic group of other retinal degenerates who'd chorus back, "Hi, Ellie!"

It was a Saturday when she finally told Jeff she was going to stop driving. She's generally not much of a crier, having gotten most of that done in the first few years of her marriage, but she was crying then. She knew she was relinquishing something that was terribly important, and yet, despite her emotion, she didn't think the decision would be anything other than inconvenient at best, frustrating at worst. Words like *humiliate*, *trap*, *infantilize*, and *marginalize* didn't crop up till later.

But that day, as she sat crying with Jeff, she also felt the slightest bit of self-satisfaction, a comfortable smugness that she was sacrificing her own vanity and convenience so others would be safe. She was noble.

Jeff was sympathetic and supportive, for which she was grateful, until it occurred to him that if she was finally giving up driving, how long had she been driving unsafely up to this point, stupidly putting herself and Hannah in danger?

Ellie was braced for this shift and the familiar ice pick in her stomach that surfaced whenever she knew she was in a losing battle with Jeff. She wearily rallied an "I'm Sorry, but I Can't Go Back in Time" defense, which, of course, made no sense, and he didn't hear it anyway. He was too intent on backing her into a figurative corner, righteously making his relentless point after point after point.

Eventually, Jeff had said all he had to say and left to get them all some Pinkberry yogurt.

Exhausted, she'd taken a nap, after revisiting in her mind all the cogent and airtight responses she should have said when he accused her of not only jeopardizing herself and Hannah but all the friends of Hannah's she'd driven while impaired, which could have resulted in a lawsuit, which would have ruined them, yada yada yada. He'd brought her back some of her favorite dark chocolate from Trader Joe's as a wordless acknowledgment that he was no longer angry at her (for now), and she'd thrust aside the ice pick in favor of the more tolerable feeling of temporary relief.

CHAPTER THIRTEEN
THERE'S A PLACE

WHATSAPP
"THE TWO HS"—HALEY AND HANNAH
OCTOBER 7, 2018

HALEY:

HOW WAS HAMILTON??!!!

HANNAH:

I. Can't. Even. It was like some out-of-body experience. I can still see it burned on my retina.

HALEY:

Any of the original cast left?

HANNAH:

No but it didn't matter, they were all Ah. MAZING. Possibly even better than on the album.

HALEY:

No way!!!!!

HANNAH:

I know, right, maybe it's just hearing it live instead of on the CD but "Burn" was like to the thousandth time more intense.

HALEY:

You should sing "Burn." You would kill it.

HANNAH:

I would. But everyone EVERYONE does "Burn" now, it's flavor of the YEAR. I'll do it in, like ten years.

HALEY:

Did Aunt Wendy like it?

HANNAH:

Oh my god, after Philip dies in the second act, we just held hands and sobbed. Like, till the show was over and then on the train all the way back to Boston. She LOVED it.

And now I have to go and be evil Auntie Spiker in *James and the Giant Peach: The Musical*. For Young Audiences! Gawd.

HALEY:

Do NOT disrespect James and the Peach to me! You will be brilliant.

H, how are you doing?

HANNAH:

H, I'm FINE. Seriously. My mom texts me just about every day to tell me to go into therapy but really: I'M OKAY. Please don't worry about me.

HALEY:

I just want to make sure you're not in denial or anything.

HANNAH:

I'm not in denial, it happened. I'm not the only girl who ever went through it and it's over. Oh, listen to this: my folks are in therapy now!

HALEY:

Good luck with that.

HANNAH:

No kidding. I *told* my mom last spring not to go back to him. Parents. They never listen.

HALEY:

So they're coming in for the show, right? That should be interesting . . .

HANNAH:

I wish they'd just stay home and deal
with their damage.

HALEY:

Listen, just smile at everything
they say and pretend you're
having a great time. Like the rest
of us do. Gotta go. Love you.

HANNAH:

Love you back.

———

Hannah smiles as her bestie signs off, then catches sight of one
of her dad's texts, which she sometimes doesn't read but just
measures (his longest was over seven inches long, back when her
mom had left him, and he was texting Hannah frantically every
hour). She feels bad for him—she does, kind of. She knows he
genuinely loves her and her mom, and she has some genuinely
good memories of her dad being goofy and fun.

But every good memory she can dredge up of Dad is followed by at least ten others that are horrible.

She grabs her pillow from her bed, smushes it against her
face, and screams, a handy tool she learned from her freshman
roommate, who left spring semester to join a Wiccan congre-
gation. She gets off three good ones and then feels guilty for
possibly injuring her voice before the show.

She hasn't told anyone about the chronic anxiety that
sent her to the Ballard Mental Health Center earlier this year.
(Was she surprised? Not really.) She doesn't like to think of the

episodes as panic attacks, because the words *panic* and *attack* make her panic, and she's come to dread the creeping, buzzy feeling in her stomach, knowing the vibration will shiver all the way up her spine to her throat, leaving her breathless and dizzy and hoarse, and *not able to sing*, the one imperative of her life that gives her focus and stability.

She sits on the pretty pale blue-and-yellow rug in her cheerful sixth-floor dorm room with the Ah.Mazing view of Boston Common. She breathes steadily and deeply, per her actor prep class, but also like her therapist, Bonnie, suggested.

Hannah ignores her dad's text, something she's been trained exactly *not* to do, for her father has made it very clear she must be available to talk with him at any *reasonable* time, and not just in case of emergency. She sometimes feels empowered when she ignores his texts, but not as often as she feels guilty or nervous, just in case this is the time one of her parents has had a heart attack or something, and she hasn't checked their texts. She sometimes feels, resentfully but somewhat self-importantly, like the grown-up called upon to give advice and comfort to her own parents. She remembers her Psych 101 class and knows as an only child she's right at the apex of her parents' dysfunction, the locus of their mutual obsession, the tiny tip on which the inverted pyramid of their family balances. Jeez—self-centered much?

She thought that being three thousand miles away from them would be perfect, far enough to avoid parental oversight but still a comfortable JetBlue flight from home. Her mom gets it—Hannah has to admit, she's been good about only checking in once a week, during which she jokes at least once about losing her regular mani-pedi buddy (God, give it *up*).

But Dad was still Dad, the tentacles of his control less physical now but still profound, still the catch in her mind, prompting her to ask, *Is this safe? Should I be doing this? How will I explain it to Dad?* Ah, the eternal question of her life, *how to explain it to Dad*, who demands to hear her thought processes (always wrong) for buying a new pair of jeans ("You really think those are flattering?"), or why she still can't figure out the fucking hospital corners he goes on and on about whenever she makes her bed at home. She hates his micromanaging and hates that when he's not there, she does it to herself, or worse, her friends ("No, don't take the T. It might be cheaper, but you'll have to walk five blocks; take an Uber or Lyft. Lyft is better. Do you have the app?"). She wonders if she'll ever hear her own true thoughts, or will she forever have her dad as her constant internal Siri.

She once told her mother, as they miserably huddled together in the kitchen after Dad slammed out of the house in one of his rages, "Every time you talk to him, you have to plan out what you say so that it's close enough to what he's thinking that it doesn't set him off." (Maybe that's why she likes being in the theater—someone else writes what she has to say, and she doesn't have to take responsibility for it.) She'd expected her mother to say, "Don't be silly. He's not like that," but Mom had shocked her by saying, "No kidding. It's exhausting."

Hannah remembers parts of that particular night vividly, parts of it not at all. She remembers grimly how jovial they all were as they arrived at the California Pizza Kitchen to celebrate the start of the winter break in eighth grade: herself; Haley (always cooler and more comfortable with the adults than Hannah was); Aunt Wendy, who'd come in from Boston for a visit; and her parents. They'd laughed and joked, Dad and Haley having fun drawing competitively with the crayons and paper left on the tables. And then, suddenly, as she likes to think when she retells the story in her mind, it all got dark. Aunt Wendy and her mom were going to the Santa Cruz Boardwalk the next day, and Wendy invited Hannah and Haley to join them. Haley was happy to go, but Dad reminded Hannah that that was the day they had agreed he would take her bike shopping.

"Well, she'll be home for three weeks," said Aunt Wendy, who didn't live with them and didn't know a storm was a-brewin'. "She can come with us tomorrow, and you can go bike shopping another day."

"That's not the point," Dad said, quietly ominous. "The point is, Hannah, you and I made a date, and now that's not as important to you as going out with"—air quotes—"'the girls.' What about me? Maybe I want to go to Santa Cruz Boardwalk too."

Hannah and Ellie both chimed in enthusiastically that Jeff could go with them too, just as Wendy said, "Nah, this is a girls' day! You don't want to come with us. You get to stay home and have the house to yourself!"

"I have the house to myself every day, since I work from home," Jeff countered. "And I was looking forward to spending some of Hannah's vacation with her, just the two of us. A father-and-daughter day."

Hannah closes her eyes and breathes as she recalls the inevitable downward spiral of that long-ago evening, the waiter bringing the check, her dad going ballistic because there were two extra orders of Szechuan chicken dumplings, which Aunt Wendy had ordered while Dad was in the bathroom. The whole inescapable unspooling of yet another shit show that in any other family would have been a happy, forgettable evening at the start of a nice vacation.

Hannah can't remember if they all went to the boardwalk. But she never got her damn bike.

Someone knocks on her door, and Hannah freezes, pillow in hand. She's the RA on her dorm floor, a brilliant move on her part (she must admit) that got her free board and a single in one of the very few Ballard dorms, thus relieving her of having to find her own apartment in Boston. She didn't think she could handle looking for an apartment in a big city and second-guessing Dad every step of the way. (She has friends who went and got apartments with friends. They just went and got apartments with friends. She marvels at that.)

"Hannah?" the girl's plaintive voice comes through her door. "It's Amaya. Do you have a second? Kendra had the sock on the door last night till four this morning. I mean, what am I supposed to do?"

Shove a pillow in your face and scream into it, Hannah thinks but doesn't say, smushing the pillow back over her face so she won't laugh at poor Amaya and her amorous roommate. She glances at her phone for the time and is relieved to see that she only has a half hour until rehearsal, until her real life.

CHAPTER FOURTEEN
DON'T LET ME DOWN

DIVORCED WOMEN OVER FIFTY CHAT ROOM
OCTOBER 15, 2018
8:23 P.M.

SuzyQ:
The hospice folks are back, they've got momma on a nice morphine drip wish I could have one too!

Mairzydoats (DWOF Moderator):
Oh, Suzy! I'm sorry. I know you're gone through this before. It takes a lot of strength.

Freeatlast:
We had the hospice come for my dad when he went. They're good people. They know what they're doing, and you won't have to be alone, Suzy.

SuzyQ:
Yeah they sent a real sweetheart nurse this time I feel like Mommas in good hands.

LORELEI:
I know "thoughts and prayers" can be meaningless, but I'm sending both to you and your mother.

SUZYQ:
Thatnks, Lorelei, you are so sweet. Whats going on here? I need distracionton, LOL!

GINGERBEAR:
EB, what's happening with you? Did you leave the Fucker again yet?

ELLESBELLES:
Ugh. No. Maybe getting closer, though.

LORELEI:
It's like therapy—you can't go till you're ready.

FREEATLAST:
You guys are in therapy, right? I remember therapy. They never kick your husband's ass enough, if you ask me.

ELLESBELLES:
Therapy's okay. We've had a few sessions, and he's got us doing this exercise where we have to say what's bothering us about the other person, and then they have to repeat what we said. Jeff's pretty abysmal at it and truth to tell, I kind of like to see him squirm when our therapist calls him on his shit.

GINGERBEAR:
Squirming's good.

LORY:

But he must be at least trying, right? I mean, he does the exercises, doesn't he?

ELLESBELLES:

Yeah, he does them as best he can. This is not a man with a lot of emotional resources. He tends to fight the therapist on it and try to go off on his own tangent.

LORY:

How's that exercise supposed to help your marriage?

MAIRZYDOATS (DWOF MODERATOR):

It's a fairly standard exercise, Lory. It's about learning to listen to one another carefully. Can't do a marriage without good communication. Actually, you can't really do a divorce without it either.

LORELEI:

I haven't communicated with my please-God-soon-to-be-ex-husband in ages. It's been divine.

ELLESBELLES:

Yeah, the exercises are great, but you know what would go a long way with me? A fucking apology. I don't think he's ever apologized to me in our whole marriage. Or even said, "Hey, that's okay, don't worry about it." I'd just like an inkling that he can actually see what kind of ass he's been to me, and to Hannah, too.

GINGERBEAR:

Not to be a downer here, but honestly EB, the Fuckers never learn.

FREEATLAST:
Not in my experience. You know what I bet would help them, though? A morphine drip!

SUZYQ:
C'mon down SMKL!

CHAPTER FIFTEEN
WE CAN WORK IT OUT

OCTOBER 18, 2018

Ellie has warily agreed to go with Jeff to the Palms, one of their favorite restaurants, though only for dessert and coffee; a whole dinner seems like too much of a commitment. With therapy ongoing but her own plans for leaving still muddled in her head, she figures she may as well be as pleasant as possible (in an un-Stepford Wife way), hoping for a harmonious homelife in the interim.

This evening has something of an agenda, because they're about to make their plans to go visit Hannah at Ballard next month and see her perform in the main-stage play, *James and the Giant Peach*. They've never missed a performance of hers yet.

"I vote for not staying at Wendy and Lacey's," Jeff begins. They usually stay with Wendy and her wife, Lacey, who live about a half-hour drive from downtown Boston. "What if we get a room in a nice hotel in Boston, so we don't have the commute from Weston, and then we can walk wherever we want to go? It might be nice to have a bit of a vacation ourselves, now that you're back."

Ellie can't help herself: "*Back in the USSR . . .*" she sings.

He shoots back, "*You don't know how lucky you are, boy . . .*"

The line hangs there for a minute. Suddenly, Ellie gets tired of being all starchy and uptight and starts to laugh. In a second, so does Jeff, and she's pleased to read a bit of relief in his eyes. She remembers, years ago, when she was starting to complain about Jeff, before she decided she couldn't stand it anymore, Wendy had asked her (much as Lorelei had asked Suzie, she realizes), "Do you love him?" And Ellie had replied, truthfully, "He's my companion of choice." And it was true: against the rising tide of Jeff's increasingly intolerable behavior there had still been times that they made each other laugh, that they finished each other's sentences, that they were content to cuddle on the sofa and watch the chick flicks that Jeff enjoyed just as much as Ellie. She misses those times and wonders if they could possibly be resurrected, if she maybe eases back on her emotional distance and the therapy takes hold. She'd be open to that kind of change, but she's wary.

Ellie left her marriage in a rage, and she returned still mightily pissed off, but what could she do? The fact was, she'd run out of money. She'd had a small legacy from her mother's late sister that she'd never told Jeff about, and she tore through that money in six months, paying both her apartment rent and the mortgage. Since Ellie never saw a lawyer or even really thought about the legal and financial aftermath of leaving, she and Jeff hadn't spoken about finances, and quite frankly, she didn't want to. Conversations about money—or anything that required bipartisan cooperation about something important—were always impossible with Jeff, who questioned everything she said, seemingly out of sheer contrariness.

When Ellie first arrived at the apartment, her sister asked, "Can you afford this?"

"Not sure," Ellie replied, not caring at that point. Then, when Wendy voiced her concern, Ellie snapped, "Wendy, I know my financial situation, okay? My bank balance is burned on my retina."

"Yeah," Wendy shot back, "and we know how reliable *that* is!"

But Ellie had assumed, back then in the first flush of her independence and fury, that an equally outraged Jeff would throw the rest of her belongings out their bedroom window onto the front yard, that he'd vigorously fight her in divorce court, that he'd vindictively try to turn Hannah against her, and that he'd ruin her in a legal battle. But to her surprise, he didn't. After a few weeks of self-righteous blame and recrimination, he took a step back and started a charm offensive that, even though she saw through it, allowed her to come home with the illusion that things might be better than before.

She knew she had to be prepared for the crap of a separation, but she also knew she'd never be prepared for that crap—so she didn't really prepare for any of it. Even the thought of cleaning out their garage and its accumulation of twenty-two years of *stuff* made her want to go right to bed and nap. And when Jeff didn't actually take any legal action against her, she didn't take any either. She lost her momentum and then her money, and at that point she had to slink back to the big house. There was even a kind of relief in that return, because better the devil you know, right?

But she'd made her point, and now they go to therapy regularly—she had to give Jeff credit for that—even if he still seems resistant, four sessions in.

She'd been trying to get him to go to couples therapy for the last ten years, so this is actually quite a bit of progress. There was a part of her that was willing to give her marriage a another shot, because she'd much prefer to leave for Hannah a legacy of forgiveness and loyalty rather than the usual divorce detritus of bitterness and anger.

"This trip is not about us—you and me," Ellie points out

once they've tucked into their crème brulés and decaf cappuccinos. "It's about Hannah. And her show."

"Well, of course. But it's also about the three of us, and how our marriage now makes us a stronger family."

"Uh-huh. Okay. Well . . ." Ellie has a feeling that Hannah would respond to this with an unladylike snort.

He continues, his blue eyes earnest, "I just don't want you to hate me, Ellie. 'Cause that's not fair, especially since I love *you*, and that has never changed."

They sit in silence for a moment. Ellie doesn't know what to make of this. Not for the first time, she wonders what life would be like if she were a different kind of woman, not so willing to give the benefit of the doubt, or to consider giving him another chance. What would life be like if she were a bitch? She hates that word, thinks it's low-rent, dismissive, a *Real Housewives* level of classlessness, but what if she were what that word implies at its best: Strong, confident, self-serving, indifferent to the pain of those who've caused her pain? Would she be long gone? Over the worst of it? In a new marriage? What about Hannah, who would then be a child of divorce—no, that was always the line she wouldn't cross while her daughter was growing up. They would have had to split custody. She couldn't imagine saying to a young Hannah, "I can't live with him, but you have to."

Ellie contemplates Jeff, sitting across from her in the restaurant. He's staring into the inside of his coffee cup as though he's reading tea leaves.

What would happen if she said, "No, this isn't going to work for me. I want you out of my life. Hannah's an adult; you can make your own arrangements with her. I'm going on this trip, but I'm not going with you."

Her eyes fill with tears. Goddamn it. How do you rip apart a marriage without being sad? She sighs. She is who she is.

"Well, we'll try to make it a good trip. We'll have some fun," she says.

Jeff's eyes light up. Again, that flash of the man she fell in love with, and there's an absurd frisson of wanting to take his hand (she doesn't). She feels a little better.

They talk of things other than themselves—their good friends Laurie and Wyatt, whom Ellie thinks of as being on Jeff's "Approved Friends" list (Jane does not make the cut); politics; the latest novels they're reading. Ellie relaxes. She came back to her marriage with a combination of resignation and resentment—but maybe there is another option? Maybe it *is* possible to salvage this relationship, and her leaving was the catalyst for, as the DWOF girls would say, a whole new chapter.

Jeff lifts his coffee cup and makes a toast. He always makes a toast at gatherings of friends and families, and always gets emotional, which everyone gives him shit for (he loves that).

Ellie smiles, embarrassed.

"To my beautiful wife, my Ellie," he says, and sings a few lines of the Beatles' beautiful, simple ballad "And I Love Her." He gazes at her, blue eyes moist and sincere, at least as far as she can tell. Ellie wracks her brain for a suitable response, but all she can come up with is:

"Why don't we d-do it in the road?"

Jeff falls off his chair laughing. Ellie sees a glimpse of the man she loved and laughs too. Could this work, this new and improved Jeff?

The waiter overhears as he comes up to them with the check, saying, "Well, I see it's getting very romantic over here . . ."

Ellie laughs up at him before catching a glimpse of Jeff's face, suddenly not smiling anymore. The temperature drops as Jeff picks up the bill folder and, without looking at it (or her), drops his credit card into it and hands it off to the waiter, who clearly realizes he somehow has stepped in it and takes off.

"What?" says Ellie, but she can take a guess. She's been down this road many times.

"He was flirting with you."

"Are you insane? He made a comment. About the stupid song."

"Yeah, and you thought it was funny. You flirted back."

She ignores the rage inside her; it's not worth it.

"That wasn't flirting. What, I can't laugh when someone, a man, makes a funny comment?"

"See, you admit it. You thought he was funny. And you did that thing with your mouth. That flirty thing you do with your lips."

"Yeah, it's called smiling. Listen, I don't know what you think you saw, but I was not flirting with the goddamned waiter."

The check has somehow made its way back to their table, but Ellie's already up, cane out, spitting out one last salvo: "This right here, Jeff? This bullshit? It's why I left. And this is why I will be leaving again."

She whips her cane forward and marches through the restaurant, waiters and patrons parting like the sea as she bears down on them.

She slips into a coffee shop two doors down and calls herself an Uber.

Yeah, this was the man she fell in love with, all right. The dozens, maybe hundreds of nights out that ended just like this, almost from the time they started dating. Nuh-uh. She's outta there. She'll go to Boston with him, but then she's done.

CHAPTER SIXTEEN
DR. ROBERT—PART 2

OCTOBER 19, 2018

"I get it," says Jeff.

It's the day after their disastrous dinner at the Palms. They're in Joseph's office after a rather frosty night at the house. Jeff slept in his home office, and Ellie, feeling the momentum of her anger, emailed Jane and got the name and number of a family law attorney who had successfully steered a friend through a messy divorce.

Jeff is leaning forward, hands wrung, brow furrowed, staring at the Navajo rug on the floor. Ellie's sitting at the other end of the couch from him, a handwoven bolster en garde at her side between them.

"I get . . . that my behavior . . . was . . . impossible."

Ellie raises an eyebrow, glances at Joseph, who meets her glance, then focuses on Jeff. "Go on, Jeff," he says.

"I see it . . . I can see that all that stuff I did—the controlling, the taking over, getting angry at Ellie for stupid little things, jeez . . . I'd hate it if anyone behaved like that to me."

Ellie eyes him warily. Who is this guy?

Joseph says, "Jeff, this is new from you. Ellie, any thoughts?"

Jeff goes on, still looking at the floor: "But I would like

to say, in my defense, it only came out of a place of love and concern—I guess a lot of concern—"

Jeff straightens up and looks right at Ellie.

"Ellie. I was such a jerk to you. All those years. And Hannah, Jesus. I don't know what to say. Except—I'm sorry. I apologize."

Hell freezes over for a second as Ellie stares at Jeff in disbelief. Jeff is gazing right at her, his blue eyes focused and steady. For a split second, she goes back in time again, sees the man she fell in love with. She has to stop doing that.

"Ellie? Do you want to respond?" says Joseph.

Ellie ponders her response, then remembers she's not at home right now.

"No," she says.

Joseph nods. Jeff gazes at her, a flicker of something in his eyes—respect? Humor? Annoyance?

"Ellie. I'm gonna work on this. I get it—I have a lot to compensate for, but . . ."

His eyes fill with tears. Ellie doesn't buy it, and her initial impulse is to snort in derision. She does.

"Ellie, words can be helpful here. Anything you want to say to Jeff?" says Joseph.

She says the first thing that comes to her mind: "I don't believe you."

Jeff nods, like he expected that.

"That's okay. Don't worry about it," he says.

Ellie is silent. She can't imagine where this is going.

"Ellie, I would like to turn back the clock, but obviously I can't do that. I can't undo years of hurt and stupidity, but I would like to maybe try a fresh start. I only want . . . to get our marriage back on the right track. To make you happy that you came back to me."

She peers at him, trying to penetrate the humble blue of his eyes, relishing the feeling of being the one on top for a change, the one doing the hurt instead of hurting. She remains silent.

"Jeff," Joseph says, "you've said your piece, and I can see it took some courage and self-revelation on your part. That was good work. But you have to understand Ellie's been pent up for decades—it may take her a while to respond positively to you, and you can't rush her. You need to give her space, give her time to finally speak up after years of keeping silent. And then listen."

Ellie and Jeff look at each other solemnly. Ellie feels the gravity of the situation, quickly followed by the absurdity, the conventionality of the married couple in therapy speaking the lines they learned from dozens of TV shows and movies. A totally inappropriate giggle wells up. Was this really her life now? Seriously?

Jeff meets her smile. And sings: *"Who knows how long I've loved you,"* making them wait as he sings all the way to the end of the Beatles' "I Will," rather smugly, she thinks.

Ellie can't believe he's pulling this again; she feels like he's showing off for Joseph. Unlike the time at the Palms, Ellie doesn't want to flip this conversation off, and rapidly goes through her mental Beatles catalog. Ah. She shrugs and flings him a line from the middle of "I'm Looking Through You":

"Love has a nasty habit of disappearing overnight."

She turns on her heel and walks out.

Jeff hurries out after his wife, leaving Joseph, jaw dropped, holding open the door.

"Good work," calls Joseph.

CHAPTER SEVENTEEN
ALL I'VE GOT TO DO

DIVORCED WOMEN OVER FIFTY CHAT ROOM
OCTOBER 21, 2018
7:05 P.M.

ELLESBELLES:
Big news!

ELLESBELLES:
Okay, not BIG news, but progress!

GINGERBEAR:
Spill it.

FREEATLAST:
Drumroll!

ELLESBELLES:
I have an appointment with a divorce lawyer. I got a referral from a friend, and I'm pretty excited.

ELLESBELLES:

I guess you can tell I haven't had too much to do with lawyers in my life, LOL!

MAIRZYDOATS (DWOF MODERATOR):

This is a terrific step, Ellesbelles!

MAIRZYDOATS (DWOF MODERATOR):

It seems like you have a good therapist, so now if you can get yourself a good attorney, you're on your way!

GINGERBEAR:

Not that there's still not a lot of misery ahead, but at least you've got your team.

LORELEI:

Don't let Gingerbear scare you, EB! Let the lawyer deal with the misery, you just get yourself out.

LORY:

Wow. This sounds serious.

ELLESBELLES:

Well . . . therapy took a sort of unexpectedly good turn the other day, but I don't want to be lulled into a false sense of security. So, even if I do nothing with the legal stuff, I figure at least I have it in my back pocket.

LORY:

That's encouraging, that therapy's going well! I'm happy for you!

FREEATLAST:
When's the lawyer appointment?

ELLESBELLES:
Wednesday morning. I have a plan for getting there without my husband knowing. Kind of cloak-and-dagger but since I don't drive, it's not as easy as just hopping in the car and not going to work for a few hours.

MAIRZYDOATS (DWOF MODERATOR):
You have a friend helping you?

ELLESBELLES:
Yes. Not for the first time! She's literally my "ride-or-die." She's coming to pick me up early for work that day and then taking me to the lawyer.

LORY:
Gosh. That's a good friend.

LORELEI:
EB, I think it's grand! You'll be surprised how empowering it will be to have a good lawyer by your side. I hope she's a woman?

ELLESBELLES:
She is.

GINGERBEAR:
It's good she's a woman, but you need a barracuda.

ELLESBELLES:
Good to know. I'll ask her! She has her own practice and she's a mediator, too, so that may come in handy.

MAIRZYDOATS (DWOF MODERATOR):
And relax, Ellesbelles. You don't need to jump if she says jump. You can take in the information and live with it for a while.

LORY:
That sounds like good advice.

MAIRZYDOATS (DWOF MODERATOR):
Remember, you're paying her (oh, you won't be able to forget THAT!) so she works for you.

LORY:
Yeah. Don't get pushed around, Ellesbelles!

ELLESBELLES:
Got it. Those days are gone, I hope!

LORELEI:
Here's to freedom, Ellesbelles!

GINGERBEAR:
To freedom!

FREEATLAST:
To freedom!

ELLESBELLES:
You girls ROCK!

CHAPTER EIGHTEEN
HERE, THERE, AND EVERYWHERE

OCTOBER 24, 2018

Ellie felt better as soon as she'd made the appointment with the attorney, and the enthusiastic approval of the DWOF sisters calmed her nerves and bolstered her courage. Enough wallowing in her own shit; it's time to take her life back into her own hands and at least start the process of ending her marriage, Jeff's big "change" notwithstanding. She's got a little money left in the Escape Account that funded her first foray into freedom and feels confident a session with a good lawyer is the right way to spend it.

She made all the arrangements from her phone at work, in between clients and claims, and Stephanie—the lawyer—understood perfectly the need for discretion and accommodation.

Jane, her trusty steed, will pick Ellie up early in order to get to work on time herself and will either come pick her up afterward, if she can, or arrange an Uber for her on her account (Ellie doesn't want to call her own Uber and have Jeff see the payment on their bank account).

So here she is, sneaking around again, just like last time. She doesn't like it, but carless and nearly sightless, what else can she do?

As they eat dinner on Tuesday night, she casually mentions to Jeff that she has to go in early to work the next day because the office is having a special meeting to go over their new health insurance plan. Jane is going to pick her up tomorrow morning at eight, instead of the usual nine.

She's surprised at how casual *he* is at the news. Jeff usually views all changes in schedule not approved by him as an insurmountable affront that can only be accepted after a combination of grilling and stony silence.

"Oh yeah?" he says mildly. "You guys never have early meetings. Why now?"

She shrugs. "Dunno. Maybe it's the only time the insurance lady can make it in to explain it to us."

He lifts an eyebrow. "You getting paid for this extra hour?"

She rolls her eyes. "Yeah, of course."

"Well, that's fine," he says to her. "I'm gonna be playing tennis early tomorrow with Wyatt; he's going to get one of the courts at the park. I'll probably be leaving before you."

"Okay," Ellie tells him. *Good*, she thinks, *keep him occupied*.

True to his word, Jeff is out of the house the next morning by seven thirty. Ellie enjoys being in the house by herself for a half hour, remembering how much she liked being alone in her little "divorce apartment" last spring and hoping she can look forward to a Jeff-less life in the future.

Jane picks her up and safely gets her to Stephanie's office, which is in a modern building, the number clearly marked, with a nice, wide, well-lit entrance. Ellie breezes right through with her cane, locates the elevators, and lands on the eighth floor, where she finds #826, with its glass door and cozy waiting room. The receptionist, Vicky, offers her water, and Ellie settles into the plush sofa, enjoying being on her own and taken seriously. She takes a breath as she braces for the meeting.

———

Stephanie, a young attorney of perception, compassion, and a briefly glimpsed killer instinct (her "barracuda," Ellie figured), let Ellie stay over her billable time so they could make sure she understood what she has to do next.

"Look," Stephanie told her, "you've got about a year, year and a half, of real crap ahead of you, no question. But we'll work it out, and you will be fine. And when the dust settles, you and your husband might even find you can be amicable, maybe even friendly. I've seen it happen."

Friendly with Jeff—what a concept. It would certainly make life easier with Hannah.

Over an hour and a half later, Ellie strolls out of Stephanie's office, empowered, confident, relaxed. Stephanie has her back. They have a plan.

Ellie's assignment: Put together a financial profile of her and Jeff's assets, savings, income, etcetera, and start to figure out an arrangement that is workable for both of them. Once she's got all that together, she'll see Stephanie again, and they'll work out the legal details.

This is so much better than last time, when Ellie left in a rage, not thinking beyond the necessity of just getting the hell out. This is long term. This is practical. How she's going to pay for all this is a bridge she'll have to cross later, though it may very well be a bridge too far, as Ellie thinks about the consultation hours racking up at Stephanie's $500 per-hour fee, not to mention that it nearly doubles if they, God forbid, wind up in court. She refuses to let that sober her up. Now she's on top of this thing.

Ellie takes a moment to call Jane, who's going to take a very early lunch so she can come get Ellie and hear all the details. Ellie then gets the Tiffany-ringed restroom key from Vicky, the nice receptionist. As she tap-taps her cane down the hallway, she allows herself a time-out for a moment, to think about nothing after an hour-plus of hard listening and processing. She reiterates Stephanie's mantra: *I will be fine.*

As she heads back to the office to return the key, she hears a strange sound behind her, a very quiet sort of *tfft, tfft, tfft* that stops as soon as she does. Smiling at the faint scent of the Mrs. Meyers lavender hand soap that she uses at home, she stops and moves to the side, thinking she's holding someone up with her slower gait. She half turns and looks behind her, but though she senses movement in the remnants of her periphery, she doesn't see anyone there. She hears a door closing down the hall, so that's probably who it was. It's just her in the hallway now, and she doesn't see anyone else as she walks back to Stephanie's office, where she hands the key to Vicky and once more says thanks.

Ellie steps inside one of the elevators, alone, locates the buttons, and is just about to push "Lobby" when she realizes, scrabbling in her huge purse, that she doesn't have her phone. She must have left it in Stephanie's office. Great. Can't have a good day without screwing something up. She pushes the open-door button and, still fumbling in her purse, cane banging ungracefully against her leg, starts down the hallway.

She looks ahead to the glass doors of the waiting room and sees a tall figure, a man, engaged with Vicky at the desk. Shit, now she's going to have to wait to get back in to find her phone—which she suddenly grasps from the bowels of her bag, safe and sound. Good! Onward.

Ellie casts a glance at the glass door, and the man suddenly solidifies in her vision, his identity clear.

No. Fucking. Way.

It's Jeff.

Who should be playing tennis right now. Who should be thinking she's at work, in a meeting. What the hell . . .?

Suddenly, she notices that, oddly, he's not wearing tennis sneakers—he's wearing . . . slippers? What? In a flash, she has a sense memory of Jeff in his slippers at home, quietly heading to the bathroom or down the stairs to the kitchen early in the morning so that he doesn't make any noise: *Tfft, tfft, tfft.*

She watches him for a minute, trying to imagine what he could possibly be doing. Is he asking Vicky if his wife was there? How would he know? She left no phone or bank account trail, as far as she knows. He seemed to buy her story about the early morning health insurance meeting at work. Did he actually follow her here, like, in the car? And then sneak around her in his fucking *slippers*?

Or wait—could he be a *client*?

No, she told Stephanie his name, and she'd never have taken Ellie on if she were also representing Jeff. Right?

Ellie assumes there's absolute client confidentiality with a lawyer, so—even if he's demanding that Vicky tell him if his wife was just there (she imagines him doing his charming "my wife is vision impaired, and I'm here to help her" spiel)—she has good reason to think Vicky will say nothing.

But what will Jeff say, to her, at home, later on? He obviously followed her; he obviously knows she's seen a family attorney. He'll confront her about it later, and it won't be pleasant. And what's she gonna do? Deny it?

Wait—that's a good idea. She's not ready to tell him she's lawyered up, and she doesn't want to let on that she lied to him. What if she just steadfastly denies it? He followed her, for Christ's sake! She could probably even get her boss, Martin, to say she was there at work the whole time—that'd really fuck with him, wouldn't it?

Ellie considers this. She knows from experience that every time she'd try to one-up Jeff before, he'd always win the round, hands down, simply wearing her down with endless haranguing and bullying. But maybe now, empowered by her lawyer and her game plan, she can pull it off. She hurries out of the building. Wait till Jane hears about this.

———

"So how was tennis with Wyatt?" Ellie casually asks Jeff over dinner that night.

"Great. I beat the pants off him. How was your insurance meeting?"

Ellie pauses for a nanosecond. *Oh, it's like this, is it?*

"Good," she says. "We have a really good plan this year."

She looks up at Jeff and sees him eying her over his pad thai. She meets his gaze.

Stalemate.

CHAPTER NINETEEN
TOMORROW NEVER KNOWS

DIVORCED WOMEN OVER FIFTY CHAT ROOM
OCTOBER 27, 2018
6:15 P.M.

SuzyQ:
Momma died.

Mairzydoats (DWOF Moderator):
I am so sorry.

Ellesbelles:
How are you doing?

SuzyQ:
I'm good. Momma's at peace it was bad at the end, the hospice girl didn't come in time and she went hard, but she's in heaven now and I feel happy for her.

Gingerbear:
Suzy. It's gonna be okay.

FREEATLAST:
It's always hard when your parents die, no matter how old or young you are.

LORY:
I'm new here but want to offer my condolences. It's terrible to lose a parent.

ELLESBELLES:
Suzy, I remember the very first thing you ever said to me on this chat room: "We are all for one and one for all here." So, even though we're not literally with you . . . we're with you.

SUZYQ:
That is so sweet EB. I'm very tired, been sleeping a lot.

MAIRZYDOATS (DWOF MODERATOR):
Do you still go to your therapist? If you stopped, this would be a good time to go back.

SUZYQ:
Can't afford a therapist, could barly get Momma buried, but I'll think about it.

ELLESBELLES:
Do you have people near you who are there for you? This is a hard time to be alone.

SUZYQ:
Well Id tell you theres chas but you'd get mad at me.

GINGERBEAR:
No we won't.

FREEATLAST:
Nope. We understand. Who better?

SUZYQ:
just seems like the same old same old though, getting tired
of it.

FREEATLAST:
We know.

MAIRZYDOATS (DWOF MODERATOR):
You just have to push through this bad time, Suzy. Allow
yourself to grieve but believe that things will get better with
time. You must have faith in the future, even if you can't see
your way to it right now.

ELLESBELLES:
Here's another wise thing you once said, Suzy, to Lorelei:
Where there's life, there's hope. So don't give up hope!

GINGERBEAR:
Too bad Lorelei's not on. She'd want to know about your
mom, Suzy.

SUZYQ:
You all have always been so good to me.

———

PM FROM MAIRZYDOATS TO ELLESBELLES, GINGERBEAR, FREEATLAST, MOREOFME, LORELEI, LORY, AND OTHERS 6:35 P.M.

Hi, All. You've all been on to chat recently and so you're aware that Suzy's mother has died. I feel that we all share considerable concern for Suzy's situation, and so I've started a GoFundMe account for her to defray funeral expenses or for therapy or just to give her a bit of a breather. I figure it's more practical than sending flowers or a wreath. Here's the link: www.gofundme.com/suzyq.

No pressure, you can contribute anonymously, and no donation is too small.—**MAIRZYDOATS (DWOF MODERATOR)**

I'm in.—**GINGERBEAR**

Me too.—**FREEATLAST**

I am too.—**ELLESBELLES**

Great idea, Mairzydoats, count me in!—**MOREOFME**

Great idea—**LORY**

. . . where's Lorelei?—**GINGERBEAR**

CHAPTER TWENTY
I'LL FOLLOW THE SUN

DIVORCED WOMEN OVER FIFTY CHAT ROOM
NOVEMBER 4, 2018
8:07 P.M.

LORY:
Maybe she's just on a vacation somewhere?

ELLESBELLES:
Just got on. What's happening?

MAIRZYDOATS (DWOF MODERATOR):
Ellesbelles, SuzyQ has disappeared. She apparently went for a hike by herself last week and no one has seen her since then. Suzy's therapist contacted me.

ELLESBELLES:
. . .?

GINGERBEAR:
Seven days. You said it was seven days ago. That's a long damn time.

ELLESBELLES:
So—police? Search parties? Do they think something's
happened to her? Are there any clues?

MAIRZYDOATS (DWOF MODERATOR):
From what her therapist wrote me, she always goes hiking
in a pretty big park near where she lives in Kentucky, and
they found her car in the parking lot after dusk, when
the park closes. I guess Chas called the police when he
couldn't get in touch with her, but by that time it was 48
hours later.

FREEATLAST:
Yeah, why'd he wait so long?

ELLESBELLES:
But they searched for her?

MAIRZYDOATS (DWOF MODERATOR):
Yes of course! They sent out search and rescue teams, and
dogs. They had the neighbors walk a grid around the park,
but it's 26 acres, and there's lots of woods as well as the
trails. I think Chas is still going out to look but at this point . . .
it's hard to tell what to think.

FREEATLAST:
Chas should be in custody.

MAIRZYDOATS (DWOF MODERATOR):
There's no reason to think Chas has anything to do with her
disappearance. Anything could have happened.

FREEATLAST:
Did she stick to the trails? They'd have found her if she stuck to the trails, but if she wandered off . . .

LORY:
Could she have been kidnapped, or run into some nutcase or something? It's not the safest thing for women to go hiking alone.

MOREOFME:
Oh, God forbid.

ELLESBELLES:
This is a horrible thing to say but—does anyone think she maybe walked into the woods and . . . did something to herself? She sounded so terrible last time she was on the board.

MAIRZYDOATS (DWOF MODERATOR):
I'm a little worried about that myself.

MOREOFME:
You mean take her own life??? No. I don't think for a minute that Suzy would do that.

GINGERBEAR:
I just can't see any way there's a good ending to this story. Unless she hit her head, got amnesia, wandered off and was taken to a hospital by some good Samaritans.

MOREOFME:
I like that. I'm going with that.

ELLESBELLES: ·
Are they still looking for her? Is there a time limit when they just call it off??

MAIRZYDOATS (DWOF MODERATOR):
Her therapist told me they haven't yet called off the search, but they're not feeling optimistic. They're having a vigil for her sometime this week.

GINGERBEAR:
We should go to Suzy's Vigil. Where is it, Kentucky? Is that crazy? It'd be like a meet-up. With an agenda.

MOREOFME:
That's a good idea. It could be very healing.

FREEATLAST:
I'd like to go and kill Chas. That would be healing for me.

ELLESBELLES:
Maybe we're maligning Chas. She did say he was there for her when her mother died.

GINGERBEAR:
EB, Chas is a bad guy. I don't know anything about him other than what SuzyQ said about him, but I don't get a good feeling about this guy. Plus, anyone named "Chas" is bound to be a fucker.

ELLESBELLES:
This seems so—weird. I feel like any second she's going to pop on the board and make us all laugh about how she's been on a . . . I don't know . . . spa week or something.

LORY:
She's such a big presence in this chat room. You notice when she's not here.

MOREOFME:
Lorelei hasn't been here in a while, either. Hey, maybe they're together! Isn't that a nice thought? Maybe Lorelei paid for Suzy to go visit her on a movie set or something.

FREEATLAST:
I wish Lorelei would sign on, she needs to know about this.

GINGERBEAR:
I really think we should go to Suzy's Vigil.

FREEATLAST:
Mairzydoats, can you get any info on when/where? I'll go.

ELLESBELLES:
I'd love to but I don't think I can. We're going out of town in a few days to see our daughter in her show at Ballard.

FREEATLAST:
"We?"

ELLESBELLES:
Yeah. I'm going with my husband.

LORY:
That's great! Sounds like it'll be fun!

GINGERBEAR:

Do you need reinforcements? As long as we're traveling, we can go back you up too.

ELLESBELLES:

No, thanks, LOL, it'll be okay. He's really trying to turn things around, so I think we'll be okay for the trip.

LORY:

Good news! Hey, maybe you won't need that lawyer!

ELLESBELLES:

I feel like we should be focusing on Suzy, not talking about me.

ELLESBELLES:

Sorry, Lory, I didn't mean to step on your comment. I appreciate it.

LORY:

No worries.

MAIRZYDOATS (DWOF MODERATOR):

I need to point out that we have a certain amount of anonymity on the board here. That goes away when we have a meet-up. Are you all okay with that?

GINGERBEAR:

Are you kidding? I'd love to meet you guys, get some faces to go with the names.

MOREOFME:

I can be the meeting point, I'm easy to spot at 250 lbs, LOL! Seriously, I'd love to go. To support Suzy.

FREEATLAST:

Me, too. For Suzy. But also to meet everyone in person. I got nothing to hide.

LORY:

I haven't been on long enough to really know her that well, so I'm going to pass.

MAIRZYDOATS (DWOF MODERATOR):

Okay, then. If you're sure. I'll get back to Suzy's therapist and find out the details and then let you all know.

GINGERBEAR:

Any chance you can reach out to Lorelei as well? I tried sending her a PM, never got a response.

MAIRZYDOATS (DWOF MODERATOR):

I will.

LORY:

Well, if you all go, safe travels. And to you, too, Ellesbelles. I hope you have a good time on your trip with your husband and daughter.

ELLESBELLES:

Me, too!

ELLESBELLES:

SMKL . . .

CHAPTER TWENTY-ONE
LET IT BE

Hannah doesn't want to talk about what happened—doesn't want to think about it. She just wants to go back to her room and smoke the joint she's been holding for just such an emergency.

She sits across from her parents at Jacob Wirth's, which is already roaring with the influx of families and students for parents' weekend, not to mention all the postshow theater people, who are bouncing from table to table, idiotically, loudly pleased with themselves.

A fellow cast member pops up next to her, gives her a hug. "Awesome show, Auntie S!"

"Thank you! You were ah-mazing!" she says.

Hannah's a trooper, on- or offstage. She smiles brilliantly as three more cast members come up for hugs and congratulations. Of course, they're all thrilled to meet her parents, who came all the way from *California*! Ellie and Jeff do their part (they love this stuff), raving about the show and how excellent everyone was, making sure to point out specific moments in each person's performance. Everyone thinks her parents are awesome as they head back to their own tables and their own families, who, she has to believe, are just as fucked up as hers.

Hannah turns back from her last enthusiastic well-wisher and takes in the high beams of her parents' concerned gaze, a headache starting. She breathes. She wishes she were twenty-one, though her dad would get her a glass of wine if she asked him.

"Hannahbananarama," Jeff says and gets right to it. "Honey, hardly anyone noticed, and if they did, no one will ever remember. Your performance, the whole show, was that good. And everyone forgets their lines now and then; you told us you've done it yourself."

"We're so, so proud of you," Ellie chimes in. Hannah grits her teeth, waiting as her mother adds her inevitable, annoying coda: "And you should be proud of yourself."

Proud, schmroud. Everyone was missing the point, and she didn't feel like enlightening them. She'd gone up on her lines before—it happens to all actors, no biggie. She remembers that time in high school, in *Our Town*, when her brain suddenly stopped providing her lines, but somehow her mouth kept moving, and the words came out perfectly until her brain caught up. She'd found it a comforting lesson, to know that even if you forgot a line, your muscle memory would automatically take over, like your autonomic nervous system would keep you breathing even if you lost consciousness. She'd felt proud then, like a real actress.

But she hadn't "gone up" tonight; she'd had a panic attack. Onstage.

She was fine backstage the nanosecond before her entrance, focused, alive—never so alive!—relaxed, or so she thought. She pondered the seconds before her entrance, trying to find a reason. Why would she get a panic attack before her entrance, a move she'd made a hundred times in rehearsal till she could do it in her sleep? Maybe she wasn't breathing? That happened sometimes. When she was really focused, she held her breath.

So was that why, when her cue came, and she Aunt Spiker–walked her way onstage, she suddenly got the bad tingle, the lights turning to a pinpoint in front of her (*Shit*, some part of her thought, *am I getting RP, like my mom*, right now?), and she felt the stage start to slide down before her. *No, no, no*, some other part of herself thought. *You can't go down; you're onstage.* She had the sensation of somehow being held aloft as she waited for her vision to clear. She had no idea what her first line was, or if she'd remain conscious to say it. *How bad could it be*, some other part of herself thought, *to pass out in front of everyone, including your parents?* This was no split-second brain fart synapse; she was aware of the quiet around her under the buzzing in her ears, and she felt herself start to sway. Was there a murmur of concern from the audience? James was a little tiny ferret in front of her, the brightly colored set a rainbow wash in what remained of her periphery. *Fuck me*, she thought, just as Tara, the girl who played Aunt Sponge, decided she'd waited long enough for Aunt Spiker's first line. In character, she strode over to Hannah, clamped a hand on Hannah's shoulder, and dug in her nails, folding her other hand over her head mic as she quietly commanded, "Breathe, bitch."

"You've already wasted four minutes of daylight," popped out of Hannah's mouth, and she was back, shaky, but back. Aunt Sponge kept her hand on her shoulder till she was sure Aunt Spiker would remain upright.

The rest of the show went without a hitch. Tara, backstage, whispered, "You okay?" and Hannah tossed it off. "Yeah, just had a weird feeling for a second. I'm fine." Tara nodded, concerned (but not as concerned as Hannah. Shit, she was in therapy for it—what more could she do?).

So, the big question: Will it happen again?

Oh, great. Let's put *that* in the hamper with all the other anxieties.

"Hannah, you want a glass of wine?" Jeff said. "I'll order it for you. I hardly ever get carded anymore."

A dad joke, so lame. She nods. She wants to change the subject.

"So, you guys are in therapy now?"

Jeff leans forward as Ellie casts a wary glance in his direction. Well, their body language sure ain't new.

"Hannah," Jeff begins earnestly, "I know you've been upset and disoriented by what happened last year . . ."

Hannah nearly laughs. If he only knew.

He continues, "And you're probably not going to believe this—but I understand what your mother has been trying to tell me all these years."

He turns to smile at Ellie, who fingers the stem of her wineglass, not giving him anything.

"I have to say, this therapy stuff has really been an eye-opener for me. I just—I never could see my behavior before, how I've been, with both of you. I've apologized to your mom, and she's been really great. I don't know if she's forgiven me, or if she even can, but we're here together, so that's at least something."

Ellie remains silent. Hannah wonders if her dad wrote all this down beforehand.

Jeff continues: "And now—I'd like to apologize to you. For all the stupid stuff I've done, the times I've been on your case, and overbearing, and controlling, I guess—"

Jeff gets a little emotional.

"I just love you so much, Hannahbanana. I think—I know—you're a solid, smart, talented, amazing young woman with a good head on your shoulders. Listen, parents make their kids crazy. We embarrass you . . ."

Yeah, you can check that box. Hannah looks around a bit, hoping no one can see her teary-eyed father having his own little drama-camp moment here.

"But I want to apologize for all the times I was stupid and wrong. And in the future, feel free to tell me off if I'm out of line. I want to do better, and I promise you I will."

Jeff is finished, looks proud and expectant. Hannah turns to Ellie, who shrugs. Hannah can still catch a whiff of Jeff's characteristic aggrandizement, the pomposity behind the humility. Was he, maybe, enjoying this?

For sure, he seems sincere, and Hannah has never heard him talk like this before. She feels a mean-girl urge to tell him he's an asshole, and she doesn't believe him, which is basically the truth. Is he really giving her, and her mother, immunity to say whatever they want to him? She feels a spurt of vindictive energy.

"You won't make me feel like a slut for wearing a tank top in July? No bitching me out for not answering your texts within thirty seconds? Oh, wait, let's see, what else . . .? Oh—I know . . ."

Jeff resolutely meets her gaze. Hannah swings her eyes to Ellie, sees her mother give another shrug as if to say, "Go for it," as Hannah leans in for the kill.

"I had an abortion last summer," she says, and hears her mother's sharp intake of breath.

———

AUGUST 18, 2018

Ellie is folding laundry on a Sunday afternoon and trying to block out the argument between Hannah and Jeff in Hannah's bedroom.

Hannah is just about to go back to Ballard for the fall

semester, and she's gotten her bangs cut—she usually goes with a straight part down the middle—and Ellie thinks she looks adorable. But now she can hear Jeff saying, "Bangs? At your age? You like looking like you're in fifth grade?"

A minute later, Hannah swings around Ellie's bedroom door and announces, "Dad is an asshole. And my nails are dis*gusting*!"

"Okay," Ellie says, not bothering to scold her for talking that way about her father.

"Let's tell Dad we're doing the mother-daughter mani-pedi thing. We always get points for that, and then we can go to that place at the mall."

The fact that Hannah has her license is liberating not only for her but for Ellie as well, since Jeff very much approves of "his two girls" going off together to shop or get a mani-pedi or whatever, and Ellie loves spending the time with Hannah, away from him.

Hannah hops in the front seat of her little silver Honda Civic as Ellie more carefully makes her way to the passenger side, folding up her cane as she maneuvers into the car.

Hannah starts the car and silently starts to drive, slowly pulling away from the curb, dutifully checking her rear- and side-view mirrors for oncoming traffic. Ellie clocks a tension coming off her, a set of her jaw that makes her tense as well.

"Hannah? You okay?"

Hannah drives in silence for a few more minutes as Ellie starts to get nervous.

Finally:

"I'm pregnant," Hannah says flatly as she moves onto the freeway. Ellie thinks she's kidding, and says so.

"I'm not kidding. I'm pregnant. Do not tell Dad. Do not. Tell Dad."

"I'm not an idiot, Hannah," Ellie snaps back. The word

pregnant hits her brain but takes a minute to reach her solar plexus.

"What happened?" Ellie is lightheaded.

"I've been seeing this guy . . ." Hannah begins.

"Guy?" Ellie is alarmed. "How old is he?"

"Jeez, he's my age, okay? He's in my acting class, and he lives in Santa Cruz, so we always travel back home together. He's a good guy. We've been dating since spring break."

Hannah puts on her turn signal and reduces speed on the exit ramp. She's a good driver even in a crisis.

"Does he know?" Ellie's brain is starting to overheat.

"No. And I'm not going to tell him."

"Why not?"

Hannah is quiet. Ellie doesn't press.

"Hannah, I have to ask: Was it consensual?"

Hannah snorts.

"Jesus. Of course it was. You think *I'm* an idiot?"

"Do you love him?"

Hannah just shakes her head, rolls her eyes.

"It was just a thing. It's over. And now I need to deal with *this*."

Ellie, a mother, cringes at the callousness, born, she knows, of bravado and fear, a world of hurt beneath.

"What do you want to do?"

Silence.

"Hannah, I will support any decision you make. But you have to promise me you'll listen to me and think about—"

"Mom, I'm going to have an abortion. Okay? I'm not happy about it, but I can't derail my life right now."

"How far along are you?"

Ellie chews her lip nervously as Hannah drives into the mall parking lot and smoothly pulls into the first space she finds. Hannah takes off her seat belt and turns to face her mother.

"Like, maybe not even a month. I knew I screwed up, and I started testing right away. It's really, really early."

Ellie is ready to grab Hannah as she pitches forward and sobs in her mother's arms.

"It'll be all right, Hannah. It will be all right. You made a mistake. You're human."

Hannah soaks Ellie's T-shirt with her tears.

"Mommy, I just can't love a baby right now."

"I know. I know."

Ellie soaks Hannah's T-shirt with her own tears as she clutches her girl tight and wishes she could weep it all away for her.

But she can't.

But she's goddamned if she's going let Jeff bulldoze Hannah about this. Ellie isn't even tempted to tell Jeff. Some postfeminist momma tiger thing kicks in, and she does not feel one iota of guilt at keeping such a secret from her husband. After years of placating and mollifying, when faced with a real emergency, Ellie suddenly finds herself a backbone. No way will she let Hannah go through this thing with the Wrath of Jeff making everything more traumatic than it already is.

It's a confederacy of women. Wendy immediately agrees to fly in from Boston and stay at a nearby hotel. Ellie takes three days off from work without telling Jeff but pretends to go in every day, walking to the corner to secretly meet Wendy instead of Jane, her usual ride. Haley, of course, is on board, and her mother, Annie, who's known Hannah since the girls were twelve, agrees to help however she can.

Wendy provides rides, moral support, and also the money so Jeff won't notice any payments to Planned Parenthood coming out of his and Ellie's account. Haley and her mom keep the recuperating Hannah at their house for three days, citing a long weekend to celebrate the end of the summer, and a week later go with her to the doctor for the postcheckup, while Ellie stays at work chewing her nails until they call her to tell her that everything is okay.

And Jeff never knows a thing.

———

NOVEMBER 10, 2018

Till now.

Hannah looks at her father. He's pale; there are tears in his eyes. Her mother's expression is harder to read; Hannah thinks she sees pride, compassion (for who?), a kind of toughness that could pass for strength. She wonders if Ellie will do the conciliatory grovel or stand her ground.

She's not as glad as she thought she would be to hurt her father so badly.

"How could you not tell me this?" says Jeff, his eyes big with hurt.

"Because I wasn't about to let Hannah get harangued into a corner by you over this," Ellie says firmly.

Hannah is surprised by her mother's cogency, by her lack of apology.

"I wouldn't have—"

"Oh, knock it off, Jeff." (*Whoa. Who is this woman?*) "You give Hannah shit for cutting her bangs. Do you seriously think I'd ever let you know about something like this?"

Hannah's eyes are wide as she watches her parents go back and forth.

"How could you keep this from me? This is probably the most tragic, most important thing that's ever happened to this family, and you didn't tell me?"

"What about, how is Hannah? How is she physically? How is she psychologically? How did she get through it? This isn't about you, Jeff. Well, actually, it is, because it's about how you were such an asshole that we didn't want to tell you. You would have made a bad situation worse."

Jeff stares at her. Hannah's mouth is open.

Jeff says, "I don't want to be with either one of you right now."

"Whatever," Ellie says. She flips open the dessert menu as Jeff stands up and shakily walks away.

"Whoa," Hannah says to her mother, eyes wide, nodding. "Aren't you the cool bitch!"

Ellie lifts her wineglass to her lips, then puts it down because her hand is shaking.

"Thank you," she says.

CHAPTER TWENTY-TWO
HEY, BULLDOG

DIVORCED WOMEN OVER FIFTY CHAT ROOM
NOVEMBER 12, 2018
11:05 P.M.

LORY:
Hi, Ellesbelles. How was your trip?

ELLESBELLES:
It was . . . fine. What happened here? Looks like we're the only two on tonight—do you know if people went to Suzy's Vigil?

LORY:
I don't—this is the first time I've been on myself in a few days. Was your daughter's show good?

ELLESBELLES:
Wow, you have a good memory! Yes, the show was wonderful and she was wonderful! It was a musical adaptation of "James and the Giant Peach" and she was the evil Aunt Spiker.

LORY:

I remember reading that to my son when he was a little boy.

ELLESBELLES:

Yes, we read it as well!

LORY:

How did things go with your husband? Is that too personal to ask?

ELLESBELLES:

On this board, LOL? Well, things were . . . interesting.

LORY:

That's an old Chinese curse, isn't it? "May you live in interesting times."

ELLESBELLES:

Well, I will say that there was a certain . . . honesty between all of us that wasn't there before. And . . . I feel like I was able to finally speak up for myself and not get bullied. So that was good! How are things with you? Did you ever get your husband to go to therapy?

LORY:

I did. I think it's going well. He's a great guy, works hard, and I love him but he kind of drives me crazy.

ELLESBELLES:

He's a man—comes with the territory. They're like a whole different species sometimes.

LORY:
Does your husband drive you crazy, too?

ELLESBELLES:
Oh yeah. Right round the bend.

LORY:
But you still love him, right?

ELLESBELLES:
If we were in person, I would probably just sigh right now.
I know you love your husband and, you know, it's perfectly
fine to love someone who drives you a little crazy. You just
have to make room for everyone's eccentricities.

LORY:
Exactly! I feel like I've made accommodations for his
eccentricities but he's too stubborn to accept mine.

ELLESBELLES:
Probably a mutual acceptance of eccentricities is essential to
a good marriage.

LORY:
That's well put! I love him warts and all, but apparently, he
has a lot to complain about regarding me. At least, that's
what I'm getting in therapy.

ELLESBELLES:
I find it much easier to talk to my husband in therapy. Like
Freeatlast says, it's good to have a referee in a marriage.

LORY:

I was afraid my husband was seeing someone, but he's not, thank God. But he still is keeping secrets from me. I hate that. There shouldn't be any secrets in a marriage.

ELLESBELLES:

I agree. You should be able to speak openly about anything.

LORY:

Yes. You should. But I found out he went to see a divorce lawyer. Secretly, behind my back.

ELLESBELLES:

Oh. Well . . . nothing's final till it's final. And even then, people get back together. I mean, it's happened to people here on the chat.

LORY:

Do you think so?

ELLESBELLES:

Sure. But if you think your husband is holding secrets from you, maybe you should confront him.

LORY:

Well, he gets defensive and then I get mad and then we fight. I wish I could just tell him that I don't mind what's going on with him, I won't get mad, as long as he's truthful. All he has to do is tell me the truth and we'd be fine.

ELLESBELLES:

People never do what we think they should do, do they, LOL? The world would be a better place if everyone just listened to us!

LORY:

Well, my marriage would be, anyway.

CHAPTER TWENTY-THREE
THINK FOR YOURSELF

NOVEMBER 12, 2018

Up in her bedroom, Ellie closes her computer, disappointed that there's no news of SuzyQ's vigil or the meetup. She wonders if she's addicted to DWOF, because the first thing she did when she came home from Boston was boot up her computer and check out the site. Since she discovered DWOF back in September, she's been conscious of her increasing dependence on it, checking in at least once, twice, even three times a day to see who's on, what they're talking about. Even when they're just rambling, it's a comfort. Ever since she started grappling with the decision to leave or not leave Jeff, she's been aware of a kind of sad loneliness lying just under the surface of her usual even-keeled self, and the connection to the warm, welcoming group on DWOF seems to keep it at bay. More than just lines of type, these women are real to her, and she feels she can relax and be herself among them, as if she's talking to her girlfriends. She decides there are worse addictions, and she's not going to worry about it now.

She's more wired than tired, even though she's still on East Coast time, and her body thinks it's two o'clock in the morning. Jeff is downstairs in his office on his computer, and she's happy to be back in the house rather than the hotel room she shared with Jeff for three days. The New and Improved Jeff, as she calls him to herself, is less horrible but slightly unctuous, as if he feels he has to overcompensate for years of being an asshole by being excessively nice. Obviously, it's better than having him be an asshole, but she's wondering how long this will last and if it even matters to her. She still hasn't done her "assignment" from her lawyer, to put together a financial plan for her upcoming divorce, but the thought of all the math makes her mind go blank, and then again, there's the worry of where the money to fund all of it will come from. If Jeff has had thoughts about what he found out that day he followed her, he hasn't mentioned them, and maybe he hopes that, with his new good behavior, the whole divorce thing will be a nonissue.

Unpacking in her pretty, calm bedroom with its "beach sand" paint and bright white trim helps her process what happened in Boston, despite the interruptions by Snowball, their all-black cat named by Hannah in a fit of high school irony. Snowball does not like that they went away and left her alone to deal with the indignity of being fed by a neighbor, and she stretches out languorously over the still-unpacked clothes in Ellie's suitcase to make her point.

Scratching Snowball's ear, Ellie muses about how well Jeff had recovered from the abortion revelation. She'd been expecting the mother of all blowups, and she was impressed when she'd returned to their hotel room after the Big Reveal to find that he was sitting quietly, without the aura of sulky, self-righteous outrage that usually wafted off him in buckets during one of his long-term snits.

"I'm heartbroken," he'd said, and she understood. As proud as she was of Cool Bitch Ellie, who cavalierly told him off in the restaurant, she had to feel for the parent who shared a child's heartache. As a master compartmentalizer, she kept the memory in its box most of the time, but every once in a while, it would climb out, and she'd be gutted all over again. She wondered how Hannah was handling it and thought about her panic attack onstage. Well, there you go. After Jeff left the restaurant that night, Hannah had confided in her that she'd been having panic attacks at school and was seeing a therapist. Ellie was saddened and relieved. What else could she do? "Looks like we're all in therapy now," Ellie had said.

"About fucking time," Hannah said.

As Ellie puts her things away, she reflects on the conversation she just had with Lory on DWOF, and what Lory wrote about keeping secrets in a marriage. Ellie was surprised at the pang of guilt she felt when Lory shared that her husband had secretly been to see a lawyer. Lory seemed quite adamant that secrets were damaging to a marriage, and Ellie has to agree— well, any counselor or psychiatrist would tell you that. Yet Jane has told her with breezy nonchalance that she frequently keeps secrets from her husband, mostly things that have to do with their four horrible children, who are always being suspended from school or getting their heads stuck between banister spindles. Jane's husband, Dale, a busy prosecutor, doesn't really want to hear about, as Jane puts it, "the quotidian shit of life," so it doesn't materially affect Jane's relationship with him. Ellie knows they have a stable, good marriage.

So who was the better model: Lory, with her insistence on a kind of emotional purity, or Jane, who didn't seem to give a fuck? Yet Jane is happily married, and Lory's marriage is obviously in trouble. *Shit*, Ellie thinks wearily, moving a protesting Snowball out of the way and shoving her makeup into her bathroom drawer, *couldn't anyone just be a person?*

Ellie was looking forward to debriefing with Jane tomorrow on the ride in to work.

Jane and Ellie met years ago in New York City, where Jane was installed at the TriState Insurance Company as a broker when Ellie started there, right after Jeff stopped working. Ellie liked the crew at the New York office of the TriState Insurance Company, which they called Sicko ("the *T* is silent"), and she found a kindred spirit in the wry-humored and überconfident Jane.

Both Jane and Dale are Northern California natives, and when her parents left her their family house in Santa Cruz, they decided to move back there. Dale got a job with the DA's office, and Jane, pregnant with number four but still a sales manager, moved to the West Coast office of TriState and invited Ellie to join her as a sales rep.

By that time, Ellie was starting to feel trapped, though she would never have used that word. She loved Hannah, of course, but the nonworking, PTSD Jeff was getting worse and worse, and their two-bedroom, one-bath condo was shrinking in proportion to Hannah's growth spurts and Jeff's escalating meanness. It got so bad that at times Ellie pretended her co-workers—good-humored, predictable, and respectful—were her family, and that her home was her job, where she had to suffer an ornery boss and less-than-satisfactory working conditions.

It never occurred to her to get divorced. Or, rather, it did, but with so little money coming in, the question was always, "And do what for childcare?"

To Ellie's surprise, Jeff agreed to move to California and to use part of his 9/11 workmen's comp settlement as a down payment on a nice townhouse in Los Gatos, an upscale little town at the foot of the Santa Cruz Mountains in Silicon Valley. Jeff loved being able to say he lived in Silicon Valley and liked to imply, to their friends and family, that the move there was not just for Ellie but so that he could put his hedge fund acumen to work as a venture capitalist. Much to Ellie's relief, he didn't—the kind of money blowing around Silicon Valley made her very nervous—but he did settle down to work his own family finances every day as if it were a real job. "I'm managing the Smalls Family Mutual Fund," he'd tell people importantly, and as far as Ellie was concerned, as long as the fund was solvent and paying dividends (or whatever a fund was supposed to pay), she was okay with that.

The cross-country move blew the cobwebs from their brains and briefly instituted a new era of harmony and ease. They had a few good years at first, as they enjoyed the California sunshine and frolicked with Hannah on the gorgeous NorCal beaches. But Hannah grew older, and Jeff reverted to type, and here they all are.

Plopping herself in bed with her computer, Ellie goes to CNN.com to catch up on the news, though she skips politics and world affairs and heads straight to the entertainment stories.

Idly skimming a story headlined "Actress Watson's Estranged Husband Dies," Ellie suddenly has an odd sense of déjà vu. "Actress Watson" is, of course, the beloved English actress Claire Watson, whose performances on *Masterpiece Theater* and in quirky but important European independent films have delighted Ellie her whole life.

Ellie knows very little about Claire Watson's personal life, other than that she had several children with her manager-producer husband, presumably the "estranged husband" who'd just died. But something about the story rings a distant bell.

"Anthony Caxton-Smythe, the wealthy Yorkshire real estate developer most famously known as the manager-producer for his third wife, English actress Claire Watson, died Tuesday in his sleep while aboard his yacht, which was moored at the Marina del Rey near his Malibu home. He was eighty-two."

Ellie looks up from her computer for a second. Ding, ding, ding. She reads on.

"Independently wealthy, Caxton-Smythe went on to make an additional fortune with his canny choice of projects for Watson, whose career skyrocketed during their thirty-year marriage, though they have been legally separated for seven years."

She scans on, reading about Caxton-Smythe's other marriages, other children, and controversial real estate developments. This line catches her attention.

"Watson, recently returned from a film shoot in Sweden, sent this statement via her representatives: 'Tony was a brilliant father and a force to be reckoned with all his life. We who loved him will miss him terribly.'"

Sweden.

No way. Ellie's head spins. Way. Why not? Of course, she knew that DWOF's "Lorelei" was a "famous actress," according to—who was it? Moreofme?—and that she was shooting a movie in Sweden—or maybe it was Switzerland?

Ellie listens for a minute to see if Jeff is on his way up. She doesn't want to risk being caught on DWOF, so she takes her computer and goes into the en suite bathroom, vaguely trying to think up an excuse in her head in case he comes in and wants to know why she's in the bathroom with her computer.

Once ensconced on the toilet, Ellie goes to the DWOF site, pauses to figure out how to get where she wants to go. In a second or two, she has a list of all of Lorelei's posts, up until her last one on the thread of October 21, 7:05 p.m.

Yes, Sweden. She was shooting a movie in Sweden. She said so in Ellie's second-ever post on the board.

Ellie scans the rest till she finds what she thought she remembered.

"Lorelei: I kept hoping that once they were adults they'd perhaps give me another chance. But they can't be compelled to spend time with me now, and he seems to have upped the vitriol against me. And it's hard to argue with a doting father (*in* his dotage, I profoundly hope, the man is eighty-two) who has limitless cash, a seventy-foot yacht and vacation houses in Malibu and Lake Como. So they remain gone. The rest is silence."

Wow.

Ellie isn't quite sure how or what to feel. In a very real sense, she feels she knows Lorelei, whom she's pretty sure is Claire Watson (though she could be wrong, maybe?), yet she doesn't really *know* her; as she's learned from SuzyQ, you can't really know someone from a chat room. And yet she feels somehow connected to this news about Lorelei's late husband. Should she send a condolence card? Or possibly a card congratulating her for outliving the bastard, for maybe now having a chance at reuniting with her children, whom Ellie privately considers little shits for not communicating with their mother. Although, what does Ellie know about Lorelei as a mother? She might be a self-absorbed, neglectful monster. She might be someone else altogether.

Without thinking, Ellie PM's Marilyn, who answers on the first ring, as it were.

———

PM TO MAIRZYDOATS FROM ELLESBELLES
11:25 P.M.

Hi, Ellie! Are you writing me about the situation with Suzy? Many people on the board are having difficulty processing

that information. It is troubling, I know.
—**MAIRZYDOATS**

I actually PM'd you on an impulse, about something else.
—**ELLESBELLES**

Okay. What's going on?—**MAIRZYDOATS**

This may be inappropriate.—**ELLESBELLES**

Oh, goodie! I love inappropriate, LOL!—**MAIRZYDOATS**

Have you seen the news about the death of Anthony
Caxton-Smythe?—**ELLESBELLES**

The husband of the actress? Claire Watson? Yes, I did.
—**MAIRZYDOATS**

So—I'm just going to ask this. Is Claire Watson Lorelei?
—**ELLESBELLES**

Ellie. Come on. Even if I knew the answer to that, which
I don't, because how would I, I absolutely would not tell
you.—**MAIRZYDOATS**

And quite frankly, this is why I was not happy about
Freeatlast, Gingerbear and Moreofme going to Suzy's
vigil, though of course it was their decision. The
intersection of DWOF and, let's call it Reality, can often
be problematic. On the board, anonymity is the best
and often safest way to express ourselves.
—**MAIRZYDOATS**

I get it. Sorry about that.—**ELLESBELLES**

Meh, I'm over it. How's it going with you? How was your trip?—**MAIRZYDOATS**

Not horrible, surprisingly enough. Therapy seems to have had some effect on Jeff and our trip to Boston was—well, honest, if nothing else. I was pleasantly surprised.—**ELLESBELLES**

That's good to hear! Just remember, Ellie—you must do what's best for you.—**MAIRZYDOATS**

Thanks. I'm trying.—**ELLESBELLES**

—

Ellie signs off. What did she expect? And what would she even do with the confirmation if Marilyn had given it? Ellie thinks about Lorelei's recent lack of presence in the chat room. This probably explains it. But wait, of course it doesn't—Anthony just died a few days ago, and Lorelei's been gone for several weeks now. Ellie feels a stab of longing for Lorelei, for her warmth and humor and bitterness. She misses her, just like she misses SuzyQ.

Ellie suddenly hears Jeff start up the stairs. She hastily gets out of the bathroom, puts her laptop on her desk, and slips into bed next to Snowball, pretending to be asleep so she can mull over undisturbed what she's just learned.

CHAPTER TWENTY-FOUR
I ME MINE

DIVORCED WOMEN OVER FIFTY CHAT ROOM
NOVEMBER 13, 2018
7:15 P.M.

ELLESBELLES:
So—did anyone go to Suzy's Vigil?

ELLESBELLES:
Are you guys there? I can see you lurking . . .

ELLESBELLES:
Hello???!!!!

FREEATLAST:
EB—SuzyQ wasn't exactly . . . who we maybe thought she was.

ELLESBELLES:
What? What does that mean??

GINGERBEAR:
Free Googled "Woman Lost in Kentucky Park" just before we left.

FREEATLAST:
It was actually all over the news. Her real name was Suzanne Decrosse.

ELLESBELLES:
. . . okay . . .

FREEATLAST:
Dr. Suzanne Decrosse. Google her. We'll wait.

ELLESBELLES:
Oh my God.

FREEATLAST:
Right?

ELLESBELLES:
Is this OUR SuzyQ? Are you sure?

GINGERBEAR:
We're sure. We were there.

ELLESBELLES:
Holy crap.

ELLESBELLES:
Okay, well—maybe this isn't so strange. She certainly could have been a poor southern woman who got herself educated and then worked her way up. To become the biographer of Flannery O'Connor.

MOREOFME:
And Eudora Welty.

FREEATLAST:
I can't even spell Eudora Welty.

GINGERBEAR:
And the Dean of Students at Kentucky College.

ELLESBELLES:
So—but then why would Suzy pretend to be . . . a person who couldn't use a comma to save her life? I mean, I love her—at least, who I thought she was—but her sentences would make an English professor keel over.

FREEATLAST:
Did you see her picture? Doesn't she kind of remind you of Jackie Kennedy?

ELLESBELLES:
Yes!

ELLESBELLES:
Wow. My head is reeling.

MOREOFME:
It was a really lovely vigil, they had it at one of the entrances to the park. Suzy—Suzanne—seemed to be very loved and respected.

GINGERBEAR:

A bunch of faculty and her students were there. The Chancellor gave a speech about her. It did sound like Suzy grew up rough—in a holler somewhere without running water—but she sure did reinvent herself.

ELLESBELLES:

Was Mairzydoats there?

GINGERBEAR:

No, she wanted to stay anonymous, which I guess makes sense. So Free, Moreofme and I represented.

ELLESBELLES:

So . . . and . . . Chas? Was Chas there? Is there a Chas?!

FREEATLAST:

Well, we figure "Chas" is actually "Charles Blackwell Montross" and he was most definitely there.

ELLESBELLES:

????

FREEATLAST:

He's the college provost.

ELLESBELLES:

I have no idea what a provost is. Or does.

GINGERBEAR:

Basically, he's Suzy's boss.

MOREOFME:

Suzy's therapist, Jeannie—who's a real sweetheart, by the way—she came right up to us, because Mairzydoats had told her that three of us from the chat room would be there.

MOREOFME:

So, Free asked if Suzy's ex was there, and Jeannie seemed kind of confused by that, but she pointed out Provost Montross to us as her husband.

ELLESBELLES:

So? Was he Manson-esque or just run-of-the-mill creepy?

MOREOFME:

He was Gorgeous. GORGEOUS. I about fell over. Oh my!

FREEATLAST:

He was seriously, seriously hot. Like, George Clooney-hot.

FREEATLAST:

He got up to speak about how much he loves her, and he'll never stop looking for her and then he got all choked up and started crying. I wanted to call "Bullshit" but I was a guest, so I didn't.

MOREOFME:

I kind of thought he was sincere.

FREEATLAST:

Pffht.

ELLESBELLES:

Did you guys talk to him?

GINGERBEAR:
Well, I was afraid Free would kill him and More would take him back to her hotel room, so I kept everyone away from him.

ELLESBELLES:
Did you talk to the therapist? Did you tell her that Suzy was different on DWOF than she was in real life?

GINGERBEAR:
Yeah. We told Jeannie that on DWOF Suzy was like a country bumpkin—we didn't say exactly that but you know what I mean—and she listened really carefully. She seemed very sad but interested.

FREEATLAST:
Jeannie didn't seem too shocked by it at all. She said Suzy-Suzanne was complex.

ELLESBELLES:
She wasn't surprised? Do you think maybe Suzy had some kind of multiple personality thing?

GINGERBEAR:
Well, we couldn't ask her THAT. We were pretty shell shocked by the whole thing ourselves. I mean, this was our Suzy, but all this stuff kind of made her seem like a stranger. It was so weird and sad.

MOREOFME:
We asked Jeannie about how Suzy and her husband met.

GINGERBEAR:

So Jeannie says that he was from a really wealthy family and Suzy's mom, who just died, used to clean for them, and that's how he knew Suzy. Suzy/Suzanne grew up dirt poor in this tiny town called Somebody's Something, but she was smart and she went to Kentucky College, which is where she and Charles—Jeannie never called him Chas— fell in love. They went to grad school, then they both stayed in academia, and she wrote books and they both rose through the ranks yada yada yada. You can find all this on Suzanne's Wiki page, btw, so Jeannie didn't tell us anything new.

FREEATLAST:

Yeah. No way you can get any good dish from a shrink.

FREEATLAST:

Bunker's Mill. The town she grew up in was called Bunker's Mill.

ELLESBELLES:

Why would Suzy do that? Pretend to be so different on the board? I feel sort of betrayed by that. Like maybe she was laughing at us for believing she was what she pretended to be.

MOREOFME:

Maybe she wanted to be who she was before she grew up and got all professional and important. Maybe her new personality was uncomfortable for her and the chat room was the place she could go that she didn't have to be the bigshot writer and professor. She could just be easy peasy breezy Suzy.

ELLESBELLES:

That makes me sad. We would have loved the real Suzy, whichever one she was.

FREEATLAST:

Well, people present different faces in different situations. Everyone does it.

LORY:

Really? You think everyone is different with different people? That's not right, to be someone different depending on circumstances.

FREEATLAST:

Well, are you the same person with your husband as you are with your son?

LORY:

I am always the same person. Of course, I behave differently with my spouse than with my child! But it's always me.

ELLESBELLES:

I was bullied by my husband for years till I learned to speak up for myself and I know he didn't see the real me. He saw the person I pretended to be to protect myself or make myself agreeable to him.

LORY:

You can't have been a different person with him for all those years! Are you saying your husband doesn't really know who you are?

ELLESBELLES:
Yeah, now I think about it. That's exactly what I'm
saying.

LORY:
That seems incredibly deceptive, to play a part for a
decades-long marriage.

ELLESBELLES:
Sometimes you become the part you're thrust into without
realizing that you're changing. I think a lot of women survive
marriages/relationships that way.

MOREOFME:
Maybe with us, Suzy was trying to get back to a happier time
in her life, maybe when she and Chas were good and things
were simple.

FREEATLAST:
I feel like I'm grieving for Suzy all over again. Like we lost Suzy
when she disappeared and then we lost her again because
there really wasn't a SuzyQ to begin with.

ELLESBELLES:
I hope wherever Suzy is, that she's okay and at peace. I
mean—whatever personality Suzy put forth on the board, it
was real to all of us. She was dear and sweet and funny. And
I miss her.

GINGERBEAR:
Like Mairzydoats said, everyone's more or less anonymous on the
board. We might none of us be who we appear to be on here.

LORY:
Well, that's the beauty of the internet, isn't it?

ELLESBELLES:
You guys have been here for me through a really tough part of my life. I'd be freaked out if you weren't who you said you were.

GINGERBEAR:
Well, Free, More and I all met. I can attest that we are who we are.

ELLESBELLES:
And I've always been a "what you see is what you get" type of gal. Even if you can't see me!

LORY:
I've got nothing to hide.

ELLESBELLES:
But still—I guess you can never really know someone . . .

FREEATLAST:
Yeah. Till you're married to them.

LORY:
And even then . . .

CHAPTER TWENTY-FIVE
GOOD DAY SUNSHINE

NOVEMBER 18, 2018

It's a beautiful day, and they're going on a hike.

Ellie feels like Jeff's been on his best behavior recently, and Ellie's responded good-naturedly in kind.

It's a short two-mile hike near their house, an easy trail they used to do all the time with Hannah when she was young. Ellie's not up to anything much more challenging but figures a little fresh air and change of scenery might do them both good, and Jeff was enthusiastically on board when she suggested it.

The day is clear, with a bright blue sky, and has that fresh NorCal autumn crispness. As they walk, she can see there are a lot of other hikers out on the trail as well; it's just as popular as she remembered.

Ellie and Jeff talk amiably as they saunter up the trail—about the weather; Jeff's new sneakers, which he's wearing for the first time; their plans for Thanksgiving. Ellie and Jeff are going to Wyatt and Laurie's, while Hannah will be in Boston with Wendy and Lacey and Ellie's parents, Betty and Mort, since she'll be home in a few weeks for her winter break. It's a nice outing. Jeff's funny and laid-back, and Ellie feels her brain unwind a bit as the pleasant day takes hold.

Ellie has to choose what she looks at, since she can only see things within the funnel of her vision, and she divides her time between focusing on the solid, nicely tamped-down trail beneath her feet, and taking in the wildflowers along the way, though there are low-hanging tree branches that she has to navigate as well. She's doing pretty well for herself, she thinks, when suddenly Jeff yells, "Look out!" and she stops, frozen in her tracks.

"What?" she croaks.

"Whoa—you just missed a big, jagged rock, right in the path. Would've gone straight through your sneaker."

She peers down and around. She doesn't see anything. But, of course, she probably wouldn't.

He sees her looking.

"It's all right. I kicked it off the path. You're good. Let's keep going."

She walks more carefully after that, her eyes glued to the ground.

She wonders if Jeff is going to take this relatively peaceful time to bring up the lawyer's office visit. She wonders if *she* should. She doesn't want to ruin the lovely day, so maybe they have each privately agreed to a détente of sorts, at least for the duration of the hike. In the spirit of the Cool Bitch from Boston, she's decided she'll meet him head-on if he brings it up, but she's certainly not going to mention it herself, at least not till she's decided if she's in or out, so to speak.

They travel without incident up the small hill till they stop at the view of the lake, which quiets them both. It's lovely and peaceful, and it's so nice to stand next to Jeff for a minute, to have his solid presence at her side; if she gets divorced, she reflects, it'll be a lot harder for her to find someone to go hiking with (and to stand by her side), and she certainly can't go it alone. She's happy to be happy for a moment.

They follow the loop that will take them back to the parking lot, warmed up from the exercise despite the fact that the late-afternoon air is turning colder. There are fewer people around too, which is good. With fewer people, Ellie can see more of the landscape of the trail, more "nay-tcha" (nature), as they like to say in her family.

They walk a bit faster with the momentum from the downward slope, Ellie concentrating hard until Jeff yells, "Oh shit!" and manhandles her brusquely off the trail and into some side brush.

"Ouch!" she yells as he twists her arm.

"Snake," he says breathlessly, looking back at where they just were. "Rattlesnake. Just rolling down the side of the hill there . . ."

She knows rattlers are a frequent visitor to the trail and they've seen them before (their first time on the trail was cut short when they saw a rattler sunning itself on a rock, and six-year-old Hannah, a New York City girl born and bred, said, "Nuh-uh!" and ran back to the car).

Ellie, of course, can't see the rattler, but she's not happy about the way Jeff grabbed her, and rotates her arm a few times around to get the blood flowing back into where his grip cut off the circulation.

"Next time," she says to him evenly, "just say, 'Go to your left,' and I'll get out of the way."

"You don't want to get bitten by a rattlesnake," he tells her (like he would know), "believe me."

The cooler temperature is reflected in her attitude toward Jeff as they continue to walk.

Not far from the trail's end, Ellie hears another "hold on!" from Jeff, and though she's tempted to just turn to him and say, "Jesus, now what?" she doesn't have a chance, as he literally tackles her around the waist and shoves her aggressively off the path, so much so that she loses her balance and falls against a Mexican sage-type bush that's pricklier than it looks.

"What the *fuck*, Jeff?" she yells in a rage.

"You don't see stuff, Ellie!" he yells back. "You're a danger to yourself and others! You went right over a gopher hole; you could've broken your ankle! I'm trying to keep you safe!"

She doesn't even do him the courtesy of looking. There might be a gopher hole, there might not be. She's never had Jeff put his hands on her like that before, and she doesn't like it. Suddenly, she looks around and realizes, though they're close to the parking lot, they're alone on the trail. Of course, someone could come around the bend at any moment, but she no longer feels safe on the path with Jeff.

She twitches out the kinks in her back, shakes loose her legs and ankles, and starts marching determinedly ahead of Jeff, swiveling her eyes from her feet to the sides and up above so she doesn't miss anything.

"Ellie! C'mon!" she hears Jeff call behind her, but she really doesn't want to deal with him right now. She tries to calm down by telling herself that she has a choice: she can move out of the house and into her own life, and that knowledge buoys her, gives her a little kick that sends her trotting down the rest of the hill toward the parking lot, enjoying the feel of the unfettered movement of her body, which she usually has to keep so confined and circumspect.

Which is probably why she takes a real header over *something* on the trail—a dip in the path, a root, maybe even Jeff's fucking foot, for God's sake—which sends her tumbling down the remaining few yards of the trail. She sees the dirt road coming up fast to her face but winds up sideways, rolling over a few times until, dizzy, scraped and very frightened, she comes to rest, panting and crying.

Jeff skids down to her in a second, gathers her up in his arms, and sweetly cradles her, smoothing her hair and murmuring, "It's okay. I've got you. I've always got you, Ellie."

Ellie sinks back against his familiar, comforting, smothering presence and thinks to herself, *In or out, Ellie? In or out?*

CHAPTER TWENTY-SIX
GETTING BETTER ALL THE TIME

NOVEMBER 23, 2018

Jeff settles himself in his comfy chair in his office, while Ellie, who has the day off, naps upstairs. It's the day after a very nice Thanksgiving with Wyatt and Laurie and their family. He hopes Ellie can see how much their friends love and value him, and also what a rich and pleasant life they'd have if she just got over this stupid phase and began to deal with reality.

He is, in fact, seeing some improvement; she doesn't seem as sad and angry and aloof as she had been when she first came back. As far as he can tell, she hasn't been to see that divorce attorney again, though God knows he was at DEFCON 1 for a while after he'd tracked her down to that lawyer's office. He couldn't believe they wouldn't tell him a goddamn thing, even though it was obvious she'd *just left there.* He's the one who really should be talking divorce. After the betrayal both she and Hannah are guilty of, he's the one who's got every right to be furious, and he is; he's just keeping it in abeyance for now, until he feels his marriage is on safer ground.

He gives himself all the credit for her turnaround, due to his pivot after that thing at the Palms restaurant.

This second chance stuff is brilliant.

He's exhausted but also exhilarated—triumphant too. "Change" is tiring, and he's been doing it for, what, about a month now? Honestly, he sees her point sometimes—after all, you can't ride herd on someone the way she claimed he did to her. It's untenable—but he has emerged, he feels, not so much humbled as enlightened. The care and handling of a woman, a wife, requires much more finesse than he'd been aware of before she first left. He gets that now. How long he can continue is anybody's guess, but he's willing to bet he can keep it up for a good while yet.

The therapy, which is about as bad as he'd anticipated, has gotten bearable over time, and he has to admit, since he's mastered the role of repentant reprobate, he almost relishes it. He doesn't care what the therapist says so much—for God's sake, he, Jeff, figured out most of the stuff Joseph talked about after fifteen minutes on the internet—but the effect on Ellie, who bought into the whole thing, is nothing short of miraculous.

He remembers with satisfaction an incident a few days ago, when Ellie banged into the coffee table in the living room, which had only been there for the entire time they'd lived in the house, and he couldn't understand for the life of him why she couldn't remember that and steer clear of it. He'd thrown down his newspaper in disgust and had just said, "Jesus, can't you—" when he stopped himself. "Sorry," he said to her, clocking her hurt, angry eyes. "That was dumb. I need to be more"—he privately flinched but said it anyway—"mindful about stuff like that." There was a pause as both of them registered this new take on the situation, and after a second, Ellie nodded, a glint of approval and gratitude and maybe relief in her eyes. Then she smiled at him. God, he was a genius!

So, basically, it's just a matter of going with the script. Throw in a few watchwords, like *mindful* or maybe *personal space*, a little self-flagellation, and you're done. But he feels it's time to kick Joseph to the curb because it's a hell of an expense—*that* guy makes $225 an hour?—and he's determined to show Ellie that he's learned his lesson so they can get that off the table.

Because it's not as though they'd only been married for five years or something. Twenty-two years was nothing to sneeze at, certainly nothing to throw away, as Ellie seemed intent on doing last year. She is his wife, for God's sake. In the eyes of the law, their family, their friends—that's who she is. They took a vow, an oath, but obviously he takes it a lot more seriously than Ellie does. Plus, he loves her! How can she not get that? He's human; he's made mistakes, sure, but she isn't perfect either—something he doesn't feel that therapist has ever really considered—and still he cares about her. He worries about her, wants to protect her. That's natural, especially since it's obvious to everyone that her vision is getting worse. She tries to cover it up, by moving fast with that cane, or pretending to fish for something in her pocket to slow herself down when she's unsure of her footing, but he can tell. She's missing things all over the place, and she can't see that she is because she can't *see* that she is. She is vulnerable. It only makes sense that she shouldn't live alone at this point in her life.

But Ellie is stubborn (another thing the therapist glossed over), and he knows the vision thing is a delicate issue for her. But on the other hand, what is she supposed to do, just give up and sit in a corner for the rest of her life? That wouldn't help anybody, particularly him. Of course, she has to keep plugging away at her idea of independence, no matter how stupid and unrealistic it is. He ponders for a moment what it would be like to have a totally blind wife. He imagines himself cutting up her meat for her, imagines her sightless face turned toward the sound of his approach, wonders if she would learn Braille to read her millions of books. He shudders. A disabled wife is not an attractive prospect. But then again, he'd be phenomenal as her caretaker, and the world would recognize him as her support and her savior. There is something to be said for that.

He allows himself a brief daydream, seeing himself at her side at a family get-together—her family, so they can see how he helps her with her chair and her purse, how he makes sure she knows where her wineglass is so she won't knock it over. He'd pretend not to hear them as they whisper, "He's so devoted to her! She wouldn't be able to function without Jeff." It would be nice to be needed, after all this separation and therapy bullshit. Well, he never pretended to be anything else but hurt and upset by her leaving, so at least he knows she knows how he felt. A little gratitude in the future would only be right.

Then he gets an idea. A great idea, if he does say so himself.

Something to get them back on track. Not therapy. Not hikes in the park or stilted dinners. Something public. Something meaningful.

He sees it before him in crystal clarity: Ellie and him, dressed up, standing close, looking into each other's eyes, their friends and family surrounding them in loving approval as they *renew their vows.*

Of course, Jeff has known couples who have renewed their vows in New Agey bullshit ceremonies, and he frankly thought them cringeworthy and ridiculous. You make a vow when you get married. It is a vow: by definition, it's supposed to last. To renew a vow is redundant, he had felt.

But now he can see the appeal. Their renewed vows certainly would not be cringey, but rather, powerful, emotional, life-affirming, and would show the world the strength of his marriage to her. It would be a very public way for Ellie to recommit to him and to their marriage, and to remember what she promised twenty-two years ago. The incentive to stay married after that would be even greater, since to fail after a vow renewal would be horribly humiliating.

He likes it. He isn't going to google a caterer or an officiant or anything right now, but he can see the event, the day, shining before him like a golden vision of the future.

Jeff is startled out of his reverie by the sudden commotion of Ellie coming home from work, fumbling with her cane at the door, bashing her enormous purse around as she starts up the stairs. He goes to meet his wife and seems to surprise her by his tender care as he helps her—blind and flawed, but still his—into their home.

CHAPTER TWENTY-SEVEN
OH! DARLING

NOVEMBER 25, 2018

"Just for, like, a tune-up." Ellie knows it's a hot-button topic, telling Jeff she thinks they should touch base with their therapist, Joseph. They've been navigating their refurbished marriage fairly successfully, sorta-kinda, on their own for a few weeks now, but it's been on her mind, and isn't the result of all their previous therapy that she can now say whatever's on her mind to her husband without fear of a counterattack?

After a total of about eight sessions, Jeff and (a somewhat unconvinced but game) Ellie decided they could take a break for a bit, particularly as it's so expensive. In one of their last sessions, Joseph warned them both that Jeff might backslide, falling into the comfort patterns of his "maladaptive behavior," and Ellie should be aware of this. Jeff acknowledged that he'd try to be, in their new parlance, "mindful," employing his new coping tools when dealing with issues, rather than his old fallbacks of blame and harangues. Ellie also agreed to be less of a doormat, to stick up for herself and hold his feet to the fire.

They're sitting at their kitchen table, eating Ellie's fresh-baked rosemary bread with some wine and cheese.

"Why? Haven't I been the epitome of the perfect husband?" Jeff says, jokingly mispronouncing *epitome*.

"Of course, you are the apotheosis of the perfect husband." Ellie mispronounces *apotheosis* too, chuckling. "It's just . . ." She can't, or doesn't want to, articulate the tiny nagging doubt, the sense that maybe an hour's correction might prevent a future train wreck.

"What?" He's not annoyed, but close.

"What's wrong with just going in to talk about how we're doing? We can show off how great we are," Ellie jokes.

"At two hundred–plus bucks an hour? Are you kidding? Why don't you just tell me what's on your mind instead of wanting to run off to Joseph to get your opinion validated."

See? She wants to say, *That right there. That response is what makes me want to run right off to Joseph to be validated.* But then maybe she's being too sensitive? Does she need Joseph every time she thinks there's an issue in her marriage, rather than tackling it herself? She wishes she was better at handling things in the moment, because Jeff is, annoyingly, right: she is pissed off about the brief round they had a few days ago, when she saw an ad for a concert at a music college for the blind and suggested they go.

"Sorry," he'd said, barely looking up from his phone. "Not interested."

She'd been hurt by his brusqueness, but she wasn't quite sure she had a right to be. He didn't have to want to go—but then again, she'd wanted him to want to go with her. So, she'd said what she thought. "That kind of hurts my feelings." It had sounded wimpy, even to her.

"Why? I'm being honest. I don't have to go if I don't want to, and I don't have to pretend about it, right? Doesn't 'being mindful,'" he'd said, with the finger-quote thing, "go both ways?"

She had tried to express what she was really feeling.

"Well, sure. But we have an extenuating circumstance here. I'm not asking you to go to a fashion show or something like that. This is about me being blind and a related thing I want to do. I'm looking for support," she'd said. There. That was pretty much it right there.

"Well, I appreciate that," he'd said, following the formula. "But don't I support you and your vision issues in a million ways, every day? I drive you, help around the house, clean up after you, and listen to you when you want to vent. You have my arm all the time, Ellie, every single time you need it, not to mention my sympathy. So, please don't say I'm not supportive. That hurts *my* feelings."

He'd turned back to his phone.

She hadn't known how to deal with that situation.

He has a right to his feelings and to choose not to go, but isn't there another way to say, "Sorry, that's not my thing," without making her feel like shit for asking in the first place?

It still bugged her, but if she's bad at speaking her mind in the moment, she's even worse at dredging something up days later. She'd decided to let that one go.

"Yeah, it is a lot of money," she says, realizing she doesn't have the fight to push for a therapy session.

"And anyway, I'm cured, right?" He's grinning. "I'm cured! I can walk again! I can play the violin again!"

She laughs and joins in, "I can see again!"

"Hallelujah!" Jeff throws his hands up in the air, and they both laugh.

Then he gets serious.

"Listen, I filled my part of the bargain. I went to therapy, and I obviously got a lot out of it—we both can admit that—so I see no need to go back. Maybe we can just enjoy the fact that I've changed, and you're back home where you belong, in a nice house with your loving husband, instead of in that crappy little apartment all by yourself. "

"That apartment wasn't crappy," Ellie says with some spirit. "And I *liked* it there."

"Why?"

She clears the plates and glasses off the table and flings back over her shoulder as she heads toward the sink: "Because it was mine."

She puts the dishes in the sink to soak and shuts her eyes. She briefly gives herself a mental time-out by imagining her Phantom Husband, the cheerful, kind, unflappable guy she should have married, who never would have belittled her or spied on her or pushed her off a hiking trail, the one who would make her laugh and comfort her and always know what she was talking about. The guy who would have cherished Hannah and not smothered her.

Ellie drags herself back to reality and studies the kitchen countertop. She can't find the large bread knife she just put down so she could wash it. She takes a breath. This happens a lot. It's just out of her range of vision, but with her vision narrowing, she sometimes takes minutes to find something she'd set down a second ago. Ellie pats her hand in ever-increasing circles on the counter, the way she was taught by the orientation teacher who'd trained her to use the white cane years ago, but the damn thing is still apparently just out of reach. She feels the irritation rise up. The space isn't that big. Why can't she just *see* it? She gives up patting and slaps her hand crankily around the surface, still can't find it; it feels like it's deliberately moving away from her. All she can see is countertop. She curses, frustrated by this simple task made that much harder by her damaged sight. She steps back from the counter, pissed off, and startles as she turns to find Jeff, knife in hand, the sharp end pointed toward her, the handle in his hand.

"Looking for this?" he says wryly. She looks from his face to the serrated knife edge glinting in the afternoon sunshine. Is her husband pointing a knife at her?

In a heartbeat Jeff has righted the knife so that the handle is toward her (as they always taught Hannah), the blade loose in his palm.

She could cut him if she grabbed it the wrong way. Slice right through his hand.

She doesn't, of course. Trust! It's what makes a marriage work.

"Thanks," she says casually, gently taking it from him and tossing it into the sink. Misaimed, it bounces off the edge and lands on the floor, where, of course, Ellie can't find it. Once again, Jeff picks it up. He takes her place at the sink—not quite shoving her out of the way—and rinses it off under the water.

"See?" he says. "It's good you came back."

CHAPTER TWENTY-EIGHT
WHAT YOU'RE DOING

NOVEMBER 25, 2018

Jeff settles into his chair with a glass of wine and a sigh, having finished cleaning up in the kitchen for, or rather, after, Ellie, as usual.

He was damned if he was going to go back to therapy. He went. He changed. He's done. Maybe she doesn't see it, maybe she hasn't changed as much as he has, but he's a new man, and it pisses him off that she can't appreciate it.

It's wearing him out, but not nearly as much as trying to figure out if she went back to the divorce attorney. He's been checking phone records and bank accounts like crazy (since he can't get on her phone anymore), but she'd slipped through his net once before, and he couldn't be sure she wouldn't do it again.

He thinks for a second about his vow-renewal plan, the image of which still seems like an attainable goal, even if the going is clearly going to be a little rocky, until he gets her where he wants her. The conversation they'd had this afternoon about going back to therapy had its lighthearted moments, and he knows that's what charmed Ellie and drew her to him years ago. He just has to keep a lid on his annoyance about the dozens of things she does that irritate him. He sighs. Good behavior, or someone else's definition of it, is hard.

At least she's under his roof. And like they say, possession is nine-tenths of the law.

CHAPTER TWENTY-NINE
NOT A SECOND TIME

DECEMBER 1, 2018

Ellie waits for the door to slam as Jeff goes off to a Giants game with Wyatt. Then she settles down in their bedroom with Snowball for a good cry, allowing herself the luxury of letting it all out because she honestly doesn't know what the fuck to do.

She cries until Snowball, who is uncomfortable with untrammeled displays of emotion, daintily steps out of her grasp and disappears down the hallway. Then she sits up and tries to take stock of her situation.

After Jeff's "change" and the trip to Boston, Ellie thought she could maybe make a go of it with the New and Improved Jeff, but now, she realizes, she was just kidding herself.

This afternoon at lunch she'd navigated a minor kitchen skirmish. As she'd poured honey into her tea, the cap had fallen off, and when she put it back, it had dribbled down the side and made the bottle sticky. She'd left it that way and drank her tea, then, of course, forgot about it. When Jeff brought it up, she admitted she was guilty as charged and scrubbed the plastic honey bear bottle with dish detergent as best she could, though he still felt he had to do it over again himself.

Which irritated her and kicked off an argument that soon

spiraled into one of their labyrinthine fights, which resembled nothing so much as a verbal Rube Goldberg machine that she could never successfully reconstruct in her memory afterward. Somehow Jeff suddenly pivoted and got into Hannah's abortion and how they deliberately kept it from him.

Ellie was thrown off-balance. She'd thought this was old news, but for some reason Jeff had been stewing about it for some time, and it became the issue of the hour, as fresh (for him) as if it had just happened. Ellie tried to rally her therapy tools and her own compassion for his pain, but Jeff threw her attempts back in her face and retracted all the "psychobabble" he laid on her after they had just completed therapy. Dismissing "all that mindful crap," he made it very clear he was the wronged party, and both she and Hannah were complicit in what was "like a dagger to the fabric of our family."

Ellie remembered that Joseph had warned them both that someone like Jeff, who'd gone through a lot of changes, might backslide, and she tried to use their new vocabulary: "That's not working for me," "Let's stay on topic," and her favorite, "Martha My Dear," which was their watchword for stepping back and taking a break from the fracas.

"Oh, really?" Jeff was so confident in his anger, in his right to be angry, and she felt all over again the feelings of lassitude and despair she'd endured for twenty-two years. "Well, guess what? This bullshit doesn't work for *me*." And just like that Ellie realized the door had slammed on any change she might have hoped for, and she was trapped. Again.

In a final attempt to get back on track, she reminded him of the promise he'd made not to fall back into old patterns. He snapped back that she'd promised she wasn't going to be a door-mat anymore, and how was that working out for her?

So they fought, and not mindfully.

Then she crept upstairs with the tatters of her dignity as Jeff got ready to go to the game. She knew that by the time he came back he'd be fine and assume she was too, and life would go on.

And on and on.

Ellie shifts restlessly on her bed as all the excuses for staying come flooding back. She inventories the good times they've had, the times they've connected. Then the reasons to go: the times she felt belittled, blindsided, bewitched-bothered-and-bewildered, and just plain bad. She knows marriage is a combination of taking the good with the bad, but what kind of life can you have if you feel deep in your bones that you are being wronged more often than not? She thinks of funny, sexy, controlling, demanding Jeff as she first knew him, all the signs there for the seeing, but, of course, she's vision impaired.

She knows it's time for her to go back to her divorce lawyer. But she won't think about that now. She'll think about that . . . tomorrow.

Ellie boots up her computer and visits DWOF, for the first time since before Thanksgiving.

———

DIVORCED WOMEN OVER FIFTY CHAT ROOM
8:22 P.M.

MAIRZYDOATS (DWOF MODERATOR):
But you don't know that this guy is Suzy's Chas.

ELLESBELLES:
Hi.

MOREOFME:
HI!!!!!

GINGERBEAR:
EB! Welcome back!

MAIRZYDOATS (DWOF MODERATOR):
Good to hear from you, EB!

FREEATLAST:
Have you left him again?

ELLESBELLES:
LOL, nope, not yet! Just missed you guys. What's going on?
My God, I'm such a horrible person, what's going on with
Suzy/Suzanne, I haven't even checked the papers! Is there
any word?

MAIRZYDOATS (DWOF MODERATOR):
Sadly, Suzy/Suzanne is still missing.

FREEATLAST:
But Chas is dead.

ELLESBELLES:
WHAT?

GINGERBEAR:
Free and I have been checking the local papers near where
Suzy lives, just to see if maybe she turned up. It seems
unlikely but still, we're praying she will.

FREEATLAST:

So I see this article that just catches my eye, "Local Man Found Dead From Vaping" and I read it because first I think, what kind of moron dies from vaping, then I see his name is "Chas" so of course I think, Suzy's guy was named Chas AND this guy died in Bunker's Mill, the town where Suzy grew up. But this guy obviously isn't Charles Blackwell Montross. If the provost of Kentucky College had died from a vaping accident it'd be a bigger deal.

ELLESBELLES:

How do you die from vaping?

GINGERBEAR:

According to the article, he was using a device he'd customized himself and it exploded and blew his head off. I guess that's a thing.

FREEATLAST:

The guy was a rocket scientist.

ELLESBELLES:

So Chas definitely isn't Suzy's husband, the Provost Charles Montross, but how do we know he had anything to do with Suzy?

GINGERBEAR:

His real name was Chasem "Chas" Beaverspil and he worked at a Discount Tire store. I remember once Suzy said he was "selling tires in Canada," whatever the hell that meant, but still . . .

FREEATLAST:
And how many people named Chas could there be in
Bunker's Mill, Kentucky?

GINGERBEAR:
Holy shit holy shit holy shit holy shit holy shit

FREEATLAST:
WHAT?

MOREOFME:
WHAT?

ELLESBELLES:
WHAT?

MAIRZYDOATS (DWOF MODERATOR):
I rarely say this, but you all need to calm down. These are
real people and there are tragedies here.

MOREOFME:
Sorry.

GINGERBEAR:
So I've been googling Chasem Beaverspil and you know
how there are sites that tell you if someone's had any police
trouble or outstanding lawsuits? Chasem Beaverspil had a
restraining order taken out against him three times in the last
four years. By guess who?

FREEATLAST:
Suzy.

GINGERBEAR:
Suzanne Decrosse.

MAIRZYDOATS (DWOF MODERATOR):
I'm deleting this post.

———

Ellie sits back, blinking. It seems a little draconian of Mairzy-doats to delete the post, but it *was* starting to feel a little weird. She scrolls backward through the last few pages of the board and indeed the thread is gone, as if it had never happened. Of course, the facts are all there for anyone to look up online, and she's pretty sure she might be googling Chasem—what was his name? Beaver-spil?—herself. *Bless the board*, she thinks. *It's always a distraction.*

Then she catches herself. Suzy is still missing, or, God forbid, worse, and unless her disappearance is due to something entirely unexpected, she is, as Mairzydoats said, a real person who could be caught in a real tragedy. Ellie's not a praying person, but she sends out a small prayer for whatever version of Suzy/Suzanne is out there and perhaps in harm's way.

She wonders if Free, Ginger, and More will log on again like chastened children and decides this conversation isn't for her. She's too weary to parse out someone else's heartache. She hesitates for a moment, then PM's Mairzydoats.

———

PM TO MAIRZYDOATS FROM ELLESBELLES
8:35 P.M.

Marilyn, are you here, or are you still on the board?
—ELLESBELLES

I can be in two places at once, LOL, I'm magic that way!
—**MAIRZYDOATS**

So how are you doing? Is it going well?—**MAIRZYDOATS**

Honestly? No.—**ELLESBELLES**

Oh, Ellie. I'm so sorry.—**MAIRZYDOATS**

I know. I'm scared.—**ELLESBELLES**

You left before. You can do it again.—**MAIRZYDOATS**

Money though. How can normal people afford to get divorced? That lawyer I saw, whom I liked very much, said to me, "Freedom has its price" but that's easy to say when the check's being made out to *you*.—**ELLESBELLES**

There's always an economic price for freedom and it's usually the woman who pays it.—**MAIRZYDOATS**

Yeah. I can just hear Gingerbear right now: The Fuckers!
—**ELLESBELLES**

God give me strength, I love our DWOF sisters but they do dig up some shit.—**MAIRZYDOATS**

I sometimes wonder about Lorelei and Suzy. Moreofme wants to believe they're hanging out together, and I love that thought, the two of them getting drunk and cackling over their husbands' bitter ends. I expect Lorelei is just laying low but I still hope that maybe Suzy will just pop up again. SMKL.—**ELLESBELLES**

It must be nice to have the biggest problem in your life go away.—**ELLESBELLES**

Ellie—Jeff isn't going to change, and you need to decide what you're going to do.—**MAIRZYDOATS**

I know.—**ELLESBELLES**

CHAPTER THIRTY
I'M ONLY SLEEPING

DECEMBER 1, 2018

It takes Ellie a few seconds to realize the call is not about Hannah, and she's so relieved she literally loses her hearing, so it takes her almost another minute to understand that Jeff has been in a car accident, that it's bad, and that she has to get to the hospital as soon as possible.

Shaking, she picks up her phone and orders an Uber. Thank God it's Saturday, 2:00 p.m. Daylight. She can see. Mostly.

Gingerly, she approaches the hospital entrance, tapping with her cane. The hospital is small and rather quiet. When she tells the receptionist who she is and why she's there, she's kindly told to take a seat, and a doctor will be with her shortly. She doesn't know whether or not to ask if Jeff is still alive. Would that sound . . . gauche? Or is that the very thing she should be asking?

The doctor, younger than she expects—ever since she turned fifty, doctors are always younger than she expects—is tall, thin, going bald, and with kind blue eyes. He invites her to sit in his "office," a tiny room off the ER. He starts out by saying, gently, "I'm sorry, but . . ." and Ellie drops her jaw and stares at him.

Jeff had lost control of the car after a tire blew out on

Highway 17, a road they traveled all the time. The car had tumbled down the hillside several times and came to land upside down, a tree speared through the back window, which injured Jeff in a way that the doctor didn't seem to want to describe to her.

Jeff died shortly after arriving at the hospital.

The doctor says again he's very sorry, and indeed, he seems to be. Did she need water? Could they call anyone for her?

Ellie sits still, not showing any emotion, because the one emotion she's conscious of is . . . joy. A heart-pounding, relief-flooding, walkin'-on-sunshine joy.

Oh, she is officially a bad, *bad* person. Her husband has just been killed in a grisly accident, and she's *happy*. But more to the point, she's free.

Then she thinks of Jeff, the man she spent almost exactly half her life with, the father of her daughter, the man who once "loved her so naughty he made her weak in the knees," the man she'd come to hate and pity. Sadness hits her like a sandbag in her gut, the weight of the years she'd wasted for herself—and for him too—by not getting the hell out and giving them both a chance at something different, something better, something right.

"Can I see him?" she manages to croak out.

"Yes, of course." The doctor stands and summons a nurse outside the door. A comfortably large woman, older than Ellie, for which she is grateful, guides Ellie to a small room, where a man is lying on a gurney, a blanket over his body.

This is so much like what she's expecting from watching TV medical procedurals that she stops in the doorway, overcome with a sense of unreality.

Just like on TV, the nurse pulls back the blanket covering his head and steps back, respectfully. Whatever trauma his body endured, his face looks mostly like him, though pale, slack-jawed, the skin drawn over his cheekbones giving him a noble look, like a Roman warrior on a coin. Ellie is moved, not by the singular aspect of her dead husband but of the dignity of that stilled body, a recognizable husk now void of the violent imperatives of life. She can feel her anger, her familiar, rouse itself half-heartedly before folding in on itself and going to sleep.

You fucker, she thinks, but she whispers out loud, "Thank you."

She steps back to begin the rest of her life.

———

**PM TO MAIRZYDOATS FROM ELLESBELLES
9:02 P.M.**

Jesus.—**MAIRZYDOATS**

I know.—**ELLESBELLES**

That's . . . detailed.—**MAIRZYDOATS**

Yeah. I've sort of been honing it over the years. That's it in its current incarnation. Sometimes I call my sister Wendy and tell her, "Jeff is dead," and the first thing she says is, "Did you kill him?" 'cause that's Wendy's sense of humor.—**ELLESBELLES**

I mean, this is just a fantasy, I don't want Jeff to really die. Obviously.—**ELLESBELLES**

Obviously. I do feel obligated to weigh in here and say that having fantasies about your spouse's death is not indicative of a healthy relationship.—**MAIRZYDOATS**

Marilyn—you don't have to call anyone about this, do you? I mean, I know if a shrink hears that someone's going to harm someone else they have to report it, but, this isn't that. It's purely fantasy. You get that, right?—**ELLESBELLES**

Yes, of course! I'm not going to turn you in because you have a fantasy that your husband dies in a car crash! You're not the only woman to have that fantasy. Believe me. *Believe me.* —**MAIRZYDOATS**

Yeah, well. There's just no feasible way I can pay for a divorce anyway right now, so fantasy is a good outlet. But he's twelve years older than me, so I figure when he does die maybe that means I'll have twelve good years left by myself.—**ELLESBELLES**

You know, you're not alone feeling trapped in your marriage. If you got a lot out of DWOF, you might want to check out this other chat room called—you're gonna love this—*I Am the Walrus* (believe it or not, the moderator is also a Beatles fan). There are women on there in exactly your situation—trapped in a marriage for economic or physical or emotional reasons—who may have some creative solutions for the problems that you're facing now.—**MAIRZYDOATS**

Well, clearly, these are my people.—**ELLESBELLES**

So, are you interested?—**MAIRZYDOATS**

Yes. And curious!—**ELLESBELLES**

Okay. This has a higher level of security than DWOF (more high-profile women with a lot of reasons to keep their identity hidden) so you're going to have to install a special browser on your desktop. I'll send you the link.—**MAIRZYDOATS**

Um. Okay . . . you're not sending me to the dark web or anything like that, are you?—**ELLESBELLES**

Therapists don't generally send their clients down THAT rabbit hole, LOL!—**MAIRZYDOATS**

But yes. This is a site on the dark web.—**MAIRZYDOATS**

???????????—**ELLESBELLES**

Again, I must stress that this gives these women, and you if you so choose, a level of absolute security and anonymity.
—**MAIRZYDOATS**

You have got to be kidding me.—**ELLESBELLES**

Isn't it dangerous??? Isn't it the equivalent of going down a dark alley in a bad part of town in the middle of the night all by yourself in a sundress and strappy sandals?????—**ELLESBELLES**

LOL, no, not at all. It's just another part of the web that you can access without Google and Amazon and Facebook tracking everything you've done and sending you a million ads for things you don't need.—**MAIRZYDOATS**

And this is just a women's chat room. It's not like they're selling drugs or babies or anything like that.—**MAIRZYDOATS**

I'll send you the link, and I'll also send you info on how to get a reliable VPN, which you'll need.—**MAIRZYDOATS**

Oh My God. What's that???—**ELLESBELLES**

Ellie. Calm down. It stands for virtual private network. You can get one through Norton Security. It's about $40 a year and frankly, everyone should have one. It's another way to hide your internet footprint so your cyberhistory can't be traced. In fact, if you've ever used your phone or laptop at an airport or a Starbucks or even a grocery store parking lot, which have unsecured Wi-Fi, you're at risk of being hacked. A VPN ensures that you can't get hacked. Look it up on Google, it will explain how it works. There's nothing sinister about it.—**MARILYN**

This whole thing sounds sinister. I'm happy on DWOF, thank you very much.—**ELLESBELLES**

That's fine, but the women on DWOF are divorced or separated. That hasn't been a successful option for many of the women of IATW, and they may have some particular wisdom about ways to handle a dysfunctional marriage that might be of value to you.—**MAIRZYDOATS**

I get that the dark web part is unnerving, but nothing will happen to you if you use a VPN and only visit the chat room.—**MAIRZYDOATS**

If you send me the link, will my computer be compromised?—**ELLESBELLES**

No. Nothing will be compromised. That's the point.
—**MAIRZYDOATS**

Ellie?—**MAIRZYDOATS**

———

PM TO MAIRZYDOATS FROM ELLESBELLES
9:35 P.M.

Okay. Send me the link. I'll think about it.—Ellesbelles

Good. You deserve to be happy, Ellie. But you have to have courage.—Mairzydoats

———

9:40 P.M.

> From overit@protonmail.com
> To: fullfathomsfive@protonmail.com
> Subject: Newbie

> Hi,

> I'm sending you someone. Big Beatles fan.

> She's a little freaked out, might take her a while.

> Take care.

> M

From: fullfathomsfive@protonmail.com
To: overit@protonmail.com
Subject: Newbie

Hi, yourself,

I'll watch for her.

Thanks.

You take care, too.

D

CHAPTER THIRTY-ONE
WITH A LITTLE HELP FROM MY FRIENDS

DECEMBER 4, 2018

Ellie lies at the foot of the stairs, her ankle throbbing where she twisted it on the way down after a misstep involving Snowball, perched on a step and stoned out of her mind after a session with her catnip toy. Ellie's annoyed; everyone in the family knows that Snowball gets catatonic with that damn thing, and they are never to leave it on the stairs because someone, most likely Ellie, could trip and fall over the corpse-like cat. *Fuck Jeff*, she thinks furiously, because she sure didn't do it.

The cat, having staggered down the last few steps, is now upright and nonchalantly giving herself a facial. Ellie irritably wishes they'd gotten a dog instead, a nice golden retriever, who'd be kissing her face right now and wagging his tail in doggy concern for her. She gingerly sits herself up, takes an inventory—no head injury, thank God, hips and spine seem to be okay. She didn't fall from the top of the stairs, just the last three or four at the bottom. Maybe her ankle will work itself out if she walks around on it. She's glad Jeff's not here to witness her fall. Though she'd like to blame him for leaving the toy there, she knows he'd probably lob the blame right back at her. He's off playing soccer with Wyatt and the guys.

She hobbles back up to the kitchen. They live in a trilevel townhome, which sounded so cool to her when they bought it, but within weeks of moving in she realized that it was, as she jokingly told Jeff, "a deathtrap," with flights of stairs from the entryway, from the kitchen and dining room, and then up to the bedrooms, not to mention the four steps up from the garage, where, of course, the washer and dryer are. As she ices her ankle, she thinks for the two-billionth time about her diminishing options and her also diminishing eyesight and wearily tells herself to just forget it. She's fine the way she is. Jeff is fine, when handled correctly, and she'll try to ignore the rest of it.

She thumps her way up the stairs to her computer in their bedroom, after giving Snowball a make-up scratch under her chin, because she loves her cat even if she nearly killed her. Once in her room, she props her aching ankle on a chair, pops a couple of Advil, and opens her computer.

She's been ignoring Marilyn's last email to her, the one with the link to the dark web. Marilyn might be right; there might be some "particular wisdom" on that I Am the Walrus site (and the name alone intrigues her), but the dark web—she's not sure she's ready for something like that. She prefers to stay on the light web, and so she goes to her comfort zone, a place she'd very much like to stay in.

———

DIVORCED WOMEN OVER FIFTY CHAT ROOM
10:17 A.M.

MOREOFME:
I don't want Mairzydoats to shut us down again.

GINGERBEAR:
She's not on.

FREEATLAST:
And this is harmless.

ELLESBELLES:
Oh, no, are you guys going to get in trouble again???

MOREOFME:
Hi, Ellesbelles!

ELLESBELLES:
What's going on here?

GINGERBEAR:
Well, we were "speculating" again. About someone who's not on the board.

MOREOFME:
But who we love and are excited for!

ELLESBELLES:
. . .????

GINGERBEAR:
Remember Lorelei, our famous actress, who was doing a movie in Sweden?

FREEATLAST:
So I just went to the movies the other night, saw Rough Night, about a group of women friends who go out for a bachelor

party and accidentally kill a male stripper. Laughed my ass off. Anyway, there was a trailer for a movie that was set in Sweden in the 1800s or something, about a woman whose husband says she's crazy and sends her to an insane asylum.

LORY:
Oh yeah. That happened a lot in the 1800s.

MOREOFME:
Really?

LORY:
Well, I think it was legal. And there wasn't anyone there to stop them.

GINGERBEAR:
The Fuckers.

FREEATLAST:
So the movie was called—hang on, I have to look it up . . . give me a second . . .

FREEATLAST:
Here we go. The movie is called Persephone, I guess that's the name of the woman who was put away, and there were a couple of scenes with that English actress, Claire Watson, who plays the warden of the asylum, or whatever you call it. And she was in Sweden. So I'm thinking . . .

MOREOFME:
Lorelei.

MOREOFME:
I always knew Lorelei was Claire Watson.

GINGERBEAR:
You did? How? Just because she's English?

MOREOFME:
I don't know. I just knew. I mean, I could be wrong. But I think it's her.

ELLESBELLES:
We have to go see that movie.

GINGERBEAR:
Field trip!

MOREOFME:
We have to swear never to mention that we know Lorelei is Claire Watson.

MOREOFME:
In case she comes back.

FREEATLAST:
Or in case Mairzydoats sees this thread. Which she probably will. And probably delete . . .

ELLESBELLES:
It's all positive stuff, though. I'm sure when Lorelei gets back—actually, I don't know how to finish that sentence.

FREEATLAST:
So Ellesbelles—what's going on with you? There's been so much drama here we haven't checked in.

ELLESBELLES:
Oh . . . it's okay, I guess. In a way. Sort of.

GINGERBEAR:
That's a compelling endorsement of a marriage.

ELLESBELLES:
I know. I think I'm just weary. Sometimes it's fine, sometimes it's not, but my overriding feeling is it's not fine, and I've got to get moving on whatever I decide to do.

FREEATLAST:
We get it. It's a shit-ton of work. It's not just thinking about divvying up all your stuff from a hundred years, it's all that money crap. Believe me, I've been married and divorced and married and whatever, you'd think I'd have gotten the hang of it, but I still get nauseous thinking about it.

MOREOFME:
But there's something sort of clean about it, when all the financials are laid out in front of you. You know where you stand.

ELLESBELLES:
I think that's what's making me drag my feet. My lawyer told me to make a detailed financial plan of all our assets and stuff so we can move forward with a divorce settlement. LOL, I never thought I'd be saying words like "lawyer," "assets" and "divorce settlement."

LORY:
Your lawyer told you to do what?

ELLESBELLES:
It's pretty basic, I guess. Just list all our assets, like all the money in our accounts, how much the house is worth so when we sell, we'll know what we'll have for our own places, what we can reasonably afford to live on when we, you know, split. Things like that. You gals are right though—I'm getting on it. I promise!

LORY:
My husband's the money guy. I'd be no good at that!

GINGERBEAR:
Oh you'd be surprised what you can get good at when you have to.

CHAPTER THIRTY-TWO
(MONEY) CAN'T BUY ME LOVE

DECEMBER 6, 2018

Ellie's once again sitting in the en suite bathroom, her computer and paperwork in front of her on the counter between the two sinks, ears peeled for Jeff's return from playing soccer with the guys. Her ankle is much better, and she's able to think clearly. And let's face it, as fond as she is of Marilyn, getting on a women's chat room on the dark web for a solution to her bad marriage seems like a ridiculous, overreactive option.

So, galvanized by the advice of her DWOF sisters, Ellie has finally settled down to what she promised Stephanie she would do. She got out once before, she keeps telling herself, and she can do it again. Only this time she has to go all the way. After some hard number crunching, she has her figures written out on a piece of notebook paper, and they make perfect sense, as figures usually do, until you get people involved.

From a preliminary Google search, she's learned their townhouse is currently worth about $1.2 million. The figure staggers her until she realizes where they're living; in Silicon Valley, that's chump change. Split two ways, that's roughly $600,000 apiece, which should be enough to buy two nice, separate two-bedroom condos, although possibly not around here. Ellie's job will keep

her afloat till she retires. Jeff has a small monthly disability payment, plus the remainder of the workman's compensation he
got from his company after 9/11, which he claims he's been in-
vesting quite brilliantly, if he does say so himself (and he does).
She has no idea what's left from the claim, which Jeff calls the
Smalls Family Mutual Fund, but it was a hefty chunk to begin
with, so even with their move to California and their down
payment on the house, there should be something substantial
left for him to live on, possibly for decades, certainly till he gets
Social Security. If he can live on that, and she can live on her
salary, then, she figures, it's no harm, no foul.

It's a workable plan that will save tens of thousands of dollars
in legal fees, but only if Jeff goes for it, and she has no reason to
believe he will. But, she says to herself, reasonably, what can he
do? He can't keep her prisoner! She wonders how other couples
handle this step—if there's always one partner who's unwilling
or if most people know when it's time to move on and make
no fuss. How would she feel if the tables were turned, and Jeff
decided to leave her when she didn't want to? She'd want to kill
him! She'd hang on to the house with everything she had! She'd
be bitter and angry and vengeful, and she'd by God make sure
she made him miserable!

Or—she'd try to remain dignified and restrained and eventually see there was no way around it and then try to deal with
the pain and shock with as much grace and poise as she could
muster.

Gosh, Ellie, which would you *choose?*

The thought of confronting Jeff with her plan to end the
marriage nauseates her, not just because it's a terrible thing to
have to do but also because, *Jeff.* She knows she got a free pass
when she left before, and she's pretty sure that every awful thing
she was afraid he'd do the first time, he'll do now, like trashing

their house, turning Hannah against her, and getting a rapacious gunslinger of a divorce attorney for himself. What's even worse, she knows there's something she's not thinking of, that'll come at her from left field and level her.

She thinks longingly of Phantom Husband. He'd be a dream to divorce. Sure, he'd be sad, heartbroken, devastated, sick with longing and self-recrimination, but eventually he would see that this was something she had to do, and they would settle down to a long-term, amicable nonmarried relationship. She sighs. She would have had a great divorce with PH.

Hearing the front door open, she gives her notes one last look and hastily tucks them into the zippered lining of her purse. She doesn't want Jeff to get an inkling of what she's doing until she's ready to deploy, whenever that will be . . .

———

Here's what Ellie would like: she'd like to be magically transported to some time, say, eighteen months in the future, when the house is sold, her separation finalized, and she and Jeff live separately.

Here's what she's got: still in the present (damn it), she has thrown her carefully laid plans to the wind because she and Jeff had another stupid fight, and the words just fell out of her mouth.

She hadn't been able to decide if she wants to broach the separation discussion when they are on good terms or when they are fighting, but the decision was made for her when he came back from playing soccer yesterday and found out that she'd paid the electricity bill when he'd told her that he would do it. Suddenly, she found herself in the middle of one of their annoying, "I *said*," "No, what you *said* was," "No, I didn't *say* that; you didn't *hear* me" arguments, so instead of sitting down and saying, "Darling, I have some bad news," she suddenly got fed with up the whole pestilential situation and screamed at him, "That's it. I'm leaving. I'm going. We're selling the house, splitting the money, and ending this." She wasn't sure if Joseph, their therapist, would be horrified or impressed, but that's the way it came out. Fuck it.

Jeff just laughed at her: "This? You're leaving over this? Now? Come on, Ellie, let's have a glass of wine and calm down."

"No. I am calm." She was, too, now. "Jeff, this isn't working for me." Jane always used that expression, because, as Jane always said, you can't argue with it.

"How is this not working for you?" Jeff argued. "We have a nice time, we get along, sometimes we even have sex," and blah blah blah.

To Ellie's amazement, Cool Bitch from Boston returned, and she felt perfectly composed as she explained that she had some figures to go over with him as part of a financial plan for their amiable (she stressed) separation and divorce.

He just laughed.

"Ellie," he said, as if to a slightly dim child, "you don't need a financial plan. The house is worth one point two million, you bring in about six thousand a month with your job after taxes, and I manage a pretty good chunk of capital in the Smalls Mutual Fund. What, were you thinking we'd split the house and each get some half-million-dollar condo? In Silicon Valley? You don't know what you're talking about."

Ellie felt like a general who's just watched the opposing army deftly execute his own meticulously crafted battle plan against him.

How did he do that? Off the top of his head?

"All that's beside the point," Jeff pronounced, "because we're not selling. I'm not done with this marriage, and neither are you."

And then, because he could drive and she couldn't, he got in his car and drove off.

She spent an hour or two just walking around till she stopped shaking, then she grabbed Snowball, a big HGTV fan, and they watched a bunch of *House Hunters*.

To her profound disappointment, Jeff came home late last night (she pretended to be asleep), and this morning he was his cheerful, postargument self, and even tried to get something going on with her in bed, which she managed to evade.

The New Jeff, she's discovered, doesn't hold grudges like the Old Jeff, where after an argument about something serious, like separation, she could expect a good three weeks of constant reworkings of the old arguments, bolstered by new ones. New Jeff has a new tactic: after his initial fury, he calms himself down and within twenty-four hours is amiable—jovial, even—as if the argument never happened.

When she comes home from work, it's to a very nice dinner that he prepared for them. There isn't candlelight or anything, but a nice bottle of wine has been uncorked, and she warily sits down with him to eat his famous chicken Tuscany with asparagus and black rice.

Politely, she reiterates her financial plan for their amicable separation.

"Hey. C'mon," he says, very sweetly, "I told you last night— I'm not selling the house. *We're* not selling the house. Listen, Ellie, we're too old for this. Calm yourself down and let's be reasonable, okay?"

Then it comes to her.

"What if I buy you out?" she says.

He snorts. "With what?"

She thinks. Her parents? Maybe she can take an inheritance early (she hates the thought of that, but any port in a storm)?

"And like I said, I'm not selling." He smugly sits back in his seat, as if he's just made a great chess move. "If you buy me out, then you get the house. If I buy you out, then I get the house. You can't afford to buy me out, and I'm not going to buy you out. So . . ."

So, here it is: The Thing from Left Field. She should have known. She gazes at him, detached, her head so abuzz with figures, options, solutions, obstacles that her heart is at a dis-connect. She nods, sips some more wine, acceding that he's won round one. She's down, but not out.

CHAPTER THIRTY-THREE
ALL I'VE GOT TO DO

DIVORCED WOMEN OVER FIFTY CHAT ROOM
DECEMBER 7, 2018
7:15 P.M.

ELLESBELLES:
Hi.

FREEATLAST:
EB! What's going on? Did you ever do your financial stuff?

ELLESBELLES:
I did. And I presented it to my husband and . . . it didn't go the way I had planned it in my head.

GINGERBEAR:
Well, yeah. That's 'cause you brought your husband into it.

FREEATLAST:
Things always suck when you bring your husband into it.

ELLESBELLES:
You'd think I'd know that by now.

ELLESBELLES:
Isn't that the definition of "insane"? Doing the same thing over and over and expecting a different result?

FREEATLAST:
Also definition of "marriage."

MOREOFME:
Boy, you all are cranky tonight!

LORY:
I'll say!

ELLESBELLES:
I guess there are some things that just can't be worked out in therapy.

FREEATLAST:
Therapy. Pffft.

MOREOFME:
Oh, I don't know. I still believe in therapy.

LORY:
We did counseling for a while, and it wasn't easy, but, I think it helped. There's always stuff to work on and be mindful about, but I think we're actually doing better.

ELLESBELLES:

That's wonderful, Lory!

GINGERBEAR:

I remember when you first came on the board and Suzy said, "Go and get your man back, woo-hoo!" or something like that. You go, girl!

MOREOFME:

I'm so glad to hear this! So are things all "Hunky Lory" now with you and your man?

MOREOFME:

Ugh, sorry, that was dumb!!! Arrgggh . . .

LORY:

LOL, no it's fine. Actually, my mother's name was Dory and whenever we wanted to drive her nuts we'd call her Hunky Dory.

LORY:

Yes, things are good. I'm hopeful!

MOREOFME:

That is so wonderful! Hey, you'll still have to check in with us on the chat—just to let us know how things are going!

———

Ellie sits back in her chair after hastily signing off, her Spidey sense tingling.

Jeff's mother's name was Dory.

Ellie had always been horrified when he and his dad jokingly called his mom Hunky Dory just to get a rise out of her
(she was quite slim, actually).

But Dory's a pretty common name, right? And Hunky Dory,
well, you could see calling someone that to tease them, or get
them riled up. Right?

She signs back on to the chat room and picks up the thread
to look at it again.

———

GINGERBEAR:

I remember when you first came on the board and Suzy said,
"Go and get your man back, woo-hoo!" or something like
that. You go, girl!

LORY:

Yes, things are good. I'm hopeful!

MOREOFME:

That is so wonderful! Hey, you'll still have to check in with us
on the chat—just to let us know how things are going!

———

Ellie starts at the screen, a sick feeling in her stomach.

She didn't imagine it. You don't imagine things like, "Hunky
Lory," jeez.

But it's for sure gone now. Deleted. Lory must have deleted it. Why?

Ellie does the math. Jeff's mother was named Dory. His
father was named Leon.

Could Lory possibly be *Jeff*?

She can't even wrap her brain around that possibility.

No, she can't be sure.

She doesn't know what to think. How, why, would Jeff get on a chat room for Divorced Women over Fifty—her cyberhaven, the one place she can best express herself and be understood—and disguise his identity, if not to deliberately follow her there? So—is he Lory? When he had to come up with a username, did he think, *I'll combine my parents' names, Leon and Dory, just to spy on her?* Seriously? Is she overreacting?

Does this mean Jeff was on DWOF downstairs in his office at the same time she was happily blabbing away on DWOF upstairs in their bedroom?

No, that's not right—Jeff has been out of the house plenty of times that she's been on DWOF. Right now, even, he's out getting groceries.

But, of course, he could be sitting in the parking lot or in a Starbucks typing away on his laptop. Spying on her through cyberspace.

He must have gotten on her computer at some point and looked at her history. The Fucker. She wonders why the hell he'd want to do that, but then, this was Jeff—the übercontrolling, fuck-with-her-phone, show-up-just-when-she-doesn't-want-him-there Jeff.

But what could he possibly hope to get out of it?

Oh shit.

She suddenly flashes to the day she told Jeff she would be going to work early the next morning for a "health insurance meeting" at her office, and her stomach plummets as she remembers how he was noticeably unphased by her plans.

He knew she was going to the lawyer's office. And he used that information to follow her there.

And then he one-upped her as she tried to lay out her financial plan for their divorce. She couldn't figure out how he'd been one step ahead of her . . . now she knows. She groans out loud as she realizes he picked up both those facts from DWOF, where she'd candidly laid out her plans for all her DWOF sisters to see, never dreaming for a minute there was a snake in the grass.

And now she remembers a session with Joseph, when Jeff had apologized and said, to her shock, something like, "It's okay—don't worry about it!" She had joked, not just on DWOF but to Jane more than once, that these were words she'd never heard from her husband in twenty-two years of marriage, and suddenly, he was spouting them with apparent sincerity.

The depth of her distress at this betrayal nearly levels her. She loves her DWOF sisters, but how can she ever think about them again except as the backdrop against which her husband had perpetrated an unforgivable deception?

She's done, she thinks. She's out. She's calling Stephanie in the morning.

She jumps as just then her phone rings. It's Wendy. It's not good news.

CHAPTER THIRTY-FOUR
HELP!

She and Jeff are making an emergency trip back to Boston to visit her parents, who are suddenly, devastatingly, not well.

Ellie shelves her rage at Jeff's DWOF impersonation as she struggles to deal with a crisis she never saw coming. At this precise moment, though not overjoyed to be with Jeff, she's mentally viewing him as "the Convenience."

Fortunately, Jeff is very good in a crisis, as he will tell you himself.

Since Ellie's move to California, her parents had been three thousand miles away across the country and safely tucked within the purview of the responsible, practical, double-income-no-kids Wendy and her wife, Lacey. Ellie didn't give Mort and Betty much thought, other than on her weekly phone calls. She loves her parents—likes them, even—but she's been preoccupied with her own troubles, which, like the good daughter she is, she's kept from them. She never dreamed they were keeping a thing or two from her as well.

So she wasn't expecting to hear from Wendy that their youthful, fit, eighty-year-old dad had just had a major stroke after a series of little ones they'd never bothered to tell her about. He's alive, but can't talk, and is paralyzed on his left side.

Panicked but optimistic, Ellie assumes that modern medicine and good rehab will get Daddy back on his feet again, and it probably will, but Wendy has a one-two punch for her when she tells her that their mother has been diagnosed with Alzheimer's and is starting a downward spiral.

Ellie *had* noticed a few odd lapses, a few non sequiturs, on her mother's part in the past few months whenever she'd spoken to her, but she chalked that up to the natural aging process, or just being on the phone, or her mother's batty sense of humor. She has friends with parents who have Alzheimer's, and it's something she'd prayed she'd never have to go through with her beloved mom and dad.

Ellie is terrified and understands that she's about to begin what will probably be a protracted grieving process. She's ashamed of how scared she is of losing them, as if she's a little child who still needs their protection, and not a full-grown woman with a husband (despite all her best efforts) and daughter. She would never burden Hannah with her own grief, and as for Jeff—well, she knows he'll be there for her, and genuinely so. But she also knows that this is one of those parts of the husband role he just loves to play, because he legitimately gets to appear self-important, supportive, and loving. He will grieve for her parents too. Genuinely. Just as Ellie genuinely grieved and stood by him when his folks, Leon and Dory (Lory! *God*!), died within a few weeks of each other back in 2013. She supposes she should be grateful, in her situation, to have a husband around for all the ways she needs support. But, married or separated, grieving or not, Jeff is not a soulmate with whom she can unreservedly be herself, and that thought makes her feel alone.

Without a better option, Ellie caves in to Jeff's solicitude on the plane, as he brings her snacks and lets her use his coveted Bose headphones and tries to comfort and distract her. She's grateful but also irritated. It's hard to hate someone who's being so nice to her, and this whole thing is throwing Ellie's game off.

They land at Logan Airport early in the morning, and Wendy is there to take them to her house, where they can catch up on some sleep before going to pick up Mom and go to see Daddy in the hospital.

Ellie and Jeff make a brief phone call to Hannah, who is in the state but can't join them, being deep in rehearsals for a play she's doing off campus, at a local Boston theater. They're doing some avant-garde updated version of *A Christmas Carol* that sounds ghastly, but Hannah is thrilled to be working with this company, which is apparently very well regarded in Boston. She loves her grandparents, but she's too preoccupied now to fully comprehend the news that Grampie and Grandie are not going to be the same as she's always remembered them.

Ellie loves her sister's house in the beautiful, semirural town-and-country town of Weston, about a half hour away from their parents' house, the same one they grew up in, in Natick. She and Jeff crash in Wendy's Shaker-inspired guest bedroom and groggily wake up in the early afternoon when the three golden retrievers—Vera, Chuck, and Dave—tired of waiting for their new friends to get up, burst in with their doggy love and doggy breath. Wendy gives them all lunch (dogs included) as she briefs them on what to expect, emphasizing that "they're not drooling, yet" while implying that drooling might be imminent.

Nervous and apprehensive, Ellie hides her cane in her oversized purse on the car ride over to get Mom. She never uses her cane in front of her parents, who know about her disease but not about its progression. She doesn't see any need to worry them about *her*. She remains calm and stoic when they pick up her mother, a tiny, elegantly dressed woman in her late seventies, whose short gray hair is well cut and whose warm brown eyes have an unfamiliar cast of vagueness that saddens Ellie.

To Ellie's relief, Betty obviously recognizes her and Jeff, and appears to be her usual cheerful self. She adores Jeff and, clueless about her daughter's misery, assumes they have the same solid, loving marriage that she and Mort have. This belief has always kind of bothered Ellie, but today she's glad her mother is getting some joy out of her delusion.

Betty has some trouble remembering that Mort is in the hospital not for his knee-replacement surgery (that he had ten years ago) but for a stroke. More upsetting is that she's not alarmed by her lack of memory, and simply seems to accept it as some new normal. Wendy had told Ellie that Betty knows she has Alzheimer's. She'd been diagnosed a year ago, in fact, and her initial panic has given way to an uncomplaining resignation.

Wendy's wife, Lacey, tall, wry-humored, and sweet, meets them at the hospital, and the five of them make their way to Mort's room, Ellie making her way around with the help of Jeff or Wendy's arm.

Ellie is unexpectedly relieved at what appears to be her father looking fairly normal, sitting up in bed, facing the door, a few pillows propping up his right side. His mass of iron-gray hair has been brushed back from his high forehead, his brown eyes alert and intelligent as always. Ellie can always see his true feelings in those expressive eyes, despite his personal preference to keep emotion on the back burner.

Wendy says, casually, "Hi, Daddy!" and goes over to give

him a kiss, followed by Lacey. "Look, Daddy, Mom's here! And Ellie and Jeff came from California!"

Jeff waits for Mom to give her husband a kiss, which he returns with closed eyes. Mort keeps his eyes on her as she gently pats his forehead and moves off so he can greet the others. He doesn't speak, or chooses not to try.

"Hey, man," Jeff says, finding Mort's hand in the bedclothes and giving it a warm squeeze. Like Mom, Daddy always liked Jeff, whom he considers a hero for surviving 9/11. Ellie feels her heart start to fall apart as she carefully approaches her daddy to give him her hug and kiss; she doesn't trust herself to speak, but she meets his eyes, sees the courage and humor there, one eyebrow cocked as if to say, "Don't *you* cry. *I'm* the one who's in the shit here," and she manages to smile. She remembers that, growing up, all their friends knew that Ellie and Wendy had the "good" parents, the ones who were calm, took them as they were, trusted them, enjoyed their company; she feels a fierce, nostalgic wave of yearning for them all as they were those many years ago, able-bodied, wholehearted, happy.

Jeff uses his considerable charm to keep the conversation—mostly about him—going, not minding that Daddy only has eyes for his wife, who sits by him silently holding his hand. Ellie realizes that Mort, of course, knows that Betty is approaching the black hole of her disease, and how that must pain him, in his current vulnerable state, not to be able to take care of her the way he would want to. Ellie feels her heart bend again, and yet there is such love here—deep, uncomplicated bedrock love, nothing like the ambiguity and anger her own relationship is mired in. *They are lucky*, she thinks.

When their visit is over, the "kids" file out first, Ellie on Jeff's arm, giving Mort and Betty a moment alone, and Betty slips out a few seconds later, quietly wiping her eyes.

They're greeted by the social worker, Valerie, who takes them into her office to talk about Mort's home-care protocol. They sit before her desk, Betty, Ellie, and Wendy up front, Jeff and Lacey behind them. Valerie explains that Mort will stay in the hospital for two more days, then will be sent home with a special bed and a round-the-clock nurse to help with his new meds, his daily needs, and coordination of the rehab specialists. She's very confident that, with time and care, he will regain his speech and most of his mobility, but they must be patient.

Betty, puzzled, speaks up. "What about physical therapy? That's what we did with the first knee."

The room goes quiet. Ellie wonders who's supposed to explain to the social worker that their mom has Alzheimer's, or maybe they're not. Is it a secret? Because of insurance or something? Ellie looks at Wendy, who's looking at Mom intently but not nervously.

Valerie seems to size things up quickly and says gently, "Mrs. Lefler, your husband has had a stroke."

Betty sighs, looks Valerie in the eye. "I have Alzheimer's."

Valerie nods.

Betty says, "It stinks."

Valerie nods. "I know."

The meeting ends with Ellie's head whirling with information, but Wendy and Lacey don't seem too fazed. They go off to get their cars, and Jeff heads to the bathroom, leaving Ellie alone with her mom for a second. Betty turns to Ellie, her gaze sharp and penetrating, no vagueness now.

"Ellie, is your vision getting worse?"

Ellie considers her options, merely nods. "Slowly though," she says.

"Get yourself a cane, then. Or a dog. Do what you have to do, but don't you become dependent on Jeff to get around."

Ellie stares at her mother, in shock. "Okay," she says.

Betty nods, pats her shoulder.

"My memory's going, but I see what I see."

Jeff returns from the restroom, and the three of them head off to the parking lot, Ellie's hand firmly tucked in her mother's elbow.

CHAPTER THIRTY-FIVE
REVOLUTION

Ellie's back home.

Sad, depressed, frightened, and lonely.

She had the thought, on the plane coming home, that she should just turn around and stay in Natick, be there for her parents and sister and sister-in-law; Hannah was only half an hour away, in Boston. But the responsible adult in her knew she needed to get back to NorCal, back to her job, and the paycheck that paid the mortgage . . . and to the marriage that made her miserable.

She can't go back to DWOF, because . . . "Lory." The very name makes her nauseous. Why doesn't she confront Jeff and accuse him of being Lory? Yeah, right. He'll just deny it. And she'll feel stupid even asking about it.

She thinks of reaching out to Stephanie, her lawyer, but with her family's resources all focused on Betty and Mort, as they should be, she's not sure she can proceed with a divorce.

So, with a weary fortitude, she figures she'll just stay the course, in her marriage, at least, for a while. Because frankly, she's out of options.

Then she remembers—that's not true.

The dark web.

Marilyn had told her the women on I Am the Walrus (and if that Beatles connection isn't a sign, she doesn't know what is) might have some "creative solutions" for staying in a bad marriage.

Fuck it, she thinks. She pulls up Marilyn's email, the one with the link to the dark web.

———

Ellie's heart is pounding as she follows Marilyn's instructions. She launches a VPN (paid for by Wendy so Jeff wouldn't see it on their bank account), navigates to the TOR browser, and finds the DuckDuckGo search engine right away. Fingers shaking, she cuts and pastes the address for I Am the Walrus: http://iatwjgkgw5soi8va.onion.

It looks very strange to her, an incomprehensible algorithm. And in a second, she's looking at a simple page with "I Am the Walrus" bannered across the top. There's a standard-issue box for registering with a username and password, and she thinks quickly, then pecks out a brand-new username, from the Beatles' song "Dear Prudence," and a password that's not like all her other passwords, which she writes down on a secret document in her Gmail files.

And she's in.

Lines of type, conversations, stretch out on the page. Unlike DWOF, there's no cozy welcome, just a grayed-out link cryptically titled *goo goo g'joob* (which she recognizes as one of the lyrics to the Beatles' song "I Am the Walrus").

Oh, for God's sake, Ellie tells herself irritably, *no one can find you here! Not even Jeff! Just go in, and if it's dicey, get the hell out.*

———

DEARPRUDENCE:
Hi. New here.

DANAIS (MODERATOR):
Beatles fan?

BTDT:
Oh God kill me now.

DEARPRUDENCE:
Guilty.

DANAIS (MODERATOR):
LOVE THAT SONG! Dear Prudence, Open up your eyes!

BTDT:
Don't. Start.

RUBY:
Welcome, DearPrudence! Lol, well, that sounds like something from Jane Austen, doesn't it?

BTDT:
So how bad is it for you? Your marriage?

DANAIS (MODERATOR):
BTDT has no filter. You get used to it.

BTDT:
Fuck you.

DEARPRUDENCE:
Okay, so we just dive in here . . .?

RUBY:
It's okay, DearPrudence, take your time.

DEARPRUDENCE:
No, that's okay, I should tell you what's going on. The person who sent me here said you guys would have some "creative solutions" about being stuck in a shitty marriage.

DEARPRUDENCE:
I'm stuck in a shitty marriage.

KORE:
How long have you been married?

DEARPRUDENCE:
Twenty-two years.

KORE:
And how long have you been miserable?

DEARPRUDENCE:
That's a good question. I think I've always been miserable and I just didn't realize that it wasn't a natural state in a marriage.

DANAIS (MODERATOR):
Oh I think many people here would disagree with that.

RUBY:
Well, typically you don't get married thinking you're going to be miserable.

BTDT:
I got married to make HIM miserable. That backfired.

LAURIEB:
Life is shot.

LAURIEB:
Short.

RUBY:
Laurie's right. Sometimes you have to act on your own behalf and not worry about anybody else.

BTDT:
Yeah. Take the bull by the dick.

LAURIEB:
Chicken?

LAURIEB:
Children?

DEARPRUDENCE:
Do I have children? Yes, we have a child in college.

BTDT:
Throw him the hell out.

DEARPRUDENCE:
Yeah, he's not the kind of guy to go gentle into that good night. He'll find a way to hang on.

DANAIS (MODERATOR):
Maybe you've already done this, but have you had the conversation with him where you tell him this isn't working for you and you want out?

DEARPRUDENCE:
Actually, yes—I left last year, went back, nothing changed, and now I'm . . . stuck. Finances . . . are an issue.

KORE:
Well, so what about just saying something like, oh I don't know, we can live together but we're going to have to lead different lives? You go your way, he goes his way. You just share the house. Like roommates, actually. Would that work?

DEARPRUDENCE:
That's awkward for me. I don't drive. I'm vision impaired, I have a degenerative eye disease called retinitis pigmentosa that's nuked my peripheral vision and my night vision's shot. So . . .

BTDT:
Please don't tell us your dick husband drives you everywhere. My head will explode.

DEARPRUDENCE:
Well, he's one of many people who drive me.

BTDT:
Shhktrhoommmblatt. That was my head exploding.

DearPrudence:
I'm just so sick of this.

Danais (moderator):
DearPrudence, before we go any further here, you should seriously investigate divorce. You don't have small children, there'll be no custody battle—find a good, reasonable lawyer and get out. Go into debt, borrow money, but do it.

DearPrudence:
I did see a lawyer—as I said, money's the issue here. Anyway, I thought this was the site where you guys have ideas on how to *stay* in a crappy marriage???!!!

Danais (moderator):
No one here advocates staying in a crappy marriage.

Danais (moderator):
But we start with the obvious. We have some legal resources here that may surprise you.

DearPrudence:
Oh. Okay—thank you.

Danais (moderator):
You can always PM us if you want to contact us, DearPrudence, but you should really set up a secure email as well. We use Proton Mail, which you can set up for

yourself on the internet, either on TOR or not. My email is
fullfathomsfive@protonmail.com. Feel free.

DEARPRUDENCE:
Thank you. I was really nervous about going on "The dark
web," but you all seem pretty normal.

BTDT:
I'M SO OFFENDED!

BTDT:
JK

BTDT:
Not really.

LAURIEB:
Fist impressions.

LAURIEB:
First.

KORE:
Yes indeed. Good God, wait till you get to know us!

DEARPRUDENCE:
I look forward to it!

_____

Ellie logs out and shuts down her laptop, leaning back in
her chair to process what she's just experienced. It was a lot

easier than she expected, probably because she was used to
DWOF; in fact, it seems a lot like DWOF—the women on
IATW could be the exact counterparts of her DWOF friends.
Maybe with a bit more of an edge, but still, there is a com-
forting familiarity.

Ellie feels good for a second—how wonderful to be able to
touch base with a whole new support system without ever leaving the comfort of your own home! She wonders once again
about the "creative solutions" that IATW will have to offer, what
Danais meant about the legal resources that "may surprise you."
What would that be? She amuses herself for a minute imagining a lawyer in a business suit threatening to break Jeff's legs
unless he divorces her. Bringing herself back to reality, she hopes
their legal help will be less expensive than Stephanie. She already feels a bit invigorated just from the experience. Hey, she
just got herself on the dark web and lived to tell the tale—who
knows what the future will hold?

CHAPTER THIRTY-SIX
AND YOUR BIRD CAN SING

DECEMBER 12, 2018

To: downunder@protonmail.com
From: thepostoffice@protonmail.com
Subject: Our Lovely Visit!

Dear Claire,

(I don't think people use the "Dear" salutation anymore, or at least not in emails. If I'm dating myself—well, tough!)

I'm sitting on my balcony in the warm(ish) sun enjoying a cup of the PG Tips you brought me. I feel so much better for your visit, fleeting as it was: more connected, less fearful. It's so reassuring to think of you sitting calmly in your English garden, sipping your Earl Grey, having successfully "jumped over the fence," and enjoying your tranquility at long last. I hope that by now Andrew has come to see you, as promised, and that he

will eventually rally his siblings to your side.
There is life after . . . all.

I am actually very happy here, in this friendly,
pretty city, but it's hard not to be able to go
back home, even when home—rather, where
I came from—has nothing for me but bad
memories. Perhaps home is here now, and can
be so without pain. There's a lot to be said for
being free.

By the way, the new woman on IATW,
DearPrudence—she has RP. Do you remember
the woman on DWOF, Ellesbelles, she had it also.
Do you think . . .?

Should we reach out?

I send love.

Suzanne

To: thepostoffice@protonmail.com
From: downunder@protonmail.com
Subject: Our Lovely Visit!

Dear Suzanne,

(The only way to start a letter, or an email, as far
as I'm concerned!)

It was brilliant to see you, even for a few hours.
There are so few women in our situation—well,
actually, we don't know that, do we, there may
be hundreds, thousands, even—that it's a rare

treat to be able to meet in person. Not sure what D would say, but if we are not the ultimate risk-takers, then who is?

Yes, I had the same thought about DearPrudence. Other details are right also— married 20something years, one child (daughter, if I remember . . . Hannah!).

I liked her very much on DWOF.

I can't quite tell if she's like us, though. Not sure she has the stuffing.

But I would indeed like to contact her. I miss DWOF. Let's give DearPrudence one more go on IATW and then see what we think.

Meanwhile, I'm off to do a turn on a rather brilliant new Netflix thing called, something something—I can't remember. Hopefully my lines are more memorable!

I loved your "friendly, pretty city," and I loved seeing you. I shall return.

Be well, my friend.

Claire

CHAPTER THIRTY-SEVEN
ALL TOGETHER NOW

DECEMBER 18, 2018

"Shit," Ellie says quietly, but she's already made a racket by accidentally knocking a china dish onto the stone kitchen floor because, gee, she just didn't see it. Jeff's always at her about keeping her arms and elbows tucked in close to her body so she doesn't, in his words, "flail about and break things," but sometimes she forgets and thinks she's normal. Besides, she's distracted. She's worried about her parents (the word is, Dad's doing better; Mom, not so much); herself (she hasn't had time to think about I Am the Walrus and what that could mean to her and her marriage); and now Hannah, who's come home for the winter break and is in some kind of relationship crisis.

She grits her teeth as, predictably, Jeff bursts into the kitchen. "Get out of the way. You're barefoot; you'll get hurt," he barks at her as he grabs the dustpan and broom from the kitchen closet.

"I can do it," she says, trying to grab the dustpan from him. He easily sidesteps her, using the outside of his arm to push her away. She wishes he'd shove her so she could fall and hit her head and then divorce him and take everything he owns, but she's not even off-balance, so there goes that idea.

"I can *do* it, Jeff. Jesus, it's my mess. Let me clean it up."

"Does that make sense? You can't see where all the pieces are, can you? I can. So I'll do it. I'll always do it. I don't mind."

Hannah enters, sleepily alert, but late to the party. "Do you need help?" she asks, her voice husky, and Ellie looks up at her quickly, noting the red eyes, the dark circles as if she hasn't slept. Ellie's sorry she woke her. She knows Forrest left early and under a cloud, and she yearns to have a moment alone with Hannah, without Jeff, to debrief.

———

Hannah came home for winter break a few days ago and brought her boyfriend, Forrest. (Ellie couldn't get a satisfactory read whether or not Forrest was the boy involved in Hannah's pregnancy last summer. A quiet question to Hannah was answered only with the mother of all eye rolls. She guesses not.) Ellie liked Forrest immediately for his obvious smarts and good humor, but also for his uncomplicated sweetness.

Ellie knows that women have a predilection for marrying their fathers and privately worries about this, regarding Hannah. Of course, Hannah's not going to marry the first young man she brings home—though she might—and Ellie feels she's young enough to play the field for a while and maybe learn something about herself and what she requires for a partner.

Personally, Ellie bitterly wishes *she'd* married her own father: kind, responsible, bighearted Mort. She sometimes wonders if instead of her lovely father, her marital prototype was some stoic Victorian ancestor, domineering and master of all he surveyed, who showed up in her emotional DNA just when it came time for her to choose a mate.

So she was relieved to see that Forrest wasn't a micromanaging, anal-retentive, control freak asshole, like Jeff, but a genuinely nice guy with, apparently, nothing to prove.

Ellie would have preferred to have Hannah to herself for the precious ten days until she has to go back to school. But what's really bothering her is that with Hannah bringing a newcomer into their family dynamic, Ellie a) can't really be herself and b) feels uncomfortable about the fact that she and Jeff have to present a united front, since, of course, she doesn't want to air the family dirty linen in front of Forrest (or Hannah). Also, they *are* united in their curiosity and observation of Forrest, and Hannah with Forrest. Ellie would like to continue to treat Jeff with a certain haughty reserve, but let's face it, who else is she going to gossip with about her daughter's boyfriend but her husband, who's right there? As usual, she can't decide if she wants to hunker down with her rage at Jeff or gratefully grasp at a few moments of congeniality.

Jeff and Ellie had privately argued about whether or not Hannah and Forrest should share her bedroom. Jeff insisted that Hannah sleep in her room and Forrest in Jeff's office, while Ellie thought that it'd be only natural for them to share a bedroom. Eventually, Ellie prevailed, mostly by pointing out how inconvenient it would be for Jeff to have a guest in his office. But then Ellie was surprised by how uncomfortable she actually was with Hannah and Forrest sharing her daughter's girlhood Pottery Barn four-poster queen bed. By unspoken agreement, she and Jeff left the fan on in their bedroom at night in the hope that they wouldn't hear any sound, God forbid, of their daughter making love with her boyfriend down the hall. Ellie wondered if that would be worse than a child overhearing their parents having sex and decided it was probably a toss-up.

It was actually kind of nice, to pretend that they were a happy, loving couple. They went out to dinner like regular folks, and

Ellie thought it was adorable when Forrest scanned the menu for Hannah to find her a hearty vegetable dish (Hannah had recently become a vegetarian) and later enthusiastically expressed his support of her decision to audition for a few shows in Boston rather than at Ballard this semester. Ellie was taken aback when Hannah appeared annoyed by his attention; she didn't actually snap at him, but she wasn't what you'd call appreciative, and Ellie could sense an underlying tension. Was there something Ellie wasn't seeing? Was Forrest passive-aggressive, and this was his way of controlling Hannah, the way Jeff picked out clothes for Ellie and couldn't stand it if she went with something else? But Forrest seemed unfazed by Hannah's reaction, letting it roll off his back and cheerfully submitting to Jeff's polite but incisive grilling about himself (a lighting designer with a minor in computer engineering. Ellie mentally gave Hannah a thumbs-up).

Then, back at the house after dinner, Hannah announced she wanted to go visit some friends of hers and nicely but pointedly told Forrest that she really wanted a girls' night with her old high school buds, and would he mind staying home? Ellie was shocked by this and wondered if it would be inappropriate to take Hannah aside like an eight-year-old to tell her that you didn't treat your guest this way. But easygoing Forrest breezily told Hannah "no worries" and kissed her goodbye as she wrapped herself in Ellie's best metallic scarf and swanned out. Jeff looked at Ellie quizzically and invited Forrest to watch Stephen Colbert with him, which Forrest politely declined, saying he was fine going upstairs to read, and told them good night.

Ellie and Jeff looked at each other.

"That was unbelievably rude of Hannah. I'm going to tell her," Jeff said, getting out his phone.

"No, you can't do that!" Ellie shushed him, but he ignored

her, intent on "parenting." "Jeff, this is her thing. Stay out of it. Besides, she's driving—"

Jeff tapped off his phone.

"She won't answer. This poor kid though. I mean, he's kind of a wuss, but she shouldn't treat him like this, in her own home, in front of us."

Ellie bristled at his description of the perfectly lovely Forrest.

"Maybe this is how they are with each other, and stuff like this doesn't bother them. They're independent of each other." She felt like adding, "You know—independent? That concept?" but that was an old fight, and she didn't feel like getting into it.

Ellie woke in the middle of the night and heard a muffled, intense conversation—an argument—coming from Hannah's bedroom. She held her breath, somewhat shamefully trying to hear what they were saying, then got scared that they'd wind up having make-up sex, so she went to the bathroom, turned up the overhead fan, and went back to sleep.

She got up fairly early the next morning to make a nice breakfast to send Hannah and Forrest off on their scheduled trip to the beach and went down to find Forrest, alone, with his bag, at the front door, checking his phone for an Uber.

He told her kindly that he'd decided he was going to go down to see his parents, in Santa Barbara, earlier than expected, and he was taking an Uber to the train station. He thanked her profusely for her hospitality and told her that Hannah was great. At which point his eyes filled with tears, and Ellie help-lessly asked if there were anything she could do for him. He shook his head, gave her a hug, and slipped out the door to the waiting car. Ellie watched the car for a minute, then went to the kitchen to make breakfast and smash a dish on the floor.

———

Ellie would prefer not to talk to Hannah in front of Jeff, but he pipes up, looking at his daughter in her PJ's, "I thought you and Forrest were leaving early for the beach?"

Hannah, with some effort, tells them that Forrest decided to go down to his parents in Santa Barbara. Jeff, never one for picking up emotional cues, presses, asking, "Why? I thought he was going to stay another few days."

Hannah shrugs, looking him defiantly in the eyes. "Plans change."

Jeff goes on, "What, did you have a fight or something? You look bad."

"Thanks, Dad," Hannah counters sarcastically. "This is pretty much how I look when I get up. And it's none of your business."

"Well, you were pretty rude to the guy last night, leaving him with us to go out with your girlfriends," Jeff replies. "He seemed like a nice guy. I looked him up on Facebook—"

"Jesus H. Christ!" Hannah explodes and walks out of the room.

Jeff looks at Ellie helplessly. "What, I can't look him up on Facebook?"

"It's a little creepy, Jeff."

"No, it's not, Ellie. It's responsible. This guy's dating my daughter, for God's sake. I have every right—"

Ellie doesn't bother to pretend to want to hear the rest of that sentence as she heads upstairs to Hannah's bedroom. She's a little surprised but grateful—jeez, she's always so fucking grateful—when Hannah actually lets her in.

Hannah's slumped under her comforter in her queen bed, which Ellie tries hard not to imagine Forrest in as well.

Ellie carefully sits at the foot of the bed, propped up against one of the posts.

"Hannah, what happened?"

Hannah shakes her head.

"He seems like such a nice boy." Ellie cringes as she hears herself.

"I know. He *is* a nice boy. He's thoughtful and patient and emotionally available and sensitive and genuine and blah blah blah . . ."

"What, did he bore you?" Ellie decides to be a person with her daughter. "I wouldn't have gone for that either at your age."

Ellie realizes her blunder too late as Hannah snorts, "Yeah, Mom, obviously you went for the assholes."

"Don't call your father an asshole," Ellie says automatically, and then both she and Hannah burst into laughter.

"I *like* him," Hannah confesses. "I really like him. I just don't . . ." She shakes her head, unable to finish the sentence.

"That's okay," Ellie comforts her. "You're so young—you have lots of time and lots of guys to go through before you find the one who's the One."

Hannah shakes her head. "But I *chose* him."

Ellie cocks her head, confused.

Hannah goes on. "You know how women marry their fathers?"

Ellie is startled. "That's a—it's not a joke, but it's not something you have to consciously worry about."

Hannah looks at her like she's nuts. "Are you serious with me right now? I know from psych class—it's classic. We marry our dads. Well, the last thing I wanna do is marry Dad, so I chose Forrest because he was so the opposite. He's like, the Anti-Asshole. I mean, he'd be perfect for me." She looks sad. "He was my preemptive strike."

"Honey, you can't feel obligated to fall in love with someone just because he checks all your boxes." Ellie has a momentary spasm as she remembers being young(ish) and having her own checklist, the way Jeff checked off so many things that ultimately just didn't add up. "No one's perfect for you just because they're generically perfect."

"Well, obviously. It's so stupid though. Why couldn't I fall in love with him? What's wrong with me? Instead, I got annoyed with him. I mean, he was *so* sweet and *so* accommodating, and . . . I started being kind of mean to him because it didn't bother him. It's like that scene in *Who's Afraid of Virginia Woolf?*, where she says, 'You can stand it! You married me for it!'" Hannah stops, suspended for a moment. Ellie knows she's seeing herself as Martha and sits silently, respecting her process.

Hannah breaks her own spell. "But we weren't married, and I just treated him like a doormat 'cause he kinda was one."

Ellie doesn't let on that she's sustained another jolt. Who else does she know who's been called a doormat?

"Honey," she says, recovering, "you have to be with someone you respect. And it may not be Forrest, but it will be someone who's just as funny and sweet but who maybe—maybe has a little more backbone, something you can push back against. Without being controlled by him."

Hannah starts to cry. "I feel so bad for him! He's a good guy, and I treated him like shit! I'm a terrible person!"

She pitches forward on her bed. Ellie rubs her back.

With her face buried in her comforter, Hannah muffles out, "And when I was with him—that shit onstage didn't happen anymore either. I was okay. I didn't, you know, freak out." Hannah sits up. "He was kind to me." She sighs. "He was even nice when I dumped him!"

Ellie sighs too. "I know. I saw him as he waited for his Uber. He was very polite."

She doesn't tell Hannah that he was crying.

"I'm just scared. I'm scared I'm doomed to marry Dad, or worse—to be like him."

Ellie's a little taken aback by Hannah's perspicacity, alarmed at the idea that both she and Hannah are destined to be defined forever by their relationship with Jeff.

She tells Hannah, "You are not your dad, not one iota. You are a smart, loving, and lovable person, Hannah, and you'll be a fine partner to someone. But you can't plan who you love. You just have to go out into the world with some trust, and some knowledge of yourself. And be aware of the assholes out there so you can protect yourself. You're lucky"—she makes a grim attempt at humor—"you'll be able to recognize dysfunction when you see it because you grew up with it firsthand."

Hannah wipes her nose on her comforter. "Yeah, you poor thing, you grew up with great parents in a happy family. You had no idea what was out there."

"No, I didn't," Ellie agrees. "I walked right into it."

They sit there for a minute.

Ellie says, "Look, you didn't choose your dad after all, did you? You made a conscious decision not to, and Forrest wasn't the right guy, but you're aware. You'll be okay."

Hannah nods. "But you know what I think," she says slowly. "I did choose my parent. I think I chose you."

Ellie's vision gets worse as her eyes fill with tears. She gives Hannah a hug, proud to be the guidepost for her daughter's future forays into love, until she remembers the words *accommodating* and *doormat*, and she stops in her tracks.

There's a pounding on the door, and Jeff yells, "Hey— what's going on? Are you guys coming out or what? I just made pancakes."

Hannah and Ellie hold each other up for a minute, each wishing he'd go away.

"Yeah, we're coming," calls Ellie, and she gives Hannah a hand up.

CHAPTER THIRTY-EIGHT
GLASS ONION

I AM THE WALRUS CHAT ROOM
JANUARY 3, 2019
8:03 P.M.

DEARPRUDENCE:
. . . but I wasn't surprised, because I knew he wouldn't go for
my idea of how to split up because he doesn't want to. I was
ready to regroup and come back with a new financial plan,
but then my parents became ill and now I can't go to my
family and ask for the money to buy him out.

KORE:
You have got to get out of there, my love. This will
poison you.

LAURIEB:
Good idea.

LAURIEB:
Poison.

LaurieB:
Him.

LaurieB:
Do it.

DearPrudence:
I mean, he said, and I quote:
"I'm not done with this marriage and neither are you." Not sure how a divorce gets through that kind of bullshit.

BTDT:
Around here, we like to say, "Divorce is what we do when we can't murder them."

DearPrudence:
Well, I don't think I could murder him. But I sometimes think how great it'll be when he's dead. Actually, I think it a lot. It soothes me. I'm a terrible person.

Kore:
No, you're absolutely not, love. You're a human person. We've all had the same thought. Exactly.

BTDT:
You can only take shit for so long.

Ruby:
The fact is, it probably WILL be great when he's dead. You'll be free. And your daughter, Hannah, she will be too.

———

Ellie logs off, the cold gripping her gut.

She knows she never told them Hannah's name. She never even told them she has a daughter; she said—and did it deliberately—that she had a "child." She knows this and doesn't even need to go back to check. She fights the panic, the anger rising in her. What an idiot, to mess around on the dark web. Should she call the police? Should she PM Marilyn? Because it's her fault. This is all her fault.

She goes to DWOF for the first time in weeks, her hands shaking.

She can't log in. It doesn't autofill, and now she's got to look up her old DWOF password. She tries to calm down as she finds it and types it in the field, trying to breathe more slowly. She'll PM Marilyn and get this figured out. Or . . . what?

Helplessly, she curses when DWOF doesn't recognize her password. She pastes it in again. No luck. She cuts and pastes it, reboots, types her username and password in once more—no luck. She can't get in. It won't let her in: "Password and User-name Don't Match." She can't get back onto DWOF.

What the hell?

Furious, not knowing what else to do, she logs back into IATW. She's not surprised to find the post has been deleted, at least the part with Hannah's name. Hannah's name! Dear God, she dragged her daughter into the dark web. What was she thinking?

She squints at a small icon at the top of the page. She has a PM.

———

I AM THE WALRUS CHAT ROOM
PM FROM RUBY TO DEARPRUDENCE
8:09 P.M.

Please forgive me. Don't panic.—**RUBY**

Who are you??? How do you know my daughter???? I'm calling the police.—**DearPrudence**

Ellesbelles, I'm SuzyQ.—**Ruby**

From DWOF.—**Ruby**

Divorced Women over Fifty.—**Ruby**

My real name is Suzanne Decrosse. I remember you from DWOF because of your RP, and I also remember your daughter's name. Please forgive me for using it on IATW. It was a stupid mistake; I meant no harm. I have already deleted it from the post.—**Suzanne**

———

Ellies sits in her chair, paralyzed. What the actual fuck is going on?

———

PM FROM DEARPRUDENCE TO RUBY
8:10 P.M.

I'm sorry—what the actual fuck is going on??!!—**DearPrudence**

No one is going to hurt you or your daughter, I promise you. —**Ruby**

How do you know about DWOF?—**DearPrudence**

I was on it for a few years. My name was SuzyQ.—**Ruby**

Yeah, SuzyQ turned out to be . . . a big fake.—**DEARPRUDENCE**

That was a big betrayal on DWOF, when we found out SuzyQ wasn't whom she seemed to be.—**DEARPRUDENCE**

I can explain. I wasn't exactly pretending to be someone I wasn't. I was pretending to be someone I used to be.—**RUBY**

I remember the first time I logged on to DWOF. SuzyQ was the first person, other than Mairzydoats, to welcome me. Do you remember?—**DEARPRUDENCE**

I don't, I'm sorry.—**RUBY**

But I do remember when my mother died, you quoted me to myself, to make me feel better. Some things I had said on the board. One was, "We're all for one and one for all here." And the other was something my mother used to say: "Where there's life, there's hope." And you urged me to have hope. —**RUBY**

―――

Ellie is startled by the sting of tears in her eyes. She's getting used to the stridency of IATW, but she misses the kinder, gentler DWOF the same way she misses her sister; now that Wendy is so absorbed in the care of their parents they rarely even speak on the phone. She remembers smiling at SuzyQ's goofy, over-the-top southern presence, and the pain she felt at Suzy's disappearance, at discovering she wasn't who she seemed to be.

Ellie doesn't want to click out of her PM on IATW, so she

grabs her iPhone and googles "Suzanne Decrosse." The Wiki page comes up.

Ellie scans it, knowing Suzanne is waiting for her response. She has the advantage over Suzanne: Ellie knows who Suzanne is, but Suzanne has no idea who Ellie is, not even her name. All she knows, she reminds herself bitterly, is that she has a daughter named Hannah. Ellie forces herself to relax as she reads the article about Dr. Suzanne Decrosse, which she'd first looked at after Ginger, Free, and More had come back from Suzy's vigil with the startling news of her other persona. The article is the same, though there's an update about Suzanne's disappearance:

"On October 10, 2018, Decrosse apparently walked into the Raven Run Nature Sanctuary outside Lexington, Kentucky, leaving her car with some personal belongings in the parking lot. She never returned. Two months of intensive searching, spearheaded by her husband, Lexington College provost Charles Montross, and aided by local park rangers and police, were unsuccessful. She remains missing."

Until now?

But Ellie doesn't, in fact, know where she is. Or if this is even her.

———

PM FROM DEARPRUDENCE TO RUBY
8:13 P.M.

I want to believe you. I loved Suzy and was heartbroken by her disappearance. But all of us on DWOF—myself, Gingerbear, Moreofme, Freeatlast—we all felt betrayed to learn that SuzyQ seemed to be very different from her real self, Dr. Suzanne Decrosse.—**DEARPRUDENCE**

I can imagine. And I am truly sorry. I had no idea that SuzyQ would engender so much love and respect on the Board. Especially when she didn't in real life.—**RUBY**

And Chas—who the hell was Chas? Was he the same Chas Beaversomething who killed himself vaping? Who was he to you, and was he the same person as Charles Montross??? —**DEARPRUDENCE**

How do you know about Chas and how he died?—**RUBY**

Ginger or Free found a local article. They kept going through the Lexington papers after you disappeared to see if you ever turned up, and that's how they read about his death. —**DEARPRUDENCE**

Suzy—what happened to you?—**DEARPRUDENCE**

All right, then.—**RUBY**

Well. Suzy—SuzyQ to her fans on DWOF—grew up in the hollers of Kentucky. Home was a shack, no indoor plumbing or 'lectricity, nestled in some of the most beautiful country you'd ever seen. Daddy was an abusive alcoholic, Momma was a kind alcoholic, and there wasn't a book to be found for miles—except at the Montross house, where Momma cleaned. She took me there sometimes, where they had one whole room full of books—a library in a house!—and I got to read whatever I wanted. That's where I met Charles Montross the Third, who was not then nor ever could be Chasem Beaverspil the Vile, aka "Chas." I won't depress you with the sordid details but the CliffsNotes version is, thirteen-year-old

Suzy gets pregnant by her boyfriend, twenty-one-year-old
Chas, marries him secretly and has the baby at home. It dies.
Chas . . . disposes of it. Grief, anger, rending of garments
(mostly hers, by him) and she never tells anyone outside the
family. Her parents know, but once the baby dies and they
realize they don't have to feed it, they're no longer outraged.
Well, that's not fair to Momma. She was excited about a
grandchild—she was only fourteen when she had me—but
when my baby died, she thought being practical was the best
way to make me feel better about it.—**RUBY**

Suzy—Suzanne—I'm so so sorry. You are an extraordinary
person to rise above that kind of deprivation and
heartache.—**DEARPRUDENCE**

Thank you. I am more lucky than extraordinary. I had a good
brain and loved books, and I got somewhere because of that.
Because of Charles Montross, actually. By the time I was
fifteen I was helping Momma clean his house and he gave
me everything I wanted to read and talked with me for hours
about the books I chose. He was a fine young man from a
good family. We, Momma and I, were treated not unkindly
but dismissively by his mother—I never saw his father in
those days—who clearly thought we were no 'count. I guess
we were clean enough to "do" her house, though.

Charles and I fell in love, his family was horrified, but his
father was a famous psychologist who probably felt that
he would fuel our passion by forcing us to stay apart, so
they never said anything and we dated through the last
part of high school. Charles is three years older than I, so he
went off to the University of Kentucky and helped me get a

scholarship to Lexington College, where I found that home could mean something other than cruelty and ignorance. I got my BA, my Masters, and my PhD in Southern Literature, fell in love with my girls, Flannery and Eudora, wrote my books, became a professor. Married Charles, that lovely, handsome man who couldn't keep his lovely, handsome penis in his pants. Oh dear, I should delete that, but I won't. Compared to where I came from, this was happiness. This was bliss. We worked our way up the academic ladder together, made our accommodations, muddled through.—**RUBY**

And . . . Chas?—**DEARPRUDENCE**

Well. Chas kept his distance for a while after the baby died because Momma tried to bash his head in with a frying pan. I was busy with Charles and school and I sometimes went days without thinking of him, but every once in a while I'd think I'd spotted him, getting off a bus, in a movie theater. In fact, every time I graduated, I'm pretty sure I saw him in the crowd, a wiry, mid-sized guy with curly blond hair and big brown eyes—oh he was adorable, Chas the Vile. You couldn't see his inside from his outside. At one point I heard he'd left Kentucky, and I relaxed, did well. Daddy died after a long battle with sheer orneriness, and Charles and I moved Momma into a nice condo in Lexington. But then Chas came back. Charles was up for the Provost position, I had just published the Eudora bio, and I didn't want anything to get in the way of our upward trajectory. Like the story of a dead baby and an underage wedding.—**RUBY**

Oh my god. He blackmailed you.—**DEARPRUDENCE**

Yes. Well—it was more complicated than that. There was something—alluring about being with Chas. It was a chance to take the path less traveled, to go back in time, to see what would have happened if I'd never been Dr. Suzanne Decrosse, if I'd just been Suzy Beaverspil. Wild, crazy-haired Suzy, who didn't have to trot out her colorful underprivileged background for the delectation of her academic admirers, but could just wallow in it. That's why SuzyQ wound up on DWOF—Suzanne didn't want to split from Charles, but SuzyQ had to have someplace to vent about what was going on with Chas.—**RUBY**

Let me be very clear: I loved being Dr. Suzanne Decrosse and every day I blessed the talents that let me get the hell out of hell. But with academia and my book fans falling all over each other about my "interesting" background—which admittedly made good copy for my own bio—I began to see the appeal myself. Chas was like an itch I had to scratch.—**RUBY**

So, SuzyQ, the woman on DWOF—she was you with Chas, and Dr. Suzanne Decrosse was you with Provost Charles Montross?—**DEARPRUDENCE**

Yes. Exactly.—**RUBY**

But I never meant to hurt anyone on DWOF by showing up in my Suzy mode. I don't know if you've ever been in therapy, but they're always telling you to "get in touch with your childhood self," your "inner child." I took it a little too literally.—**RUBY**

And I had been diving deep into the lives of such profoundly creative women. SuzyQ was my chance to be creative as well, to tell my own story from the point of view of the girl who was left behind. I didn't know I was going to default to Suzy when I signed onto DWOF, it just happened. Also, I felt it gave me an added layer of anonymity.—**RUBY**

Wow.—**DEARPRUDENCE**

I'm so glad you didn't die in the woods. We were all so worried.—**DEARPRUDENCE**

But, what WAS that?—**DEARPRUDENCE**

Well, Chas was going after me to go after Charles, who was up for Chancellor. I didn't want my stupid past to ruin Charles' brilliant future, so I . . . "disappeared myself," a phrase that sends chills down my spine grammatically as well as practically.—**RUBY**

But I am so sincerely sorry about hurting the women on DWOF. There's no way I could have done otherwise, but I regret causing them pain. Their support—YOUR support—meant the world to me.—**RUBY**

Did Chas stop threatening Charles once you'd left?
—**DEARPRUDENCE**

I was gone.—**RUBY**

I guess he died not long after that.—**DEARPRUDENCE**

Is Charles okay now?—**DEARPRUDENCE**

Yes. And he's Chancellor.—**RUBY**

And are you . . . okay? I suppose I can't ask you where you are. Can I?—**DEARPRUDENCE**

I'm here. SMKL!—**RUBY**

Are you safe?—**DEARPRUDENCE**

Yes.—**RUBY**

Does Charles know you're safe?—**DEARPRUDENCE**

I can't answer that.—**RUBY**

Will you ever come back?—**DEARPRUDENCE**

No.—**RUBY**

Can you ever come back?—**DEARPRUDENCE**

Not sure I want to.—**RUBY**

Are you happy?—**DEARPRUDENCE**

Often.—**RUBY**

When Mairzydoats sent me to IATW, she told me that the women there would have "creative solutions" for navigating a miserable marriage. Is that it? How to "disappear yourself" so that you can escape the marriage you can't otherwise escape? Are all the women on IATW "disappeared"???
—**DEARPRUDENCE**

Everyone's situation is different.—**RUBY**

I can't get back onto DWOF.—**DEARPRUDENCE**

That's hard. I miss them.—**RUBY**

Is that because I'm on IATW?—**DEARPRUDENCE**

As I say, everyone's situation is different. I can only speak for myself, and I can only speak so far.—**RUBY**

Suzy—Suzanne—Ruby—wait, who is Ruby?—**DEARPRUDENCE**

Ruby Fisher is a character in Eudora Welty's short story, "A Piece of News." You should read it—it's rather perversely relevant to our situations.—**RUBY**

Suzanne—I'm glad to have connected with you. I felt strongly about SuzyQ and I'm happy to know that she walked out of that park in Lexington.—**DEARPRUDENCE**

And your secret is safe with me.—**DEARPRUDENCE**

I know. Thank you for listening. I'll see you again on IATW. —**RUBY**

Thank you for reaching out.—**DEARPRUDENCE**

———

Ellie logs out. Mind blown. Unless she was gullible far beyond her usual paranoia, she just legitimately made contact with Suzy/

Suzanne. What a story. She thinks about Jane; her sister, Wendy, and wife, Lacey; and herself—sure, there's drama in everyone's life, to an extent, but this is some crazy shit.

Ellie doesn't know what to do with this information. There's no one she can tell, obviously. She's given her word to Suzanne that she will keep her secret. But does it have anything specifically to do with IATW? Suzanne didn't answer her question about whether the women on IATW had successfully "disappeared" themselves to get away from their bad marriages. Was that the secret of IATW, and the reason they had to be on the dark web? How did it work? Was it like witness relocation? Did you get money and a new name and passport, a new apartment in a strange city? She wasn't sure she'd like that, though she had to admit, there was something about Suzanne, a serenity, a confidence, that was appealing. Of course, Suzanne had no children—except for her little baby buried in some backwoods holler—and Ellie could not imagine herself living anywhere where she couldn't have a relationship with Hannah, up close and personal.

Ellie thinks again about the DWOF chat room she loved so much, the secrets it concealed. She wonders if she's stupid for being such an open book, for giving so much personal information away, anecdotally if not specifically. She thinks with bitterness and regret of the whole Jeff-Lory situation. She wonders if he's still logging on to DWOF and wondering about her absence. Serves him right— he joined a chat room to spy on her, and she's not on it anymore.

It's dark outside. Jeff's out somewhere, having dinner with an old college buddy who's divorced; Ellie hopes the guy loves being divorced and will sell Jeff on the idea. Not likely. Ellie sits in the glow of the gooseneck lamp on her desk. She can't

see anything outside the light—not a new sensation for her—
and the rest of the townhouse is dark. She gets up to put on
the lights, snaps open her cane; she's had to start using it at
home now at night. All those damn stairs. She sighs, feeling
the press of a big, mysterious world outside the cozy confines
of her loveless home.

———

I AM THE WALRUS CHAT ROOM
PM FROM DANAIS TO RUBY
8:47 P.M.

Well, that was a disaster. I know you did it by accident
but now there's two points of reference: she has RP and a
daughter named Hannah.—**DANAIS**

I know. I'm so sorry.—**RUBY**

I PM'd her and apologized. I told her the text was deleted. I
think she's okay.—**RUBY**

I was thinking you'd be a good mentor for her. I mean, before
this.—**DANAIS**

I will be a good mentor for her. We connected. She trusts
me.—**RUBY**

We'll see.—**DANAIS**

———

I AM THE WALRUS CHAT ROOM
PM FROM KORE TO RUBY
9:05 P.M.

Did you PM her?—**KORE**

Yes.—**RUBY**

Is everything okay?—**KORE**

I think so.—**RUBY**

So, you told her about Suzy?—**KORE**

Yes.—**RUBY**

Well—I gave her the PG-13 version.—**RUBY**

But you didn't tell her about IATW?—**KORE**

No! That's Danais' job.—**RUBY**

CHAPTER THIRTY-NINE
FIXING A HOLE

JANUARY 3, 2019

It's a cold NorCal night, but Jeff is warm in the car as he drives home and mulls things over.

He had a nice dinner with his old college roommate, Colin, a professional photographer who just got back from a trip to Vietnam. They spent a few minutes jointly incredulous that Vietnam was now a travel destination as opposed to when they were in college, when it was to be avoided at all costs.

More importantly, Colin was recently divorced, and Jeff was interested in how that was going for him, having narrowly escaped that fate himself. Colin seemed relaxed, open, so maybe he was okay with it. Jeff assumed that anyone who had an artistic career, like photography, rather than a solid career, like insurance or finance (like himself), probably had to live hand to mouth and was accustomed to insecurity in life.

Jeff was proud of the fact that he could sustain a twenty-plus-year marriage, and he even told Colin they were planning a vow-renewing ceremony, which was not exactly true since Ellie knew nothing about it. He was beginning to think the whole thing was, sadly, just so much pie in the sky. But it was satisfying to see the envy in Colin's eyes, and he certainly wasn't going to mention that Ellie left once, wants to leave again, and droops around the house like a malnourished fern.

She hadn't been in that chat room lately, and he supposes he'd accidentally outed himself with that Hunky Dory slipup. He had found it astonishing that those women, especially Ellie, poured their hearts out on that chat room to virtual (literally) strangers, and yet he'd gotten so comfortable that he went and did something stupid. Well, he's not going to beat himself up about it. The chat room was an excellent source of information, but those women are also dangerously influential, always pushing Ellie to leave him. He wonders briefly if she's going to confront him about being Lory but knows she never will.

His dinner with Colin was uneventful until, after their second beer, Colin's easy-come-easy-go mask slipped, and he started to cry, actually, in his beer, much to Jeff's horror. The whole story came out: his wife's infidelity, Colin's initial rage, feeling betrayed, how she'd left him, though not to be with the guy she'd cheated on him with. Colin was gutted, and Jeff was fascinated.

He was torn between keeping Ellie's defection a secret or telling Colin about his own experience and shattering the image of their intact marriage. As he watched Colin, red-faced and puffy, Jeff decided it was his duty as a friend to confess that he'd been through the same thing. And in fact, Jeff would look even better; he'd gone through his trial by fire and remained married. There were so few times in his life, Jeff realized, when he could give others the benefit of his own experience and the wisdom that came with it.

"Listen," he said, leaning forward earnestly toward Colin, "I know what you're going through, man. Ellie and I separated for a few months last year" (oh, that was a good spin—a mutual separation).

Colin looked up, interested. "Really?"

"Oh yeah."

Jeff enjoyed the way Colin listened raptly as he told the story, sort of based on fact, of his and Ellie's trial separation, emphasizing that it was therapy that got them through it, and how he and Ellie were able to rekindle their love and find their way back. Jeff even got a little choked up as he recounted the tale. He gave a lot of credit to his own willingness to change. He also said that Ellie had realized it was probably just a midlife crisis or something, and that may be the trouble with Colin's wife.

"We tried therapy," Colin said gloomily. "Didn't work."

"Our therapist was the best. Took me a while, but I found this fantastic guy, right in Saratoga. Joseph Robert. I'll give you his info; you should call. I'll bet he can help. At this point, it couldn't hurt, right?"

Jeff was gratified to see Colin perking up, considering his words, the promise of another therapist, another shot. Jeff remembered what a kick he got out of helping people. He felt good that he could translate his own pain and subsequent enlightenment for the good of another human being.

Jeff's own righteous glow began to fade, though, after they said goodbye, and he's been driving for a while, contemplating his own tenuous situation.

He doesn't want to think about losing his marriage in his sixties, which is Colin's age too. Of course, Ellie is younger, still in her fifties. Does she think that she'd have a second chance at a relationship? Does she think she would, or could, as the crass saying goes, "trade up?" He'd never in his life thought that he was someone to be "traded up" from, and he felt an unfamiliar stab of shame and outrage at the thought that she might not only divorce him but put him aside for another man. She was still attractive, even for her age, and smart and funny . . . but she was going blind, and who would want that? And in any event, where would she find this other guy? At work? He knew most of the people in her office, and none of the guys were a threat, that's for sure; unless, of course, they hired someone new, or she's maybe interested in someone she sold a policy to? Still, when would Ellie have the time to have an affair? And honestly, he didn't think she had the energy to be unfaithful, when it came down to it.

His car hums along Santa Cruz Avenue, which is alight and bustling in the winter evening. He loves the leased Prius and doesn't mind that everyone else seems to have one, and that he can no longer afford a BMW. It's not that he sees his marriage as a status symbol, but let's face it—divorce, especially at his age, is a very public failure, as opposed to the private failure that he's been trying not to think about.

He knows he will have to tell Ellie soon because of Hannah's tuition. He can probably limp along with what remains in his accounts, but the hit from Ballard will just about wipe him out. Of course, it isn't his fault; he had confidence in his professional investment acumen, which he'd poured into the Smalls Family Mutual Funds, and he'd been doing so well for so many years. But he'd begun to notice the leaks that sprung in the principal, and the years of Hannah's tuition, which he staunchly promised Ellie they could afford, proved to be the flood that broke the dam.

Jeff figures that Ellie will be mad at him, but they are a team (even though he feels Ellie is a poor team player), and a team has to pull together even, *especially*, when one party makes a mistake. Jeff isn't sure what Hannah's reaction will be, but he's certain they can figure out some way that she can finish her degree—maybe a junior college?—without breaking the bank. Of course, she'll be upset about leaving Ballard and Boston, but she's had three excellent years there, and that will have to be enough. The good news is that Hannah most likely will have to stay in Silicon Valley to finish her degree, and maybe even live in their house in Los Gatos. He smiles, thinking about how much he loves the idea of having the whole family living under one roof (even though he often finds them both an irritant). With Hannah living with them, Ellie will probably want to stick around too. Win-win-win!

Is he upset? Of course he's upset! But people forge through adversity! They keep their pride in the face of diminishing circumstances! *That's the spin*, he thinks to himself, becoming almost emotional as he contemplates the American never-say-die spirit that makes the most demoralized bankrupt former millionaire pick himself up, dust himself off, and start all over again. What do they think he's been trying to do since his 9/11 freak-out, when he went from being a Master of the Universe to a Hero of New York to a stay-at-home dad? He did the best he could, the best anyone could have done with the Smalls Family Mutual Fund, and besides that, he watched out for them, managed the day-to-day stuff, took some of the burden off by doing things for them all. He'd never be a Master of the Universe again, fine. He was the Master of His Family, though, and he did a damned good job.

The important thing is, they have each other. They have Ellie's salary from her auto insurance job. They have the remaining couple of hundred thousand from the fund, the interest from which he will, as always, use entirely for his family. He smiles as the Prius silently glides through Santa Cruz, and he heads toward that frozen yogurt place Ellie always likes.

CHAPTER FORTY
HAPPINESS IS A WARM GUN

JANUARY 4, 2019

Her workday over, with Jeff downstairs in his office, Ellie has settled herself in their bedroom and is finally free to contemplate her last session with Suzy/Suzanne/Ruby.

Granted, that was a lot to process, and Suzy's story seems incredible even after she reviews the PM from last night. Ellie's pretty sure Suzy was telling the truth, but she can't shake the sense that there's something fuzzy around the edges that she's not seeing (oh yes, that's so funny, of course she can't see around the edges, ha ha).

She believes Suzy's story about Chas and Charles and how she grew up. Of course, she could opt not to believe it, but her gut tells her that it's the truth. And she believes that Suzy's gone underground, that she's had to leave her life behind to live in some secret place in order to—what? Keep Chas from blackmailing Charles? But Chas is dead. Why can't she go home now?

She mulls over her theory from last night that IATW supplies new identities and relocation to new cities for women who can't stay in their miserable marriages. But still, Suzy is married to Charles, not Chas. Unless Charles was really the problem?

His infidelities? Or was she actually still in some legal way married to Chas? But why would that necessitate leaving home in such a draconian way?

Unless IATW doesn't offer that service, and that's just what Suzy did on her own.

Ellie muses that online friendships exist in a sort of ether. Unlike "real" friends, you wouldn't recognize these women on the street, you don't know what their homes are like, you couldn't say what they like to eat when you all go out for brunch. In a sense, they are all in different countries, separated by the very cyberspace that brought them together. And yet how real they all seem to her, how she misses Moreofme, Freeatlast, and Gingerbear. And Lorelei, who somehow touched her heart more than the others with her vicious "bastard" and her estranged children.

She thinks about Lorelei for a moment. Even if you can't see your chat room friends, you can nevertheless *hear* them, in a way. All the women she's met on both boards have such distinct vocabularies and rhythms to their speech, she could almost identify them by their—

Ellie sits up at her desk, her heart pounding.

She could identify every person on DWOF simply by looking at what they had written, what they had "said," as it were. Their signature style was inescapable. That's what she couldn't put her finger on, the nagging detail crowding the edge of her subconscious.

Kore, the woman on IATW.

Reminds her of Lorelei.

Ellie opens her laptop. She can't get back on to DWOF since she's been on IATW (and why? Why is that?), so she can't go back to compare Kore's speech with Lorelei's. But she knows it: they just sound the same. The breeziness that doesn't bely a genuine caring, the energy of the train of thought, the English penchant for using the affectionate "love" when making a particularly tender comment—and "brilliant," with which Lorelei liberally peppered her remarks.

If Ruby was Suzy/Suzanne, from DWOF, then why couldn't Kore be Lorelei? Ellie went from Ellesbelles on DWOF to DearPrudence on IATW, so why wouldn't they change their names too?

But Suzy was underground, as it were. If Kore was Lorelei, and Lorelei was Claire Watson, she was still very much in the world. Her latest movie had recently been released, and she'd probably attended the premiere, and perhaps was even working on a new film.

So maybe IATW wasn't some kind of relocation program for women in crappy marriages.

Of course, Lorelei wasn't exactly in a crappy marriage, since she'd been separated for so many years from the husband who had made her life miserable. But then again, he was dead, and recently. Anthony Something-Smythe died right around the time Lorelei left DWOF.

And Suzy wasn't really in a crappy marriage either. It was her ex or maybe not-so-ex Chas who was the pill in her life. And Chas died shortly after Suzy left—

Holy shit.

Holy shit.

No.

Marilyn's words come back to her: "These women may have some creative solutions for navigating a bad marriage."

"Creative solutions."

The dark web. Where you can't be traced.

Fuck me, Ellie thinks, and can feel a cold hand around her heart. These women have murdered their husbands.

And then the thought comes:
And gotten away with it.

———

Fifteen minutes later, Ellie has regained the normal function of her brain. Reality check: these women haven't actually killed their husbands.

That is not real life. Women divorce their husbands, women remain in messy, painful relationships for various reasons, but it is rare for women to kill their husbands.

Wait—is it? Maybe she can look that up? Without compromising her browsing history on her computer? Then she remembers she's on the dark web and decides to take a dive.

Ten minutes later, she decides somewhat queasily that she's not scuba certified for a dark web deep dive, which is, at best, disconcerting, and at worst—worse. But one key piece of information she comes away with is that more husbands kill wives than wives kill husbands. She probably could have figured that out herself.

But, of course, women who kill their husbands tend to be in deeply dysfunctional, violent relationships, where guns are in the house and violence has already occurred and it's no surprise to anyone.

With that in mind, she can, of course, eliminate herself and her situation and the people she knows—or thinks she knows—from this equation.

Obviously, she'd made a big, dangerous leap. These are just coincidences. Lorelei's husband was pretty old, and Suzy's Chas was a vaper, probably unhealthy. Both men were assholes, but that's irrelevant, Ellie decides.

Then she can't help but cycle back. Seriously, could this be the "special wisdom," the "creative solution" of how to manage a bad marriage? The husband dies—or is *killed*? Maybe it's like *Strangers on a Train*, where they go after each other's husbands, not their own, so the wife remains in the clear? Then her blood runs cold—does that mean that somehow Jeff will die within a month? (And is that a bad thing? Shut up, Ellie!) Will he meet some mysterious accident? Is this like some sort of perverted fairy tale, where you get what you want but then go right to hell? How does it happen? Will she have to kill someone else's husband? She thinks of the deaths of Chas and Anthony Something-Smythe—accidents, surely, but . . . maybe not? Once again, she has to ask herself, is she being paranoid? Should she warn Jeff? Or just let the chips fall? This is crazy. How could she possibly warn Jeff? What would that even sound like? "Um, I've been on a dark web chat room for women who hate their husbands, and it's possible someone's going to come to kill you." Should she go to the police? She should, shouldn't she? But she'd look like a total idiot, and in any case, she's not going to rat out these women.

Why not just get on IATW and ask what the fuck is going on?

But wait—if they can come after Jeff, can they come after her?

But Suzanne and Claire are both trustworthy, at least, if her theory is true—which, of course, it may not be.

She eyes her laptop, fingers hovering over the keyboard. She pauses. Is she getting into something really weird and possibly dangerous? (Ya think?) She ponders her encounter with Ruby/Suzanne/Suzy—though troubling, it was informative and didn't feel dangerous.

The question is, does she forget all about it? Or does she get on IATW and blithely say, *I just had the craziest thought!*

Don't think so much, she admonishes herself, and logs on.

———

I AM THE WALRUS CHAT ROOM
8:24 P.M.

IvyLeak:
Green.

BTDT:
Uggh. Who can wear green?

Danais:
Who can wear orange?

Danais:
Is it all green now? Or just Club Fed?

IvyLeak:
Let's be clear:
this was NOT Club Fed. There was nothing clubby about it.
And yeah, I think the gen pop in the higher securities wear
orange.

DearPrudence:
I can always count on you guys to be talking about something
interesting.

Danais:
Ivy, meet DearPrudence, our newest member. Doing
twenty-two years in a crappy marriage.

BTDT:
See, now THAT'S hard time.

IVYLEAK:
Hi, DearPrudence! I just did twelve months!

DANAIS:
DP, meet IvyLeak.

IVYLEAK:
Originally eighteen, commuted to twelve for excellent behavior!

DEARPRUDENCE:
Sorry—it sounds like you were in prison?

IVYLEAK:
Yup. Just got out, came straight here. They don't let you get on the web inside, let alone the dark web.

BTDT:
Just in case you're nervous, DP, Ivy wasn't in for anything violent. Just a little parental fraud.

DEARPRUDENCE:
????

IVYLEAK:
I helped my kid get into a good school, okay? I fudged a few things on some documents, beefed up the transcripts, like you'd do with any resume, sweetened the pot in a few places. I maybe went a little overboard and it became a thing. So sue me.

DEARPRUDENCE:
Wow.

KORE:
Hell hath no fury like a parent trying to get their child into a good school.

BTDT:
So, did your kid get in?

IVYLEAK:
Transferred out. Thin skinned, like his father. Oops—mustn't speak ill of the dead!

DANAIS:
DP, IvyLeak's husband died while she was in prison.

DEARPRUDENCE:
I'm sorry, that must have been awful.

IVYLEAK:
Uh-huh.

DEARPRUDENCE:
How did your husband die?

IVYLEAK:
Insulin overdose.

DEARPRUDENCE:
Oh. He was a diabetic?

IVYLEAK:
Well, yes. That was the only way it would have worked.

DEARPRUDENCE:
Excuse me???

DANAIS:
Ivy—you're on the homepage, not *goo goo g'joob*.

IVYLEAK:
SHIT.

IVYLEAK:
Well, that's the Leak in IvyLeak for ya.

DEARPRUDENCE:
Okay, I think I know how this goes now and I'm going to ask you PLEASE DO NOT DELETE THIS POST. OKAY?? TELL ME WHAT THE FUCK IS GOING ON HERE!

LAURIEB:
Don't yell. Hurts my eyes.

DEARPRUDENCE:
May I ask a question?

KORE:
You don't need to ask to ask, love, just ask!

DEARPRUDENCE:
Are all your husbands dead?

BTDT:
Dingdingdingdingding! We have a winner!

DEARPRUDENCE:
So, I may be making a leap, here, but it just occurred to me that that'd be a good way to navigate a crappy marriage. Becoming a widow.

DANAIS:
Yes. It's a long-standing and very respected tradition.

DEARPRUDENCE:
Okay. Tell me this. Do you try to . . . speed up the process?

BTDT:
Ummmm—Danais, you wanna take this one?

IVYLEAK:
Shit. I'm sorry. I feel bad now.

KORE:
Should we do this here? Or should we send her to *goo goo g'joob*?

DEARPRUDENCE:
That's that link, right? On the first page of the chat room? It's grayed out. Is that what you're talking about?

DANAIS:
Okay, DearPrudence. Per your request, and because we've all, as it were, been outed, thanks to IvyLeak, I'm not going to delete this and I'm going to tell you what we're all about here.

IVYLEAK:
I am so, so sorry.

DANAIS:

Every woman in this chat room, myself included and, from
what it sounds like, yourself as well, has found herself in an
untenable, long-term marriage. All of us have lived through
decades with men who may not have physically abused
us, but who belittled us, or controlled us, or bullied us, or
screamed at us, or in some nonviolent but very damaging
way made us feel cornered, small, helpless, trapped in our
own homes. I bet you can tick a few of these boxes yourself.

DEARPRUDENCE:

Go on.

DANAIS:

It has also been our experience that other women in the
same circumstances were able to leave, and did so. And that
the world at large either never knew about the psychic pain
we were in or couldn't believe that it was that big a deal, or
understand why we didn't just walk out. With me so far?

DEARPRUDENCE:

I don't know if I'm with you, but I understand you.

DANAIS:

For some of us, leaving wasn't an option for many, many
reasons, usually economic but sometimes emotional, sometimes
due to children, or older parents, or a lawyer husband who
could stretch it out for decades, or any number of things that
made leaving, or divorce, impossible. Utterly impossible.

DEARPRUDENCE:

It's not the nineteenth century. You can always get divorced.

DANAIS:

Yes, you can always get divorced. And a few posts ago, I urged you to get divorced, to borrow whatever you had to in order to get yourself out of your marriage. Remember?

DEARPRUDENCE:

Yes.

DANAIS:

Did you?

DEARPRUDENCE:

. . . No.

DANAIS:

Do you remember you once said something here about how you fantasize sometimes that your husband is dead? And you felt guilty about it and we all said something like, we've all had that fantasy, you're only human?

DEARPRUDENCE:

Yes.

DANAIS:

Every single one of us here has had that fantasy. It's a great solace, a little daydream sometimes that gives you a glimpse of a future in which you're free, safe, happy. But mostly—free. Much more so than in a divorce, which might not only, as I said before, drag on for years but, if you have children, doesn't really ever allow for a full separation from the one person in the world who makes your life miserable.

DEARPRUDENCE:
What are you saying?

DANAIS:
I'm saying that in this chat room, you are surrounded by women who have made their fantasy a reality. With no consequence to themselves.

DEARPRUDENCE:
How is that possible? How is it possible to do what I think you're telling me and not have consequences? If not legally, then—what about your conscience? What about emotional damage? *How do you live with yourself????*

DANAIS:
When you weigh the decades of your life with this man, who makes you miserable, against the remainder of your life—and no one knows how long they've got left, right?—there is a balance here. After all, if he'd been beating the shit out of you for decades, we'd call this self-defense, right? He's been beating the shit out of you emotionally and psychologically for decades, doesn't that count for something?

KORE:
There's a brilliant Stephen Sondheim musical—well, they're all brilliant, actually, aren't they?—called "A Little Night Music." There's a song in there about a woman in a marriage with a philanderer who doesn't love her, "Every Day a Little Death." That's what I think of when I think of my marriage.

DEARPRUDENCE:
My child was in that musical. I remember that song.

RUBY:

Dylan Thomas wrote, "After the first death, there is no other." But all of us here rather agree with Sondheim: Every day in marriages like ours brings a little death. And it adds up.

DEARPRUDENCE:

What—to one great big one that you're justified in avenging? With another death???

BTDT:

Yeah, baby!

DEARPRUDENCE:

You people are SOCIOPATHS!

DANAIS:

Yes, some of us are. Not all sociopaths are in prison. Some of us are CEOs and high-profile attorneys and politicians.

KORE:

But DearPrudence, not all of us are sociopaths. Some of us are just like you—"normal"—I have to use quotes to be PC, because, after all, what is normal, right?—but with a big problem that hinders our ability to get on with a productive, happy life.

RUBY:

Listen, none of us came to this easily.

BTDT:

Speak for yourself!

LaurieB:

Says the Sociopath.

BTDT:

Oh, and what are you?

LaurieB:

. . . same.

Danais:

DearPrudence, we're not idiots here. We know this is an
unthinkable step. And we're not talking about guns or knives
or explosives. We're talking about exploiting what we call
a preexisting condition. We find a physical weakness—like
diabetes, or emphysema, or a bad habit—and we take it to its
logical conclusion. We are all dealing with men who are over
sixty, sometimes way over. The chinks in the bodily armor
have become obvious. And we use that to our advantage.

IvyLeak:

Yeah, it's like when someone's in hospice and they give them
morphine, right? Just helping them along. No fear. No pain.

LaurieB:

Sadly.

DearPrudence:

Even supposing I can wrap my head around what you are
so casually discussing—let's be practical. How is it that you
don't get caught? At least, some of you? There has to be
some percentage of women who get caught, dear God, I
can't believe I'm having this conversation.

DANAIS:
There's never been a woman caught on my watch. And I
would know.

DEARPRUDENCE:
Are there other "chat rooms" that have this same . . . agenda????

DANAIS:
DearPrudence, this homepage is sort of a clearing ground so
that we can judge whether or not a woman is ready, willing
or even able to, as we put it "jump over the fence." We speak
in generalities here. Once a woman decides to go ahead, that
grayed out *goo goo g'joob* link goes live, and she finds herself
in her own ultra-secure cybercell, as it were, with myself
and a handpicked mentor to help her come up with the best
plan for her unique situation. We have access to medical,
psychological, legal and law enforcement specialists who will
weigh in on the plan.

DEARPRUDENCE:
You must be joking.

DANAIS:
I would never joke about this. All of our associates are
women in our network who have successfully jumped over
the fence themselves.

IVYLEAK:
A lot of times, you don't even need to be there. Why do you
think my hubby checked out when I was in prison? All part of
the plan!

DANAIS:
I'm deleting that. Ivy, watch yourself.

KORE:
Don't worry, love, it's a fair guess you won't have Ivy on your team!

DEARPRUDENCE:
I'm sorry—this is insane.

DANAIS:
Yes. Except that it works.

DEARPRUDENCE:
How many women have you helped jump over the fence, or whatever you call it? Who are still walking around as free women?

DANAIS:
100 percent.

DEARPRUDENCE:
Okay, 100 percent of how many? The five who are on this board?

DANAIS:
I'm one of many who do this work. Since the program was started ten years ago, we figure we've released over three thousand women. Successfully.

KORE:
Wow.

LaurieB:
That's all?

DearPrudence:
AT THE COST OF SOMEONE'S LIFE!!!

Danais:
DP, how many years have you been miserable with him? Isn't it the cost of your life, too? How do you tally that up?

BTDT:
Think of all the people you loved who died and you said, how come the good always die? Why can't the shitheads die? Well, here's your chance.

Ruby:
She's gone.

BTDT:
She'll be back.

Kore:
Or not.

Danais:
Her path.

CHAPTER FORTY-ONE
LADY MADONNA

JANUARY 5, 2019

Ellie hit her knee on the edge of a kitchen drawer that had been left open, and acute pain sent her down to the floor in tears, gritting her teeth.

She knows in five minutes she'll be perfectly fine, but there's something about being on the floor when Jeff comes in and looking up at him. Something primal and raw, her husband peering down at her, maybe not with contempt, or disdain, but it sure isn't sympathy. Then he says, "Well, you should have remembered that you left it open. You do this all the time; I don't get it. How do you not manage your personal space better, knowing that you're vision impaired?" It is the question that sends her over the edge.

Especially since she knows *she* didn't leave the drawer open.

In her pain, Ellie can only gaze at him in amazement—*how stupid can you be*, she thinks to herself, and honestly, she doesn't know if she's thinking about him or herself.

And this is not much more than an hour after he dropped his bomb, about how he'd miscalculated an investment that should have been a sure thing, was unable to recoup their losses, and basically pissed away the 9/11 workman's comp payout he'd gotten fifteen years ago—the one that paid for the down on their house; the one that paid for Hannah's college, or was supposed to; the one that was going to keep them solvent in their old age. He explained that he had hoped he could use his old mojo to make it stretch longer, but in the end, he couldn't. It was gone.

Ellie listened in bowel-wrenching silence to his story, clocking Jeff's patented combination of bullshit humility and smug self-assurance. But the thing that hammered home was that with this hit to his only form of income, he now has virtually nothing to live on. Ellie's blood ran cold as she remembered that his 9/11 account was a big part of her escape plan *for him*. She thought with fury that this is just another way that Jeff has ruined her life: other women who get divorced have husbands with jobs or pensions, so they can just go, leave with impunity; leave the Fucker the house, even, who cared, but they could get the hell out, get their own place, and start living their best lives.

Not her, though, thanks, once again, to Jeff.

With him in such desperate financial straits, she knew that legally she'd have to support him as well as herself, and Hannah, on her paycheck.

Of course, she thought wildly, even as he was talking, they still had the house. But even if they sold the house, he wouldn't have enough income to pay his own mortgage or rent. The figures Ellie so carefully mined weeks ago spun in her head like confetti, so thick and light she was unable to grasp them.

But this she knows: For as long as she lives, he'll be a millstone around her neck, dragging her down as he sucks off a precious percentage of her scanty-enough paycheck, eventually taking part of her even more pathetic Social Security payouts.

For the rest of her life.

Living together, though horrible, is at least financially feasible. But if she left him now? Got her own apartment, siphoned off the legal amount from her paycheck every month to finance his lifestyle, whatever it might be? Paid her lawyer, and probably his? Impossible.

She knows he won't sell the house—at least not voluntarily, he's made that clear—and now it's not a question of who buys out the other; it's a matter of putting it on the market. Her fury rising, she thought about the time, energy, and money it will take to convince him the house has to go.

With cold calculation, she voiced her thoughts: "I'm going to have to support you for the rest of my fucking life."

He said, not for the first time, "Well, you're wasting your time in that dead-end job—you should have gotten something where you could've made some real money. But you'll never do anything now."

This from someone whose only source of income is from her work and that "dead-end job." Does he think he can just upend her life through his own idiocy? That she's such a doormat she's perfectly fine with him talking to her like this?

The enormity of the colossal failure of her life sweeps in suddenly. This is her life, the only one, as far as she knows, that she will ever have. And what has she done with her "wild and precious life," spending a quarter century with a man who couldn't make her happy, couldn't earn a living, couldn't provide Hannah with the harmonious family life she deserved, and now is destined to be a permanent drain on her resources?

She stares up at him from the floor, where the pain is just beginning to subside from her throbbing knee. She sees him clearly, this person with whom she is in every imaginable way trapped for the rest of her life.

God, she could kill him.

Wait.

She *could* kill him.

With his words, "You'll never do anything now," ringing in her ears, she pushes herself to her feet with as much dignity as she can muster, shrugs off the solicitous hand he holds out for her, and walks up to their bedroom, shutting the door behind her.

She logs onto IATW. She casts a quick glance at the grayed-out *goo goo g'joob* link, then types an email:

> From: dp@protonmail.com
> To: fullfathomsfive@protonmail.com
>
> I'm in.
>
> DP

She only has to wait a minute.

> From: fullfathomsfive@protonmail.com
> To: dp@protonmail.com
>
> Well okay then.
>
> D

Ellie closes out the email tab.

———

I AM THE WALRUS CHAT ROOM
11:15 A.M.

Ellie stares at the home page banner. The grayed-out *goo goo g'joob* link suddenly turns blue.

She clicks it.

CHAPTER FORTY-TWO
THE CONTINUING STORY OF BUNGALOW BILL

I AM THE WALRUS
GOO GOO G'JOOB
JANUARY 5, 2019
11:16 A.M.
Nothing looks any different. Except there's no one there—no streams of text, no lines of conversation from the gang. It's a blank page. Ellie feels tentative.

———

DEARPRUDENCE:
Hello?

DANAIS:
Hi. We're waiting for Ruby, I just PM'd her. She'll be your mentor. I'll be here too, when I can.

DEARPRUDENCE:
I guess she's a good choice.

RUBY:

DearPrudence, hi, are you okay?

DEARPRUDENCE:

Yes.

DANAIS:

All right. You've just made a big decision. And for the next few weeks, all we're going to do is talk. This whole process will be theoretical until it becomes practical, and you can stop it at any point up till then. For now, all you have to do is live with your decision.

RUBY:

It helps if you imagine your life in the future, after all is said and done. What will your new life, that freedom, look like for you? It's good to be practical: Will you stay in your present home or move? Will you have to downsize? Are there financial considerations? But it's also good to dream a bit, because if you're like most of us, now you can. After being tamped down (or worse) for decades, now your heart and your brain can expand. You will be able to be your most authentic self. You will be able to rest.

DEARPRUDENCE:

It seems like . . . I will be looking over my shoulder all my life after this. "Rest" doesn't seem too realistic.

DANAIS:

Yes, it's an odd prospect in light of the step you're about to take. But trust us—it happens.

RUBY:

It's a process.

DANAIS:

Right now, you don't have to do anything except think of a future without your husband. Imagine the world without him in it. Think of your life if you hadn't met him. In how many ways will your everyday life be easier if he's not part of it.

DEARPRUDENCE:

I've already had those thoughts . . .

RUBY:

Most of us have. But now you have the power to make a daydream become a reality.

DANAIS:

Meet us back here in about two weeks. All you have to do is log in and click on *goo goo g'joob*. One or both of us will join you within five minutes.

RUBY:

Right now, you're just thinking. That's all you have to do. Nothing is imminent.

DEARPRUDENCE:

Can I still get on the chat room?

DANAIS:

Yes. No one there is aware of your change in status, as it were. And obviously, what happens on *goo goo*, stays on *goo goo*.

RUBY:
Danais loves saying that.

DEARPRUDENCE:
All right, you got a smile out of me.

DANAIS:
Good! See you in two weeks.

RUBY:
But you can always check in if you need to.

DEARPRUDENCE:
Got it. See you in a few.

———

Ellie signs out, closes her computer, sits back in her chair, and wonders, *Am I insane?*

CHAPTER FORTY-THREE
DAY TRIPPER

JANUARY 19, 2019

Ellie stretches her back and hears her neck crack after sitting so intensely hunched over her laptop for the past twenty minutes. She notices what is becoming a familiar sense, that her computer represents some kind of alternate reality to her real life. She told Danais and Ruby on their last chat she doesn't know if she's living a double life or a half-life: A double life because she's secretly planning to dispatch the person she lives with, or a half-life because she feels like she's in some kind of limbo, where she can't live her life fully until she does what she's going to do. *If* she does it.

Today they'd had their first real (surreal) spitball session about Jeff's habits and physical weaknesses. Ellie had a moment of giddy triumph when she suddenly remembered he was allergic to peanuts, which sent a thrill of horror up her spine as she wrote: "There it is! Anaphylactic shock—it could happen to anyone!" But Danais and Ruby were quick to shoot it down—too obvious. In a house where you know someone's deathly allergic to peanuts and someone dies from eating or breathing peanuts—that's a nonstarter.

Ellie didn't know if she felt disappointed or relieved. Danais wrote: "When it's right you'll know it. We'll all know it. In the meantime, be strong and live your life."

Or, as Ellie glumly said to herself, her half-life.

Who is she kidding? This whole thing on IATW is some kind of weird fantasy therapy for her, a sick parlor game or maybe some deeply personal first-person-shooter video game. She's not going to kill her husband, and she knows this, deep in her bones. She's a good girl. She's going to eventually rev up the energy to divorce him, with all the time, stamina, and money that entails, which she does not have, and until then—well, until then, she's sort of enjoying plotting. Or maybe just being in the company of women who know exactly how she feels.

Ellie had written Danais and Ruby about Jeff following her onto DWOF as Lory, and they were both shocked and, she thought, a little alarmed. Danais admitted to her there was no way she could prevent Jeff getting onto one of their network sites, but she would make certain that no one new would get on IATW while Ellie was working through her process; she would also get the word out to her other cybersisters in crime (well, she didn't put it that way exactly) to be aware of a male imposter. Ellie wasn't exactly relieved, but it felt better to let them know about it. She just knew, somehow, that both Danais and Ruby, wherever they are, have her back.

Ellie looks beyond the little pool of light emanating from her computer and is startled to see that it's dark already; she'd been too immersed in dreams of killing her husband to notice. She can hear Snowball thumping around, irritated at having to wait for her dinner, which she expects promptly at six.

Ellie's at the dining-room table, since Jeff has gone out for dinner with Colin, whose efforts to get back with his wife, according to Jeff, are going very well, now that they're seeing Jeff and Ellie's old therapist, Joseph. Ellie's glad to hear this and has been waiting with interest to see if Jeff suggests *they* go back to Joseph. But he hasn't, and frankly, Ellie doesn't care.

She gets up to turn on the dining-room light, stopping suddenly at a slight breeze that floats by her on the left. "Snowball?" she calls out tentatively, though she has the distinct feeling it wasn't the cat. Jesus, could someone be in the room with her? Her scalp prickles as she slows her breath, listens hard. Nothing, there's nothing there. She begins navigating carefully around the table to the other side, where the light switch sits on the wall by the archway to the kitchen. She's staggered a bit at how really, really dark everything is—probably because she's been so focused on the lit screen for so long. Yeah, that's it. Nothing to do with her vision.

She hears Snowball prowling about in the kitchen. "Dinner's coming, Snowy," Ellie calls to her as she puts out her hand toward the light switch.

Her body floods with panic, head dizzies with a jolt of fear the instant she touches the switch and feels *another hand* already there, the flesh shockingly warm and firm beneath her unsuspecting fingers, the light popping on so quickly that it blinds her as much as the dark did. Her heart crashes against her rib cage as—

"Ellie," says Jeff, "it's just me. Calm down. It's okay."

"You miserable *fuck*," she says quietly but intensely to Jeff, who steps back, arms up in a "what did I do?" gesture.

"Hey, watch the language! I got home early. You were somewhere in the dark; I could see your computer screen, so I flicked on the light. Don't yell at *me*. You nearly gave me a heart attack!" Like it's her fault.

"Don't creep up on me, okay? You don't creep up on a blind person! *I* about had a heart attack!"

"All right, I'm sorry," he says. Gosh, guess he learned something in therapy.

She walks hand over hand across the tops of the dining-room

chairs and plops herself back in her chair, her heart rate still elevated, her fury still pitched.

Jeff raises his arms again, backs off. "Jesus, you are in a *state*."

"Yeah, I'm in a *state* because you came up out of nowhere in the dark. Why would you do that? Next time, for God's sake, make a noise, announce yourself. I'm fucking blind here!"

She starts to cry, horrified at herself.

She can feel him come over to her, put a hand on her shoulder. She's so angry, and she's so sad that she can't lean into him, rest her head against his chest, and cry her heart out. Not that she ever could during their marriage, except for when they learned about Mort and Betty's declining health; that, for him, was a legitimate reason to fall apart. Not because she just had the shit scared out of her.

She pulls away, takes a breath, gets ahold of herself. And realizes with a jolt that he's staring right into her computer screen. Fuck—did she leave IATW up? She doesn't even look to see if she did, because she won't be able to find the cursor fast enough (even though she set her cursor at its largest size, she always has to hunt it down because it's inevitably just outside her field of vision), so she just snaps the laptop closed. She glances up at Jeff, catches him looking from the computer to her face.

"What was that?" he says casually. "A chat room?"

She has no idea how to react. Outrage that he looked at her screen? Well, it was open. Defensive, it's none of his business? Should she go on the offensive, which she never does, or at least, not successfully. What would the offensive even look like?

"How do you know what a chat room looks like?" she's surprised to hear herself say. "Have you ever been on one?"

She looks him right in the eye. *Yeah*, she thinks, *that's it.* He's quiet for a second.

"Sure," he says. "Yeah, every once in a while. Like, when I have a computer problem, sometimes I go into a chat room."

"Oh yeah?" she says. "That all?"

Holy shit, she thinks, she can back him into a corner. Oh, wait—nobody backs Jeff into a corner.

"Excuse me?" he says incredulously. "What do you care? If you were on a chat room just now, that's fine with me."

She studies him. Then she comes right out with it.

"Jeff. Are you Lory?"

She watches his expression carefully. Does she see something in his eyes change for a split second? Nope. Not a goddamn thing. At least, not anything she can see.

Jeff replies, "Am I what?"

"Lory. Are you Lory?"

"What does that mean? Is that an adjective—is it even a word? Jesus, are you having a stroke, like your dad?"

"It's a name. The name of a woman in a chat room I was on for a while. Lory. A combination of *L* for Leon and *D* for Dory, your parents' names? This Lory even mentioned that her mom's name was Dory, and they called her Hunky Dory, like you called your mom when you and your dad were joking around."

"I have no idea what you're talking about," he says, after what she thinks might be a split second too long.

"It was a chat room called Divorced Women over Fifty. I thought you followed me on, pretending to be this woman, Lory." *Okay*, she thinks to herself, *I'm going for it*.

"You're hallucinating."

She gazes at him steadily. "Right," she says, picking up her laptop and heading into the living room. For some reason, she doesn't want to go all the way upstairs to their bedroom. She feels, actually, afraid, as if some fissure that was safely beneath the tectonic plates of their marriage has given way, causing a shift in the ground she's walking on.

CHAPTER FORTY-FOUR
TELL ME WHY

FEBRUARY 2, 2019

He hears her bang her head against the microwave oven door, which he'd left open deliberately. Her swear words float up to him as he sits silently upstairs in Hannah's room, trying to comfortably negotiate the pain in his back from a recent soccer injury.

He doesn't know why he does it.

He's the not the type of person to pull the wings off flies, for God's sake, so why does he sabotage his own disabled wife? Joseph once said that hate isn't the opposite of love, that indifference is the opposite of love, which at the time sounded like psychobabble bullshit, but he has found that the rage in his heart against his wife has turned his love, which was real, to hate, not indifference. Does that mean he really loves her, and that when they get through this, they can get back to what they were? He used to think so. Now, not so much.

Of course, the thing with the laptop drove him nearly berserk. That was the night he came back early from his dinner with Colin, who called him at the last minute to say he had to cancel—he wasn't feeling well. Jeff went for a quick bite at Panera and then came back home early. He didn't deliberately try to be quiet, but when he walked in and saw her, so engrossed in her laptop she didn't look up, didn't hear him, obviously couldn't see him, he stopped and watched her from the small staircase leading up to the dining-room/kitchen level. He could see how intent she was on whatever it was she was reading on her laptop, saw her push it away and sigh, and worry, and think . . . whatever it was she was thinking.

He had a bad feeling.

He stood there for a minute, barely breathing. He wondered how much she could see outside the light of her laptop. He sometimes wonders how blind she really is, but, of course, he can never really know that. He slipped off his shoes and carefully walked behind her, taking care to be on an angle so she wouldn't see his reflection in the computer screen. She was very still. By way of an experiment, he very gently lifted and lowered his hand about a foot to the left of where she sat.

She stiffened. "Snowball?" she said, turning her head to the left.

She was clueless. And, so it seemed, far more impaired, or oblivious, than he thought.

So he sneaked up on her, pretending he'd just walked in, and nearly gave her a heart attack by putting his hand on the light switch just before she reached it. He knew it would scare the shit out of her. He doesn't know why he did it.

In the split second before she snapped close her computer, he could see she was clearly on a chat room. He couldn't see anything except the bare bones of it, the banner across the top that he didn't have time to make out—it looked like nonsense words, something made up—and he only saw two lines of text, one of which, he thought, said, *See you next time.*

But she shook him up with that Lory crap. She had some nerve, to accuse him of sneaking around like that when she was clearly keeping a few hefty secrets of her own, like DWOF and now whatever this was, and he'd bet there are others. DWOF was a public forum; he had every right to be on it. But he was damned if he was going to give her the satisfaction of admitting that he was Lory—at least, not then, where she had the upper hand through sheer element of surprise. He'd revisit the Lory question later, when the time was right for him.

He sighs irritably. He liked getting on DWOF, enjoyed the anonymity of it; it was a little like when he followed her whereabouts with the iPhone app, except that he could get a sense of what was on her mind, how she was with other people, as though he was watching her through a window in a crowded room without her knowing he was there. He saw an authentic side of her, uncensored and alive, in the chat room—something he hadn't seen in their marriage in a long time. It saddened him. It infuriated him.

He thought about her expression that night when she didn't know he was watching her, the worry, the deep thought, the emotions flitting across her face. It didn't come to him right away, but by the time he woke up the next morning, it was obvious. He knew what she was doing. He felt sickened.

She was on some sort of goddamn online dating site.

He remembered the dinner when Colin told him that his wife had been cheating on him. Jeff had comforted himself with the knowledge that Ellie simply didn't have the time or opportunity to cheat on him—she was either at work or at home.

It never entered his mind that she'd find someone online. But it makes all the sense in the world, now that he thinks about it. The clues are all there. Her drawing back from him, her refusal to forgive him for his financial "mishap," her irritability—hell, it could be why she wanted to separate, until it became clear that just wasn't a viable option for them.

If it was a real guy, a flesh-and-blood guy, he could maybe

force some kind of confrontation. He wasn't sure how to proceed with some sort of cyberguy, someone Ellie was chatting up,
and possibly had real feelings for, though, of course, they weren't
really real, because the guy was in cyberspace, for God's sake.
He was probably not even what or who he said he was. Jeff worried that she was getting herself involved in one of those scams,
where men prey on women by convincing them that they're in
love with them and then marry them and steal all their money,
or even kill them. Of course, Ellie has a good impediment to
that scenario—him. She's already married. Maybe she's the one
who's pretending, saying that she's free and available?

It kills him to think of Ellie betraying him like this.

He wonders if she's on some special dating site for people
who are disabled, or maybe even one for people who are blind?
He briefly wonders if she's merely on a support site for people
with RP or something innocent like that—but then he remembers the look on her face when she pushed away from her laptop,
the intensity, the sadness—that couldn't possibly be generated
by some stupid support group for blind people.

He didn't confront her then, because she caught him unaware with the Lory thing, and like the Lory thing, he'd have to
pick the right moment to tell her he knew what she was doing
in that chat room.

He wishes he could get ahold of her laptop, but she's been
taking it to work with her—another obvious sign of guilt; she's
never taken it before—and the frustration is driving him crazy.

He first got the idea of pretending to leave the house but
not really leaving from that time he came up on her unexpectedly after his nondinner with Colin. Of course, it's only on
weekends and nights; otherwise, she's at work, but he's aston-
ished at how easy it is to creep back in without her knowing
it. He's a little disappointed in her; you'd think someone with

diminished sight would hone their hearing, or the tingly sense that tells them someone else is there, but apparently Ellie is too engrossed in whatever it is she's doing to listen for intruders or, as it happens, him.

He remembers how he felt when she left him last year, how devastated and shaky and, if not quite repentant, at least willing to play her game and do all that therapy crap. He feels contempt for that weaker, vulnerable Jeff, who'd apologized for all the things that only Ellie felt he'd done "wrong." He's past that. She seemed willing to play ball back then, but now, he feels, all bets are off. Once infidelity is on the table, everything changes. He has nothing to apologize for—he's been faithful and loyal all these years, not her.

He thinks about his hopes for a vow-renewal ceremony. He feels like a chump. Doesn't like it.

Leaving open the cabinets and drawers—again, probably not his finest moment, but there's something satisfying in leaving the pots and pans drawer ajar, or the door to the area under the sink open, as hazardous as it can be to her. After all these years of catering to his disabled wife, of picking up after her, rewashing the counters that she could never get completely clean, the glasses she would always knock over by accident, which he would then have to sweep up because she couldn't see the tiny shards—now she was betraying him in the most obvious way possible, and he finds satisfaction inflicting on her a little of the pain that he's feeling.

The cabinet-drawer thing happened by accident the first time. It was the second week of his sneaking in and out, and he'd come in silently, like a cat burglar (props to Snowball, he thinks, as elegant and noiseless as a dancer as she prowls through the house), reveling in his invisible status. He saw that Ellie had left one of the kitchen cabinets open. He knew it wasn't him;

he'd always been meticulous about not leaving anything out that she'd blunder into with her limited vision. He could have shut it, but didn't. He was in the darkened corner of his office and could hear the *blam* of the impact and Ellie's bleepable language as she absorbed the blow.

He'd waited till she'd recovered and fixed herself a sandwich, which she took into the breakfast nook on the far side of the kitchen. He could hear the clatter of a utensil as it fell to the floor, apparently knocked over by her, accompanied by her "ucch" of self-disgust. When he felt she was settled, he slipped quietly out of the office, down the steps, and then silently out of the front door.

Seven minutes later, he came in through the front door, keys jangling, stomping his feet as he wiped them off, making all the noise he could think of before yelling, "Honey, I'm home!"

After that, it was easy.

CHAPTER FORTY-FIVE
SHE CAME IN THROUGH THE BATHROOM WINDOW

FEBRUARY 3, 2019

While Jeff was upstairs taking a shower, Ellie moved swiftly and quietly around the kitchen, meticulously shutting every drawer, every cabinet, the fridge and the dishwasher, so that she knew for sure they were closed. She was sitting in the breakfast nook reading her Kindle when he came down, and cheerfully said to him, "Bye, bye, have fun!" as he left to meet Wyatt for a late-afternoon movie.

He's been out a lot lately—dinners with Colin, movies with Wyatt, playing soccer with the guys even though it's dark early and cold, and a couple of weeks ago he caught a foot in his back that nearly sent him to the ER. He usually comes in very noisily and jovially, bringing a rush of the stale air from the garage with him. And she greets him with the usual wifely questions—how was the game, who was there, are you hurt—feeling only a slight twinge of vindictive glee about the fact she's privately contemplating his murder.

Now she waits till she hears the car leave the garage, then shuts off the light in the townhouse's second level, the one with the kitchen, the breakfast nook, the bathroom, and his office. Five minutes later she goes upstairs to their bedroom on the third level, turns on the light, and runs the water for a shower.

Now she's quietly standing at the top of the stairs on the bedroom level, in the darkness that for her isn't so much a cloak as a liability. She's waiting for Jeff to do what she thinks he's been doing: sneaking back into the house when he's supposed to be gone.

Like most people with impaired vision, Ellie's shins are criss-crossed with a number of old scars and some new ones from recent run-ins with open cabinet doors and laundry baskets left out where they shouldn't be. Yesterday she slammed her head against the open microwave door, the corner of which narrowly missed her eye. The other night, after Jeff had gone off to meet his soccer buddies at a bar, she ran into the low drawer where they keep the pots and pans, just below her line of sight.

She couldn't swear to it, but furniture seems slightly re-aligned, chairs and end tables off their marks, so that her natural pathways through the house, set in their ways for over ten years, seem fraught with danger. Is it simply that her eyes were getting worse, or are there more obstacles in her way than usual? She knows her vision is deteriorating, especially in low light, where images become softened and ghostly or disappear altogether. She keeps her cane with her in the house but also sometimes walks with a flashlight after dark, to use in between light switches.

She can't see into darkened corners, and Jeff knows that too. She could stare right into the unlit corner of his office and never know if it were empty or occupied.

She also knows that she's not the one leaving cabinets and doors and drawers treacherously ajar.

After that time he sneaked up on her, when she felt his hand on the light switch and nearly dropped dead, she began to get the uneasy feeling that he was in the house with her when he said he was going out. She knew it would be easy for him to stay just outside her field of vision (which is what he must have done that time he followed her to the lawyer's office) and have the run of the house. Why he would do something like that, she could only guess: To get back at her for wanting to separate, to catch her doing something on her computer? To hurt her so he could rush in and rescue her and be the hero?

She can barely hear him as he finally comes in, he is so quiet, but she recognizes the scratch of the front door as it opens and hears Snowball, who is actually a pretty good little watch cat, click across the hardwood toward it. She holds her breath but can hear nothing . . . maybe she can make out some unidentifiable noise in the kitchen that could just be the fridge.

She doesn't know if he'll go back out or stay, or where he'll wander within the house, but she decides that she'll pretend to finish up her shower and then go downstairs. After all, that's what she'd do normally. She walks softly back to the bathroom, shuts off the shower, and gives herself enough time to get into her sweats-and-T-shirt pajamas before going downstairs.

She visualizes herself figuratively keeping her terror at arm's length as she walks downstairs to the kitchen level with her flashlight, cane tucked under her arm so she can use the handrail on the way down, her bag with laptop and phone over her shoulder. She wonders where he is, if he's still in the house, playing the game the way she thinks he is. Is he going to pull a *Wait Until Dark* and spring down upon her from out of nowhere? That'd surely give her a fatal heart attack, and it'd serve him right.

She flicks on the kitchen light, takes few minutes for her eyes to adjust, and trains her vision on the upper level of the kitchen, where all cabinet doors seem shut, the way she left them. She doesn't know if it's with validation or terror that she carefully runs her eyes around the bottom half of the room and soon spots the dishwasher with its mouth yawing open. Which it certainly wasn't when she went upstairs.

So he came back.

Was he still here?

She walks through the kitchen, sits at the table. Is he waiting to hear her fall over and curse?

She leans over and very quietly tucks up the dishwasher door and considers the situation.

The open doors and cabinets, the rearranged furniture—had Jeff, like her, gone from DWOF to a dark web site like IATW, and was he doing the same thing she was trying to do to him, to exploit her weaknesses into a seemingly accidental death?

Suddenly, the blackness outside the tunneled light of her own vision is filled with menace. She no longer believes her own reassuring mantra, that everything in the dark is the same as in the light.

She should be scared, and she supposes she is, but there's also something steely and uncompromising blooming inside her.

And she's not a fool. Jeff might be in the house or not; he might be trying to kill her or not, but she knows one thing: it's time to go.

She's gotten in the habit of traveling through the townhouse carrying a large shoulder bag with her purse, computer, phone, and cane—there are just too many stairs to keep going up and down all day when she forgets something—and she clutches it to her now, her pulse pounding in her ears. She stops for a split second to listen for Jeff, wondering if he can hear what she's doing, or if he's not listening but sloppily relying on his own perfect sight.

Whatever. She suddenly has her own perfectly clear vision. Right now, she's going to call Jane, take a Lyft to her house for the night, then tomorrow get on a plane and take care of the business of divorce from the base camp of Wendy and Lacey's unremarkable, reality-grounded house in Weston. Just the thought of it makes a weight drop from her shoulders, and she breathes deeply for what seems the first time in months as she makes her way down the stairs to the front door.

The crash from above catapults her heart into her pounding head—first splintering glass, then something heavy falling, and a split second after, the thud of a body hitting the ground.

She's frozen with terror. All her theories go out the window, and she's left with the panicked realization that there's an intruder inside her house, a burglar or home invader who's come in, like the song says, through the bathroom window.

No, wait. It's Jeff. She knows it the instant she hears his voice, panicked and thick with pain, calling her name, calling for help.

CHAPTER FORTY-SIX
WHILE MY GUITAR GENTLY WEEPS

FEBRUARY 3, 2019

Ellie's in the Good Samaritan Hospital waiting room, waiting to hear about Jeff.

She'd had to call 911 when she found him spasming with pain on the floor of Hannah's bedroom, where he'd pulled down her glass-fronted armoire as he scrambled for purchase while he fell, the pain in his back like a hot zipper up the center of his spine. The paramedics had stabilized him on a gurney and carefully maneuvered him down the stairs, then taken both of them to the hospital in the ambulance. She was horrified to see him so frightened and in so much pain, and instinctively held his hand, squeezing it to give him comfort. Suffering is a great leveler, even when it's the suffering of the man you're plotting, at least theoretically, to kill.

Jeff told the EMTs he couldn't move his legs and had searing pain in his back that made it hard for him to breathe. He told them about the soccer injury he'd incurred a week or two ago, but the admitting doctor, Dr. Patmore, had said that spinal injuries weren't like breaking a knee or ankle, and they'd have to do a bunch of tests. The doctor had a reassuring bedside manner, but when he turned away from Jeff to give his orders, there was a gravity among the medical staff that made Ellie uneasy.

Ellie thinks about that story she wrote about Jeff's "death," the one she sent to Marilyn, which prompted Marilyn to send her to I Am the Walrus. In that scenario, the whole thing was over by the time she got to the hospital. Much preferable to this. She wonders if he'll die now—gosh, that'd solve a lot of things, wouldn't it? (*Who the hell thinks like this?* she asks herself)— but, of course, it's just a sports injury, and he's not going to die, which makes her feel dispirited and weary, and then guilty for feeling that way.

She tells herself to think positive: after all, it *could* be fatal, which makes her slightly hysterical, and she has to stop herself from laughing out loud, muffling her face in her hands with a moan. She knows she's not the only woman who ever wished her ailing husband would die, but sisterhood or not, it's a lousy feeling, and she's angry that she has to feel it. At least (and it is no small comfort) this incident had nothing to do with her. This was not on the list of things that she'd discussed with Danais and Ruby, not one of the "preexisting conditions" that would facilitate his exit and her freedom.

She thinks about her recent chats with Danais and Ruby. She knows she doesn't have to pull the trigger (nice image, that) unless she's 100 percent ready, and their discussions sometimes seem to her to take on a giddy unreality, like a game of How Many Ways Can You Kill Your Husband?

So as long as it's still theoretical, Ellie has to admit, it's kinda fun. Will she be able to go through with it, ultimately? Probably not, but who knows? The white-hot pitch of her fury waxes and wanes, but she has noticed it wanes when he's not there and waxes when he is, when his actual presence brings not a cessation of her rage but its burgeoning, like coals doused with lighter fluid. Sometimes just the sound of his key in the door is enough to make her blood pressure rise, her spirits plummet. She doesn't want to live with that forever.

Ellie wonders if, by denouncing her marriage through eradicating her husband, she's not only gaining her freedom but also unearthing some unsavory truth about herself. Ruby and the ladies of IATW have all extolled the virtues of the husbandless home, in which you can finally be free and be your authentic self after years of misery. But if that's so, is her true self a monster? Are all the women on IATW monsters? Well, yes, if you really think about it—aren't murderers monsters? Unless you buy the IATW company line that they are all acting in self-defense.

Ellie ponders Danais's brief overview of Murder 101, where she broke down the degrees of murder from manslaughter (accidental) to first degree (premeditated), and the possible consequences for each. Which, of course, begged the question, which Ellie asked, "Um—didn't you say your women never got caught?" But Danais believes knowledge is power, and anyway, she assured her, if it comes to that—to, God forbid, charges or a trial—her attorney and quite possibly the judge will be, as Danais put it, "in network," by which she means women who have also "jumped over the fence."

Ellie tries to get comfortable on the waiting-room chair, holding her cane at the ready just in case. She hasn't yet called Hannah, doesn't want to worry her; she's in the middle of rehearsals for an off-campus play, *Crimes of the Heart*, which Ellie remembers seeing off-Broadway when she was young. Hannah is playing the part of Babe, who shoots her husband because "I didn't like his looks." Ellie doesn't even want to unpack that one.

Ellie wonders, if her rage subsides, is there any scenario

in which she'd forgive Jeff? Possibly, if she loved him, but she doesn't, hasn't in a long time. And it's not just not loving him— loads of people live in loveless marriages that are civil, possibly comforting, maybe even successful in their own way, if they can roll along together in some sort of harmony. But hers is anything but harmonious, the daily verbal snipes and jabs like the *drip*, *drip*, *drip* of water wearing down stone. Her life with him is unbearable.

And now she's certain he attempted to injure her or worse. He *had* been sneaking in and out of the house; it's no longer a wild theory. He'd come back inside after telling her he was going out to the movies. So—is he on a dark web chat room, plotting her demise? Or is this just something he's come up with on his own? As far as Ellie can tell, there's only one person on IATW who she isn't familiar with, and that's IvyLeak, who has already dispatched her husband. In any case, Jeff couldn't possibly carry off the impersonation of a woman as uniquely irrepressible as IvyLeak. But could he be on some other site in their network, despite Danais's promise to alert other moderators?

Deep in thought, Ellie startles when she hears Jane saying, "Ellie, it's Jane. I'm just to your right," and she looks up grate-fully to see Jane, whom she'd called half an hour ago to tell her about Jeff being in the hospital. Jane settles down next to her, pulling some homemade chocolate chip cookies and a turkey sandwich out of her enormous bag.

"Sugar? Or protein?" she offers.

Ellie is too nervous to eat and says, "Neither, thanks," then takes a chocolate chip cookie, which Jane knows is her favorite food in the world.

"What's the sitch?" Jane asks, pulling out a thermos and pouring Ellie a cup of coffee. "It's decaf."

Ellie takes the cup and has a hot sip, wondering if it would be tacky to ask Jane to take her home right now—to Jane's house—and then continue on with her recent plan to hop on a plane to Wendy and Lacey's, leaving Jeff to fend for himself. She suddenly feels exhausted, but she looks up as Jane gently jabs her in her side. A doctor, not the one from the ER, is approaching, apparently tipped off that Ellie would be the one in the waiting room with the white cane, which is propped between her knees. Jane takes the coffee from her as they both rise.

"Hi, Ellie?" the doctor says, sweet voiced, with a slight accent; of course, she's maybe forty, looks twenty-two. "Let's go into the office, and I can tell you about Jeff."

Ellie gets lightheaded, remembering her fantasy of Jeff's death, when they showed her into an office off the waiting room, just as Dr. Weiss does now. She hopes fantasy and reality aren't somehow merging; she would simply have to fall at Jane's feet and go fetal if it did.

She's grateful to have Jane as an extra set of ears as she listens to what Dr. Weiss is saying.

Apparently, it's pretty serious.

(Yay?)

But it's treatable.

(Oh. Okay.)

Jeff has something called osteomyelitis of the spine, which is, basically, an infection that has traveled to the vertebrae, causing pain and the inability to stand. Dr. Weiss thinks his spine was compromised by the hit he got playing soccer, and then an opportunistic staph infection from the root canal he had a few days ago made its way to the spine.

They've tanked him up on painkillers and antibiotics, and he'll have to stay in the hospital at least overnight while they make sure surgery isn't required. When they do release him, he'll most likely have to be on an antibiotic IV drip at home for three weeks or more. They'll set Ellie up with everything she needs, and a nurse will be there for the first few sessions to show her how to safely administer the antibiotics intravenously through the PICC line in Jeff's arm.

Ellie's brain is whizzing. What does this mean? Will he recover? Will he be disabled? What's that gonna look like, both of them disabled? Oh God, poor Hannah.

She thinks, with white-hot fury, of what this is going to cost her, the hospital stay and maybe surgery and the nurse coming to the house. She has health insurance through her job, but there's still going to be the co-payment and the deductible and then whatever the excess is when they reach the limit of what's covered, or maybe it's an out-of-pocket expense she'll have to pay before any of it's covered.

Then she thinks of the misaligned furniture in her house, the doors and drawers left open, the sneaking in and out without her knowing.

The Fucker.

"Do you want to see him?" Dr. Weiss asks.

Yes, she wants to see him. She wants to go into his room and put a pillow over his face.

She doesn't say that. She merely nods, and Jane and Dr. Weiss escort her through a set of doors and down the corridor to his room. He's propped up on a bed at an angle and seems pretty out of it, despite a soft groan every now and then, which Ellie meanly thinks is simply theater on his part.

"Don't worry," Dr. Weiss says lightly. "He'll live."

"Great," Ellie says noncommittally, and with a tight smile she lets Jane take her home, where she suddenly finds a second wind.

———

I AM THE WALRUS CHAT ROOM
GOO GOO G'JOOB
FEBRUARY 4, 2019
1:05 A.M.

DEARPRUDENCE:
... so he's probably coming home tomorrow or the next day.
It won't be so bad—he can barely walk, and can't go upstairs,
so I can have the bedroom level to myself, and also the
ground floor, where the living room is. It's just a shame that
he didn't—well, you know. Anyway, he's going to be fine. I'll
be bankrupt, but he'll be fine.

DEARPRUDENCE:
Hello?

DEARPRUDENCE:
You guys there?

DANAIS:
Yes, sorry, we were DMing.

RUBY:
You'll be fine too. So, he's not there right now, right? He's still
at the hospital?

DEARPRUDENCE:
Yeah.

RUBY:
Okay. Why don't you DM me the name of your husband's exact
condition and the name of the hospital that's discharging him.

DEARPRUDENCE:

. . . you want to send him a card?

DANAIS:

LOL, don't worry. Get some rest, DP.

———

Ellie DMs Ruby the information, afraid to ask any questions. She thinks of IvyLeak, whose husband was dispatched while she was in jail and nowhere near her location. Maybe they're right now working out something just as comfortable for Ellie. She doesn't know how she feels about that. It seems somewhat heartless to kick a man, as it were, when he's down like this—as if it's somehow a fairer fight if he's able-bodied (yeah, and able to rearrange her house so she can kill herself, the Fucker). How would it feel to be awakened in the early hours of the morning to learn that Jeff had taken an unexpected turn for the worse, and there was nothing they could do . . . *Wouldn't that be something?* she thinks, as she drifts asleep.

CHAPTER FORTY-SEVEN
STRAWBERRY FIELDS FOREVER

FEBRUARY 5, 2019

Ellie sits in her kitchen, trying to stay calm and not to pop up every five minutes to check on Jeff's converted office, her cell phone, the chicken soup she's got on the stove. Jeff is coming home from the hospital any minute, and Ellie's a wreck.

She'd started the day speaking with Hannah and Wendy, who were both waiting to hear when Jeff was coming home. When she had called them the day after his fall, they were alarmed enough to want to fly out to be with her, even Hannah, despite the fact that she's in the middle of the run of *Crimes of the Heart*. Ellie talked Hannah down and felt a slight lessening of her stress just speaking with her.

Hannah understands that, with her father immobile, Ellie is going to need help, not only with driving but more importantly because, as Hannah so succinctly put it, "Dad can be a real bitch when he's sick."

Ellie reassured Wendy and Lacey that Jane was standing by, but she would call them if things got out of hand.

She understood that everyone was extra concerned because she was coping with the situation as a disabled, vision-impaired person, but it was hard not to feel that her competency was being called into question. Not that anyone thought her incompetent—well, maybe Hannah did, 'cause Ellie is her mother—but it was not an uncommon feeling, as a disabled person, to feel distinctly unempowered by her loved ones' unspoken doubts about her ability to get by. Ellie doesn't like it. She considers her sister, Wendy, an extraordinarily competent person and has always wondered if she herself didn't have RP, would she be extraordinarily competent too? Ellie sighs and files that thought away, along with her envy of people who can just walk down a street without thinking about it.

She considered telling Wendy that she was going to come back east and divorce Jeff just as soon as the sonofabitch could walk again. She knows Wendy is operating at peak capacity with their parents, though, and she doesn't want to burden her with one more thing.

Ellie was back on the divorce track as of yesterday morning, when at 7:20 a.m. she'd been awakened by a phone call from the hospital, its name emblazoned above the number on her cell phone screen. She sat up, wide awake, and said "Hello?" to Dr. Weiss, who was not, alas, calling to tell her that Jeff had taken a turn for the worse during the night, and they were so sorry, but . . .

Jeez, Ellie thought to herself sternly, *stop with the death fantasies already.* This is real life. Jeff is going to live as long as he's going to live, and you, most likely, will have nothing to do with his departure from this mortal coil. Get him well, get him ambulatory, and then spend all the twenty-seven cents you have left to divorce the Fucker and go live happily ever after in a nice hovel somewhere.

Dr. Weiss sounded cheerful. Jeff had a good night and was apparently doing very well in the hospital, where the drugs were good and the livin' was easy. Fortunately, he doesn't need surgery, and the plan was to discharge him the next day, which is today.

Dr. Weiss told her that Jeff will be on an IV antibiotic called vancomycin, twice a day for six weeks, which they will set up for him at home. The equipment and bags of the medication will arrive before Jeff does, and a nurse, Maria Estevez, will be there later to show Ellie how to administer it. Dr. Weiss breezily told her the whole IV thing is no big deal, that many patients rely on family members to give them their meds this way. Dr. Weiss was very reassuring about Jeff's recovery and Ellie's ability, even with her vision, to handle the IV.

It was very nice to hear someone finally have confidence in her ability, but the idea of administering any drug to Jeff other than Advil makes Ellie very nervous, and she's already pretty nervous about having a semi-ambulatory, injured, in-pain, and cranky Jeff in the house with her.

After the discussion with Dr. Weiss, Ellie decided she'd park Jeff in his office/den on the middle level of the house, so he'll have a fold-out couch, all the comforts of his office (TV, computer), and a bathroom and the kitchen nearby. Dr. Weiss also alerted her to make a special space, probably on the kitchen table, near a sink for handwashing (which she laughingly said Ellie would be doing a lot), where she could set up the equipment for the IV drip.

About an hour ago, Ellie had just cleared everything off the dining-room table, to make room for the bags and equipment, when she heard the doorbell ring. She carefully made her way down the stairs and opened the door to find a huge box filled with the pharmacy supplies. *Shit*, she thought, *does the vancomycin need to be refrigerated?* She decided she wasn't going to make any assumptions or do anything until the nurse comes.

She can't believe how nervous she is about this whole IV thing, but she knows that paying a nurse to come twice a day for the full six weeks will be prohibitive, so she's going to have to suck it up and do it herself. What's the worst that could happen? She could kill him? She should be so lucky.

She jumps up quickly and goes to the front door when at four o'clock Jeff arrives with much fanfare: medical transport, a noisy off-load from the ambulance, and EMTs (big guys taking up a lot of room) who trundle him in and up the stairs on a gurney and painstakingly settle him in his sick room. Like Goldilocks, the pullout bed is too hard, the sofa it folds into is too soft, but his reclining chair is, miraculously, just right, and he sinks into it with a sigh of relief. He sees Ellie, hovering ineffectually by the EMTs, and calls out sweetly, "Ellie! Honey! You look beautiful!"

Ellie raises an eyebrow to the nearest, taller EMT, who grins and says, "Yeah, he's on his 'happy pill.'"

Ellie glances at the box of supplies on the table. "Any more in there?" she asks.

"Sorry," he says, "Doc doesn't think he needs them anymore."

"I wasn't asking for him," Ellie says, in what she's sure must be a joke these guys hear all the time, like the closet jokes the wife always makes on *House Hunters*. The EMTs smile politely.

"He'll be fine," the taller EMT says. "He told us how he was in the Towers and survived 9/11. This'll be a piece of cake for him."

Now Ellie smiles politely. Suddenly, she doesn't want them to go, doesn't want to be alone with the real Jeff, who she knows is lurking in there somewhere behind the happy pill.

Thankfully, just as the EMTs are leaving, Maria, the nurse, shows up, and Ellie breathes a sigh of relief.

Maria is in her sixties, round, motherly, and chatty, with a wry glint in the big brown eyes that miss nothing. She's so sweet and comforting that Ellie is afraid she'll burst into tears from sheer gratitude that someone's being nice to her.

As Maria unpacks the box with all the pharma goodies and sets up the table for business, Ellie makes Jeff a grilled cheese sandwich and a bowl of soup. He eats hungrily, in between groans, as he tries to get himself comfortable on the chair. He also complains of being cold, so Ellie finds him blankets, turns up the heat, and makes him a cup of hot tea. He seems more alert and starts taking in the situation.

Which Maria has well in hand.

"Listen up, you two," she begins cheerfully, and leads them through the long but not terribly difficult IV procedure. She sets up Jeff's portable IV pole with the first round of tubing and clips by his chair, positions the Sharps bin for syringes in the kitchen, and washes down the dining-room table with disinfectant. She sets down an official-looking plastic place mat that is drawn up with the names of each procedure in order, with spaces for alcohol wipes, hand sanitizer, new tubing, the flushing syringe, and the bag of vancomycin, which, she tells Ellie, will be okay at room temperature for fourteen days; the pharmacy will send her another set of bags twelve days from today.

Maria deftly but slowly prepares Jeff's first IV drip, making sure that both Ellie and Jeff see what she's doing, stopping for any questions. Jeff, of course, says, "My wife is vision impaired. Is she really the best person to do this?"

Maria turns to Ellie and says, "Are you totally blind?" to which a startled Ellie answers, "No!" and starts to explain about her central vision, until Maria cuts her off to say to Jeff, somewhat sharply, "Well, my goodness, there's no reason on earth why your wife can't do this! She can see what she looks at, she seems like a smart cookie, and anyway, I'm going to train her so she can do this blindfolded. Any more questions?" to which Jeff meekly splutters a bit and then quiets. Ellie immediately falls in love with Maria and wants her to come live with them forever.

As Jeff's IV flows, and he starts to doze, Maria takes Ellie back in the kitchen to show her how to set everything out, how to wash her hands for twenty seconds each time she handles a new piece of equipment, and how to handle the prefilled syringes that contain the saline solution that will flush out Jeff's PICC line.

With a mock setup of an extra bag and extra tubing, Maria painstakingly puts Ellie through her paces, warning her with a sharp "Eh-eh!" when she's about to screw something up. They go through the procedure at least ten times, and by the end of it, Ellie feels—there's no other word for it—competent. Of course, it's one thing to do it in rehearsal and another to do it with a real person, but Maria will be coming there for the next few days, and she will watch as Ellie administers the medication. Ellie has Maria's number in her phone and can call whenever she has the slightest question.

Ellie's starting to feel better about all of this, until she remembers that her patient is Jeff, who gets angry if she makes a bed the wrong way—that is, not how he does it. *Oh well*, she thinks, *this may be a long haul, but it's the last thing I need to do in this marriage.* She feels better knowing there's a light at the end of the tunnel (and hoping it's not an oncoming train).

Maria watches as Ellie übercompetently sets out the tubing, etcetera, for Jeff's next infusion, which will be tomorrow morning, and when she's finished and looks up proudly from her work, Maria nods in approval with a big smile.

"Now," she says, "there's just one more thing I need to teach you. That's the thing you *don't* want to do."

Ellie's brow furrows. "Okay."

Maria explains that Ellie must be very careful when she's flushing the saline into Jeff's PICC line. She must squeeze all the air out of the syringe so there are no air bubbles left. Ellie's confused—Maria already showed her how to depress the syringe so that there's just one drop at the top, and then flicked it off before inserting it into the port in the PICC line.

But, Maria tells her, if there is air in the tubing, it could get into a vein. When an air bubble enters the vein, it can travel to the patient's heart, brain, or lungs and cause an embolism, which could be fatal.

Now Ellie's nervous again.

Maria says, "Here, let me demonstrate. Sometimes it's very useful to know what *not* to do."

Using extra tubing and an empty syringe, which she fills with water, Maria shows Ellie exactly what an air bubble in the syringe would look like. She does it twice, then has Ellie do it herself, two, three, four times, so that Ellie becomes very conversant with the process. "You see," Maria tells her gravely, "it's an easy thing to do."

Ellie's quite relieved, actually, and tells Maria that she appreciates the demonstration and feels more secure because of it.

Maria gathers her things, checks once more to make sure everything's ready for tomorrow morning, when she'll return to do the IV.

Before she leaves, she gives Ellie a big smile and a warm squeeze of her arm. "You can do it, Ellie," she says encouragingly. "Many women have done it before you."

Ellie rattles around the house for a bit, savoring her new sense of competency but aware that it's probably only a temporary sense of well-being because she doesn't actually have to give Jeff his dose yet. She tries to be in the moment and not worry too much about the future, or at least, the immediate future.

With Jeff still out of it, Ellie creeps up to their bedroom and logs on.

———

I AM THE WALRUS CHAT ROOM
GOO GOO G'JOOB
7:48 P.M.

DEARPRUDENCE:
Jeff's home.

RUBY:
Did the nurse come?

DEARPRUDENCE:
Yes. She was great. I feel a lot better about the whole IV thing.

RUBY:
Was her name Maria Estevez?

DEARPRUDENCE:
Yes.

DEARPRUDENCE:
???

RUBY:
Good. And I assume she was clear about what *not* to do?

RUBY:
DP? Are you there?

DEARPRUDENCE:
Wait . . . did *Maria* . . . jump over the fence???

RUBY:
Yes.

RUBY:
Twice.

DEARPRUDENCE:
OMG.

RUBY:
Take your time. Be brave. Do what's in your heart.

CHAPTER FORTY-EIGHT
CHAINS

FEBRUARY 11, 2019

Ellie's at work, marginally functional, after taking a few days off to get Jeff comfortably set up. She's trying to massage the headache out of her temples, since she can't take more Advil for at least two hours. Even with a headache, it's preferable to be here.

Mostly, she's exhausted. She had bouts of empathy because at first Jeff was truly miserable, but then the happy pills wore off, and, as she knew it would, the situation got worse.

He's always cold for some reason, though she doesn't mind keeping the heat up for him (even if her bedroom at the top of the house gets toasty). And she doesn't mind serving him meals, and bringing him hot drinks and cold drinks, and helping him to the bathroom those first few days, when he really needed it.

She minds being at the beck and call of a person who thinks it's perfectly fine for her to be at his beck and call because he's sick, and she's not. And yet he's not sick enough not to question her proficiency as someone who is vision impaired. *So whaddya want, Jeff? Do you* want *me to make you a protein shake even though I can't seem to make it the way you do, or do you want to go without it?*

She'd be okay at the beck and call of Phantom Husband, who wouldn't decide when she was upstairs and about to go to sleep that he had to have a bowl of Cheerios, just because he doesn't want to get hungry in the middle of the night. It isn't easy for her to go safely up and down the stairs, and his habit of humming the waiting tune from *Jeopardy!* doesn't make her want to get to him any time soon. ("What are you so pissed off about?" he'd say. "I'm *joking!*")

Then, of course, there is the IV. Maria, God bless her, came six more times, and the last three times watched carefully as Ellie went through the protocol, though she didn't watch her half as intently as Jeff did. Maria had been gone since yesterday morning and left Ellie in charge of the IV with every confidence, which Jeff only grudgingly seemed to share.

As he explained to Ellie while she deftly hung the bag and undid the clip, checking the line for snags, "It's not only that your eyes aren't good, Ellie; it's that honestly you're not all that competent, no offense."

That word, *competent*. Yeah, no offense taken, Ellie wanted to say, thinking that now would be a good time to get that embolism started. But she didn't. She smiled sweetly and hummed the Beatles song "It Won't Be Long Now" to herself.

So she is glad to be at work. She's going to do that thing where she pretends work is her home, and home is her work, a place where she has to satisfy an ornery boss until she can get back the next day to the people who care about her and treat her well. It's fucked up, but there you are.

"Shit," Ellie suddenly says aloud. She doesn't remember taking her laptop with her to work today and feels around frantically in her canvas tote bag for it. Not there. Not good.

She looks over at Jane, who's on the phone with a client, and considers asking for a ride home. Of course, Jane would do it in a heartbeat, but Ellie feels funny going home just to pick up her laptop.

She left it, stupidly, right on the dining-room table, where she was going to grab it on her way to work, but Hannah had called, and she got distracted and left without it.

She tries not to overreact. She knows that Jeff can't get onto her TOR browser—at least, not without her password, and he can't do anything without her VPN log-in and password either. So, really, there's nothing to worry about, other than the fact that she still doesn't know what he saw on her computer that day, the first day that he sneaked up on her. But what could he have seen in that split second? Nothing that would have made any sense; it would have looked, at worst, like another chat room, which is what he thought it was.

Calm down, she tells herself. *Jeff is barely ambulatory. His back is wrecked. He probably can't even walk into the kitchen. He's no threat.*

———

Jeff just can't get warm. He complained about it to Dr. Weiss, who just looked at him blankly and told him it would probably go away. *Doctors are morons*, he thinks. *If they can't help you, they just roll right over you.* He's tired of staying in his damned chair. It's the only place his back feels moderately comfortable, but maybe if he moves a bit he might warm up.

He gingerly gets himself into an upright position. He's on Extra Strength Tylenol, which he took about an hour ago, so it's starting to kick in. He remembers to put his phone in his sweatpants pocket, in case, he grimly tells himself, he falls and can't get up.

He painstakingly gets himself to the door of his office,

holding on to the wall, then realizes he probably will have to use the cane they gave him that he swore he would never use. It's resting by his chair—too late; he ain't going back for it now.

He moves very, very carefully through the little hallway, past the guest bathroom, and then makes a right into the dining area, giving the stairs down to the living room a wide berth.

He does feel a little warmer, but he also feels exhausted, and decides to turn around and go back to his chair when he spots Ellie's laptop on the dining-room table.

A goal.

He breathes deeply, relaxes his neck and shoulders, which have hunched in his effort. Ellie won't be home till five thirty, so he's got all day. He inches slowly toward the table, careful to stand up straight and not arch; he can feel the pain crouched like a tiger behind the Tylenol, and he doesn't want to do anything to make it pounce.

After about an hour and a half, or possibly five minutes, he reaches the table. Eying the laptop, he gingerly pulls out a dining-room chair and sits down, the computer open in front of him. It's a MacBook Air, smaller and less powerful than the larger, more expensive, more capable MacBook Pro, which he and Hannah each have.

It's an older model, so Ellie doesn't have to log-in to get started, and her desktop comes up as soon as he presses the start button; her password is already autofilled. He takes a minute to enjoy her screen photo: Hannah, four years old in Central Park, lying in the snow, her red hair vivid against the white ground, her grin huge, caught in the act of making a snow angel. It cheers him up for a second.

Jeff gets down to business, grimacing as he hunches down to see her screen, a good three inches smaller than his own. He studies her desktop icons; she doesn't have that many. There's a folder for some of her work documents, a folder for their taxes—Jesus, he thinks irritably, that shouldn't be there, right out where anyone could look and see their private information; he'd have to tell her to remove it (although then he'd have to tell her that he'd been on her laptop. He's not sure he can justify that, but he'll probably think of something). There's a folder for photos, a folder for recipes, a letter she's gotten from her eye doctor to get out of jury duty, and that's about it.

He glances down at the dock, which looks pretty much like his. He runs his eyes over the familiar Apple icons: Finder, Launchpad, Safari, calendar, photos, settings. He can see she's got Chrome on the dock as her browser; they all use Chrome rather than Safari, on Wyatt's recommendation. He sees the icon for settings, Word, Mail, iTunes, and then puzzles over two icons he's pretty sure aren't on his dock.

One looks like a padlock with a Wi-Fi signal over it; the other is a purple-and-white globe. He ponders this for a minute, not sure if he should click on one of them, what kind of footprint that might leave, and does he even care? He's beginning to get very tired and thinks about the long trek back to his office, which will take about an hour or, at any rate, at least five minutes. He fishes his phone out of his pocket and snaps a photo of the computer dock, focusing on the strange icons. He can probably find them on the internet, but he can also ask Wyatt, who'll surely know.

He creaks his way back up to standing, waving slightly like a stalk of wheat.

He's just about to pass by the stairs down to the living room when he hears keys in the front door, and he stops, alarmed. *It must be Ellie*, he thinks, but his heart is pounding, and he feels frightened for a split second, realizing that, immobile and incapacitated as he is, he's helpless if anyone tries to break in to their house.

He breathes a sigh of relief when he sees Ellie's red head pop through the open door, then catches her look of dismay as she sees him at the top of the stairs in front of her.

"What are you doing up?" she says.

"What are you doing home?" he counters.

He tracks her eyes as they go to the dining table, to her laptop.

Which, he realizes, he left open.

———

Well, it's not her worst nightmare, but it's up there.

"What were you doing on my computer?" she asks, wishing that he'd fall down the stairs to his death.

"I wasn't on your computer," he says evenly. "I found it like this when I came in to get a little exercise."

She knows it wasn't left open. She'd have closed it to take it to work with her.

"Bullshit," she says.

"Why are you home?" he says again.

"Jane had to go pick something up at her house, and I went with her to check in on you," she lies back at him.

"Bullshit," he says back at her. "You came back to get your computer."

"That too," she says. "My computer that I didn't leave open."

———

If he didn't feel like he was going to collapse with the sheer exhaustion of remaining upright, he'd handle this a lot better. He'd be angry and demanding and self-righteous, and he is all those things, except he can't express them.

"Fuck it," he says, waving his arm irritably. "Take it."

He can see she's not going to come upstairs until he's out of the way, so he moves his rickety body, shuffling back over his pathway, from the stairs past the bathroom to his office, where he lowers himself into his recliner with a groan. He's not as cold as he was before—so that's good. He shuts his eyes and listens as Ellie quietly goes up the stairs, grabs her laptop, flips it closed, and goes back out, closing and locking the door behind her.

He can't believe it—she leaves her critically injured husband alone, just like that? No "How are you doing?" or "Can I get you anything?" He's not just angry; he's disappointed—he thought she was a better person than that.

Then he wonders if he even knows what kind of a person she really is, as he sends the photos of those two icons and a quick text message to Wyatt before he falls asleep.

Later, he munches on the sandwich and thermos of coffee Ellie left in the cooler by his chair so he wouldn't have to walk to the kitchen for lunch, an excellent idea for which he gives himself full credit even though she had mentioned it first. He's about to go on his computer when he gets a call from Wyatt.

After filling Wyatt in on what happened to him, and after Wyatt expresses his sympathy and promises to come over to visit, Jeff asks about the icons he found on Ellie's computer.

Wyatt had recognized them right away. He tells Jeff that the icon with the lock is for the Norton VPN. Jeff, of course, has a VPN, has for years, but he's surprised Ellie's got one. Then he's gobsmacked when Wyatt, with a grin in his voice, tells him that the other icon is the TOR browser.

"I.e., the dark web," Wyatt announces, then waits for Jeff to get hysterical. Jeff is shocked speechless.

"I mean, I'm pretty sure your wife's not selling drugs or illegal weapons on the dark web. But the thing is, the dark web's not all that much of a big deal anymore. Lots of people get on it and just do regular stuff, like you'd do on Google. She probably just wants some privacy. And, dude, if you've been snooping around on her computer, it's obvious why."

"I wasn't snooping around on her computer," Jeff says indignantly, even though that's exactly what he was doing. "I just opened it to look for something, and I saw those weird icons on the dock."

"Sure, man," says Wyatt, laughing. "But unless you know both passwords, no way you can get in. She's encrypted up the yin-yang."

Jeff doesn't think it's funny, but he guesses it makes sense, especially if she's on a dating site and doesn't want him to know about it. He presses Wyatt a little, trying to see if Wyatt actually knows a way for Jeff to get in, but Wyatt's not only firm; he tells Jeff that even if he knew a way to override her security, which, as he said, was impossible, he wouldn't tell him. *Thanks, Wyatt, you're a real pal.*

If Jeff weren't so pissed off, he'd be hurt, but he knows now his marriage, or more specifically his wife, is spiraling way beyond his control. She had shut up about the divorce nonsense after it became clear they'd both have to live in seriously reduced circumstances if they separated, which is, of course, her fault, since she's stayed in that dead-end job all these years. What did she expect?

He wonders who the guy is she's "chatting up." Probably some artistic type, like she used to date before she found him, some writer or actor, Jesus Christ, or maybe some professor, though he didn't know why a professor would have to get on a dating site. He's getting a little winded and slows his breathing so he doesn't have a panic attack—that's all he needs with what's going on right now. And that's another thing: He's six weeks on this antibiotic, and then what? He's still going to be compromised, probably, for a while. Is she going to dump him for Cyber Guy? How could she live with herself if she left him for some guy she doesn't even know while he's sick and in need of his wife? Some guy who exists *in the ether* when she has a perfectly good flesh-and-blood husband at home? She's going *blind*, and has he *ever* talked about leaving her? Never!

What if Cyber Guy has money? He doesn't see Ellie as a gold digger, but if she snagged some guy with money she really could, then, divorce him, and he'd be living in some crappy studio apartment in Campbell, and she'd be in a nice house in San Jose or somewhere. Well, that's not gonna happen. Not on his watch.

He has to calm himself down. Most likely, the guy's a sleazebag who's pretending to be something he isn't. They probably haven't even met yet; she's probably just—what? Flirting? At her age? He dismisses that as ridiculous. Ellie isn't the flirting type, never had been.

There is no way in hell that this guy she's been talking to is better than him. So what the fuck is she doing?

He's itching to confront her, and he has to do it now, before it goes any further, and she takes advantage of him when he's down and out. (That'd be charming, wouldn't it, he thinks, conjuring a mental image of Ellie and some vague tall asshole swanning out of the house with half the furniture and leaving him all by himself, broken and sick. God, it breaks his heart.)

He thinks with longing about the last few weeks, when he was strong and on his feet, and leaving the house booby trapped for her. He didn't really think about it then, but he supposes if he'd really injured her, she'd be in the same position he's in right now. Then he'd have to take care of *her*, see how she'd like that. He knew he'd be a great nurse; he's a natural nurturer, and something of an empath.

Of course, he'd be no good right now as a nurse, but then he wonders, what would it be like if the two of them were incapacitated together? That might put a different spin on things for her. If the two of them had some quality time alone together, maybe she'd see the humor in both of them being "disabled." Maybe Hannah could come home early and take care of them, but then he thinks, it'd be more romantic if it were just the two of them and some nurse, coming and going. Give Ellie time to find her way back to her husband and her marriage.

Well, he thinks, that's another thought for another day.

For now, he has to deal with this dark web dating chat room or whatever it is.

He'll wait till she gets home. After she gives him the IV.

He's starting to feel a little better.

———

It's hard to concentrate, but Ellie's trying to bury her anxiety in her work. She never uses her laptop at the office, but on her lunch break she'd found a quiet corner and logged on to IATW. Danais and Ruby both told her there was no way, *no way*, that Jeff could override her cybersecurity, but they did advise her to change her usernames and passwords immediately for both her VPN and TOR, which didn't make Ellie feel any better, because if she were really so secure cyberwise, why would she have to change them?

She also asked them if they could tell her whether or not Jeff found his way to another dark web chat room like, IATW, and was possibly going after her via her "preexisting condition." Danais promised her that she and her sister moderators were keeping an eye out, but there could be no guarantees. This didn't help much, but what else could she do? That piece of the puzzle was out of her hands.

She did change all her passwords, which made her feel a little better. She had no idea what Jeff could have seen on her laptop, but she wouldn't be surprised if he'd found some hacker, a disgruntled IT guy, who could override everything and see all her posts on I Am the Walrus and *goo goo g'joob*, even though Danais told her that all posts on *goo goo* were expunged every two hours. But there's always a trail, Ellie knows, if you know where to look for it.

She longs to confide in Jane, who had once or twice offered to kill Jeff for her. She's pretty certain, though, that the reality of I Am the Walrus would be too much for even Jane to take . . . although it was also possible that Jane would want to sign up, herself, just in case.

Danais and Ruby advised Ellie to tell Jeff that she got the VPN and went on TOR for additional security per Wendy's advice, to prevent hacking and identity theft, *and*, by the way, to keep him from rummaging around on her computer.

And, of course, there's no way, *no way*, that he could possibly know about I Am the Walrus.

Right?

———

Ellie heats up her homemade lasagna and puts together some garlic bread and a salad for her and Jeff for dinner, which she eats with him in his office. He was cheerful when she came home, and looked pretty good, all things considered. She decided she wasn't going to bring up the open laptop and his obvious lie about it; if he couldn't get into her stuff, there was nothing to talk about, and if he did, well, she was pretty sure he'd want to bring *that* up.

But he's relaxed, though not chatty, and they have a relatively benign meal together. She clears away the dinner things, smiling

at his joking offer to help. After she's done the dishes and straightened out the kitchen, she sets up the dining-room table for his
infusion, carefully and slowly following all the steps she'd now been
doing for a few days, marking everything off against a checklist.

His eyes are shut, and he seems to be dozing as she sets up
the bag on the IV pole, connects the tubing to the port in his
PICC line, and opens the clip, making sure the antibiotic is
flowing freely. She's just about to leave the den when he says:

"I know what you're doing."

She stops. She feels every sense go on alert, but actually,
she's not surprised; rather, she feels as if this is some inevitable
fate that has been approaching from a distance the moment she
joined I Am the Walrus, and its arrival now is as expected as
the next train to Union Station. She turns to him and sees him
looking at her with eyes that are hard and wary.

"Do you?"

"Yes. Did you think your VPN and your TOR browser
would prevent me from figuring it out?"

Her heart is pounding. There may not be anything on *goo
goo* that will incriminate her, but she also realizes she never told
Danais and Ruby that she'd decided not to jump over the fence
and instead just divorce him. She wishes now she'd told them,
but she supposes she just wasn't ready yet to give up their support and confidence in her—and the fantasy they provided. She
hopes he'll believe her. On the other hand, what can he do to
her, really? Physically, he's tethered to an IV pole with a serious
back injury; legally—can he come after her for whatever it is
he found on IATW? Probably not, since she hasn't acted on it.
And if she needs legal representation, will the IATW network
provide it if she isn't going to jump over the fence?

She takes a deep breath. "Jeff," she starts, "I don't know what
you think you've found out, but nothing's going to happen."

She feels a reluctance to talk about divorce right now since the poor guy is so down and out. She'll tell him later, when he's feeling better. For now, best just make it clear she's not trying to kill him. Which she also has a hard time just coming out and saying because, let's face it, this is not a conversation you can ever really prepare for.

He gazes at her steadily. "You really think you can get away with this? Right under my nose?"

"I promise you—nothing is going to happen. Everything's okay. You have nothing to worry about."

"Uh-huh," he says, clearly not buying it.

"Listen, Jeff, let's just get you well, and then we can—"

"What's his name?" he says, lifting his chin, his eyes focused, direct.

She's confused.

"What?"

"Don't pretend you don't know what I'm talking about. I want to know his name, I want to know how far it's gone, and most of all I want to know what the hell you think you're doing?"

She can only stare at him, jaw dropped, wracking her brain to figure out what he means, if there's something on IATW that she's forgetting.

"Ellie, I know what I saw on your laptop that night I came home early. Don't play dumb; you're too smart for that, though you're not too smart for me. I saw that you were on a chat room. A dating chat room."

She feels her mind moving through molasses as his mistaken assumption starts to dawn on her.

"Don't even bother to deny it. You've been"—he makes the quote signs—"'seeing someone' behind my back, on the internet, and I want to know who he is, and how long it's been going on. Maybe you don't think it's real, because it's in cyberspace, is that it? You're going to tell me it doesn't mean anything, and I shouldn't worry about it? Let me tell you something: This is a betrayal. It's a betrayal of our love, and of our marriage, and of the vows we took twenty-two years ago. I only hope to God Hannah never finds out. Unless, of course, you're thinking of leaving me, leaving us, for this guy, this imaginary guy?"

Jesus Christ. He thinks she's been on a dating site! Not a site for killing your husband!

Her relief is overwhelming, but she can't help herself. She just starts laughing. And then she just doesn't care.

"Yeah," she says, "that's exactly what I'm doing. You nailed it, Jeff."

He's mad now.

"You think it's funny?" he says, and starts to get up, only to fall back down with a grunt as the pain and the IV get in his way.

Ellie hears a rip in the fabric of the universe, which she knows is metaphorical but which she also understands to be her, ripping herself away from this man, from her marriage, from the person she has been these past twenty-two years. She experiences a strange sense of lightness, as if a weight has been peeled away, and she stands up straighter, a line suddenly grown taut from her brain to her heart to the center of her being.

"Yeah," she says to Jeff, suddenly just so sick of the whole damn thing, "I've been talking to this guy on a dating site for people over fifty, and he's a doll. He's warm and funny and sensitive and humble. He has no problem with me being independent, or being inconsistent, or doing stuff differently than him or not always thinking *exactly* like he does."

She's got a head of steam now.

"*And* he's not some self-aggrandizing asshole who thinks the world owes him a living because eighteen years ago he walked out of an inferno and decided to call himself a hero. But you know what his biggest attraction is, Jeff? He's not you."

Ellie walks out of the room.

And then it occurs to her to be afraid.

———

Jeff's heart is broken, but his rage is alive and well; it fuels his body as he rises from the recliner, ignoring the sharp kick of pain in his back and irritably fighting with the IV pole. Fuck it—he drags it with him. Maybe he'll strangle her with it.

He squints his eyes as he leaves behind the soft dimness of the den into the glare of all the lights she leaves on, all the time, in the hallway, the dining room, the kitchen, no wonder their goddam electric bill is so high.

He follows her into the kitchen, annoyed that she can't quite get her malfunctioning eyes on him right away, that she can only look vaguely, stupidly, toward the sound of his entrance. He doesn't know what he wants to do, but he knows he's hurting, and he wants to hurt her too. He wants to hurt her, badly.

He flicks off the light switch.

CHAPTER FORTY-NINE
MAXWELL'S SILVER HAMMER

FEBRUARY 11, 2019

She has to keep all the lights on now because, unlike a totally blind person, the dark is not to her advantage. She needs as much light as she can get to broaden the edges of her vision and extend her central sight into the damaged periphery, which has closed in so much over the decades she's sometimes breathless with claustrophobia.

She stares hard, trying to keep the blackness at bay, strains her ears, holds her breath. She knows he's in the room with her. Doesn't know where.

She swings her tunneled vision around, a dim kaleidoscope of unfamiliar familiar objects—cabinet, microwave, fridge—she can see his face for a split second, but he keeps it moving just out of range. She can't see but can sense—unless she's imagining it—is that a *knife* in his hand?

No, she thinks, *that's against the rules.* But then she remembers her rules don't apply to him as he swipes down the blade toward her. It catches the sleeve on the arm she flings up to protect herself, slicing the material and her skin, sending a shock of pain through her body.

She gasps, instinctively leans back on the counter, clutching her arm against her waist. There isn't even time for her to think, *This can't be happening*, before she senses movement on her right-hand side, and his fist, or the knife, or the knife in his fist suddenly swooshes down past her, and she can hear it slam into the wooden chopping block on the counter. Without thinking, she smashes her arm around, and the block—hopefully with his fist or the knife or the knife in his fist—clatters to the floor.

Still leaning against the counter, her eyes feeling like they're literally peeled as she strains to get some visual intel of the chaotic scene, she kicks out instinctively, feeling Jeff's body close to hers but not able to see exactly which part is where. She hopes she catches his leg. She can hear him swear and hop back. Damn it, she should have kneed him in the crotch, but too late. She kicks out again; it sounds as though she's caught the IV pole and that it's tipped back against the cabinet. But then she hears the scrape on the floor as he rights it again, and she can see the silver glint of it bouncing off some wisp of light as he swivels and points it at her, like he's jousting.

What the hell kind of a fight is this? she wonders as, panting and shuffling, the almost-blind woman and the spine-damaged guy attached to an IV pole trip and curse and lock horns.

This is it, she tells herself. Broke and blind, blinded and broken, she knows her life is worth fighting for. She hurls herself out of his way onto the floor and gets down on all fours, thinking she'll trip him as he walks, maybe bite his ankle. Even better—she sweeps her arm in his path, shocked but pleased as both his legs and his IV pole easily break ground contact and swing upward, until the sickening, satisfying clonk of skull on travertine stops her in her tracks.

Shit, she thinks, her heart slamming, wracking her brain to access what Danais taught her. What would this be? Self-defense? Manslaughter? Something worse?

She hears him groan as he drags his body forward and vomits. At least he's alive. She should call 911.

Instead, she crawls out of the kitchen up the stairs to their bedroom and boots up her computer.

———

I AM THE WALRUS CHAT ROOM
GOO GOO G'JOOB
7:02 P.M.

DEARPRUDENCE:
He just tried to stab me. With a knife. He drew first blood. I'm going for it.

DANAIS:
Do EXACTLY what Maria taught you. If it's not instantaneous, you should have ten to twenty minutes to take action. Call 911 and Ellie, *play up your RP*. No one ever thinks a disabled person is capable of something like this.

DEARPRUDENCE:
Yeah. They think we're fucking incompetent.

DANAIS:
You're not. But you have to walk a fine line between appearing to be sighted enough to reasonably handle his IV and impaired enough not to be a threat. So, obviously, things got away from you, but that could happen to anyone. If you feel you need to call Maria, don't do it until after you do what you're going to do. If you have no more questions for me, log out of IATW and TOR, and shut down your computer right now. You can do this. We're here for you.

CHAPTER FIFTY
I AM THE WALRUS

FEBRUARY 11, 2019

Her computer powered down, Ellie flings her slashed shirt into the laundry basket and throws on another; she's relieved to see her cut arm is in good shape, just the slightest dotting of blood along the slash line. She cleans it up with wet toilet paper, flushes it, and heads downstairs.

———

Her hands aren't even shaking. She's never felt more calm, more certain, more empowered, more of all that bullshit that simply means she's finally taking control of her life, but right now she can't be bothered with how good it feels.

Jeff isn't bleeding, and he's not unconscious, but he's vague and not quite right when she comes back into the kitchen. He looks at her quizzically, and she puts on a reassuring smile as she helps him off the floor and gently settles him, his IV pole next to him, onto a dining-room chair, the one with the arms (the one she had to argue for two weeks to get him to let her buy because he said they'd never need it. Hah!)

Ellie disengages the antibiotic bag and gets ready to flush

the tubing in Jeff's PICC line through the port in his arm. She doesn't let her heart pound—she takes a breath, relaxes her shoulders, and focuses, breathing steadily.

She glances at Jeff, who's staring straight down at the table, then suddenly squints up at her, something unfamiliar and un-readable in his eyes—fear? Panic? Regret?

Too late. She holds up the syringe, gives it a quick shake, the way Maria taught her, and, shielding it with her hand from him, watches as a nice juicy bubble forms inside the cylinder. This is the time to depress the plunger so that one drop slips to the tip of the needle to be flicked off. But she doesn't do that.

She doesn't look at him again as she plunges the syringe into the port in his arm and sees the bubble start its journey down the pathway to his heart.

CHAPTER FIFTY-ONE
CARRY THAT WEIGHT

FEBRUARY 22, 2019

Ellie is sitting next to Hannah, and she feels at peace for the first time in—probably decades, really.

They're at Jeff's hospital bedside; once again, Ellie has the surreal experience of seeing her fantasy play out in yet another variation—but this time, it's real.

Hannah came in last week, worried and scared and ready to help however she can, though clearly conflicted because she also wants to get back to her play so that her understudy doesn't get too comfortable. Ellie took a leave from work and has spent the past week or so in the hospital with Jeff.

She tries not to think about the 911 call she made eleven days ago, when she surprised herself at how convincingly she fell apart while apparently trying to hold it together, as she described to the 911 operator Jeff's thready breath, the blue hue of his skin, the panic in his eyes. With her own panic mounting, seemingly, she explained how she was flushing out his PICC line, and he suddenly started with the shortness of breath, and then had fallen out of his chair and vomited (she thought it was a good touch to work it in; certainly, the vomit was there to back up her story since he had thrown up just before she crawled up to her bedroom). Having watched a lot of TV procedurals—but also possibly because her daughter was an actress, and it must have been in the gene pool—Ellie felt she'd hit the right note of hysteria versus control, panic vying with rational thought.

The EMTs—not, thank God, the same ones who brought Jeff to the hospital a few weeks ago—took in the scene—the IV setup, the syringe, Jeff's symptoms—and asked her a few questions as they strapped him onto the gurney and, with a sense of déjà vu, she rode with Jeff to the hospital, making sure they noticed her tapping her cane.

Once at the hospital, her sense of empowerment and control sped away like the outgoing tide, sucking her courage and resolve with it, and she began to shake uncontrollably, nearly sick with the enormity of what she'd just done. The nurse on duty assumed she was concerned about her husband, and brought her a warm blanket and some tea, though she could do little to reassure her about his condition. Ellie huddled in the blanket, teeth chattering, expecting—she didn't know what. To be taken into police custody? That was unthinkable. To get off scot-free? Almost worse.

To her surprise, Dr. Weiss was the one who came out to her about a half hour after Jeff had been admitted. Ellie knew that a fatal embolism could take up to twenty minutes to do its job, and she braced herself for what Dr. Weiss might say about Jeff, or worse, about Ellie's culpability. Ellie felt like moaning, the weight of what she'd done an almost palpable burden on her body.

Dr. Weiss took her hand and gently told her that an embolism had entered Jeff's blood stream via the PICC line and appeared to have lodged itself in his brain, putting him in a coma. She explained to Ellie how an embolism worked, which Ellie already knew from Maria, and told her that it probably happened because air got into the saline syringe and then entered the vein as an air bubble.

Ellie, in a very real state of terror, said, "So it was my fault," and burst into tears.

Dr. Weiss patted her arm. "It was an accident," she replied. Dr. Weiss held on as Ellie hiccupped her way to a kind of composure, then looked her in the eye when she was sure she had her attention and said, "You were doing what you had to do."

Ellie watched her leave, wondering how to interpret her last remark when yet another doctor arrived, to usher her into the now-familiar office off the waiting room. Dr. Li, avuncular, in his sixties, was very solicitous of Ellie and her cane, and held her arm somewhat annoyingly tight as he guided her into a seat opposite the desk and then took his own seat.

There had been an embolism, he confirmed, but it was not immediately fatal. Jeff had probably sustained some brain damage and was at this point in a coma and on life support. There was no way of knowing what would happen next, but in a few days it might be necessary for Ellie to, as Dr. Li put it delicately, make a decision. And would she like to see him?

She would indeed.

For the past eleven days, she sat alone, and then with Hannah, in Jeff's room, peacefully watching his living but stilled body, as straight and long as it would ever be, before the coma would inevitably curl him up. Ellie thought, gratefully (but not resentfully) that this was an outcome she did not anticipate, but one she could work with.

She hadn't killed him. She doesn't have his murder on her hands. Okay, if you're going to be literal, she did take his life away, but she's come around to the I Am the Walrus way of thinking: He had taken so much of her life—and yes, she was complicit in her oppression, but she was also worn down by it—that she feels that his debt to her has been paid, and she can finally forgive him.

They took Jeff off life support last night, and he passed, peacefully, without fanfare, about five minutes ago. Ellie and Hannah have been left alone by the hospital staff for a final few minutes with their dead, and when she leaves the hospital, Ellie will be able to play to the hilt her last role vis-à-vis Jeff, the Grieving Widow.

As her daughter quietly sits beside her, deep in thought, red-eyed, her hand in her mother's, Ellie remembers a remark Hannah made, in one of their conversations, about how she should never have married him to begin with. Everything, in hindsight, is twenty-twenty (*Ha ha*, Ellie thinks wryly), but Ellie wonders: If she'd married someone else, if she'd had a happy marriage, would she have appreciated it, or just accepted it, blithely unaware of the desperation of women caught in bad marriages? Marriages where the slings and arrows of marital misfortune are not the obvious ones, like drug use, or physical abuse, or infidelity, but something more nuanced and more likely to be swept under the rug or worse, attributed to the woman's own failings.

Her own marriage has taught her humility, patience, empathy for others; it's given her strength and purpose and a backbone she wouldn't have needed in a loving, nondramatic relationship with Phantom Husband, that sweet, unattainable, probably-doesn't-exist figment of her bruised and lonely heart. But then, she wonders, if she hadn't been stuck in this marriage, which sucked so much out of her, would she have been more joyful, passionate, loving, productive? A better mother to Hannah? A better participant in the world? Well, she'll never know, she thinks, but then, she stops herself. She will know. Her life isn't over. She still has it before her.

She smiles, turning her head to look at Hannah's red hair

next to her, the same flame as her own when she was that age. She remembers how on 9/11 she and Hannah waited together for news of Jeff, and how she'd privately, deep in her heart, hoped for her husband's death. It took eighteen years to make it happen. It took *her* to make it happen.

She looks over at Jeff's slack face. It's over. He'll never come home, never bother her or Hannah again.

And then the muscles of his face twitch and bunch, and with a grimace, he opens his eyes and looks right at her. Right at her.

Her heart drops.

The bastard is still alive . . .

ACKNOWLEDGMENTS

I have to thank the following people for being with me on this incredible journey.

First of all, my most profound gratitude to my friend and author extraordinaire, Sarah Skilton. You have been my main cheerleader and hand-holder since I first told you my idea for a novel about murderous women in a dark web chat room years ago. You never doubted that *For Worse* would make it to print, and I am so proud and grateful that your unflagging enthusiasm and generosity paved the way to its publication.

To my agent, Victoria Marini—formidable, compassionate, always-there-when-you-need-her—I can only say, I couldn't ask for a better agent or a better guide on this long and winding road to publication. Thank you for taking a chance on a first-time writer and answering all my panicked questions. I can't promise I won't be as neurotic about the next book!

To Dan Ehrenhaft: I am so happy that you and the other editors at Blackstone Publishing loved my novel enough to publish it. Your patience, humor, and knowledge have made my first experience with publishing one of the best "firsts" of my life.

To the extraordinary crew at Blackstone Publishing: editorial director Josie Woodbridge; publicity and marketing wizkids Tatiana Radujkovic, Sarah Bonamino, Francie Crawford, Brianna Jones, and Rebecca Malzahn; print editor David Baker; graphic designer Alex Cruz; art production manager Candice Edwards; studio director Bryan Barney; and senior producer Jesse Bickford. I am in awe of the brilliance, creativity, and passion you all bring to your work in the service of getting a novel to print. You made my book—a book!

To my developmental editor, Celia Johnson: I never had so much fun writing as when we were working on the edits of *For Worse*. Your suggestions inspired and educated me, and I hope we get to do it again!

To my first readers: Sarah Skilton, Susan Lowry, Kathy Foley, Christiane Carman (with help from Billy Palmieri on the NorCal/Silicon Valley details), Irene Arranga (with help from Julio Martinez on how to deliver IV meds to your spouse without killing him), Debbie Gyenes, Trish Doktor, Kathy Kadish, Terry Smith, Deborah Fryman, and Heidi Connolly—what would I do without you? You kept me going and made me believe there really was a book here. Thank you all—you are the wind beneath my wings.

To screenwriter Heather Ostrove: my heartfelt thanks for the hilarious car rides home from work, during which we enthusiastically exchanged ideas on how to kill off our characters.

To Bob Stayton, with much gratitude for the tutorial on the finer points of insurance agencies, which resulted in Ellie having a real job.

To the people who made up the Weekend Trifectas of Perfect Happiness that fueled my creative process: Marcia Brandwynne, thank you for the courage; Niki Saccareccio, thank you for the breath; and Maggie Wheeler, Emile Hassan Dyer, and the Golden Bridge Community Choir—thank you for the music.

To my wonderful, far-flung family, from California to Boston to New York to New Jersey to Georgia to Israel: Thank you for being a constant source of love, support, and delight. Without all of you, honestly, I just couldn't..

To everyone who lives with a disability, and to their loved ones who support them, and to those who watch us with impatience or bafflement or compassion—I hope this book will, in some way, shed a little light.